jay k. shah

a.k.a

(dadhi)

Written from January to April 2013

Re-transcribed: January 14, 2014

(MAKAR SANKRANTI – TUESDAY)

WITH GIFT PENS FROM
PARENTS OF BROOKLYN RODRIGUE
EXTENDED FAMILY OF ARHAM

First published in 2015 by

BecomeShakespeare.com
Wordit Content Design & Editing Services Pvt Ltd
Newbridge Business Centre, C38/39,
Parinee Crescenzo Building, G Block,
Bandra Kurla Complex, Bandra East,
Mumbai 400 051, India
T: +91 8080226699

ISBN 978-93-83952-46-5

DEDICATED TO "S" WITH UTMOST GRATITUDE

"To the love that is my life
To the life that is just you"

In homage to my parents, for planting the seeds of compassion and a love of medicine and reading within me.

In Appreciation

With gratitude to my two best friends, Murli in India and Madan Roy in Canada for making possible the two most loved abodes in this world for me - Vaishnavi Farms near Karnala, India and Majabira Cottage on Georgina Island in Canada.

In appreciation to them I reproduce an old poem spoken spontaneously by me over twenty years ago, sitting in my home at Sion with family (I will take the liberty to add an extra line here!)

Oh! BabuMoshai,

Karo na koi upaay

Lao ek charpai

Baaju mein rakh teepoy

Peeye ja Madan Roy!

(Jeeye ja Murli Bhai!)

March 31, 2015 Tuesday

Dearest Dr Dent (Peter)

It is a privilege and source of joy to acknowledge your request and support towards my cause.

What do I write for the very first person I met in McMaster at St. Joseph's hospital Grand Rounds one morning almost 30 years ago!

Your kindness, enthusiasm and welcoming attitude, patience, appreciation for my abilities, guiding me to Bosco, Brian and Stephanie has made my life maybe quite different from what it might have been when I first arrived in Canada on May 17, 1985!

Yes, you helped make Mac a family and a home for me and I have never regretted one moment of the choice I made thanks to you!

You are a mentor, a friend and your caring for me always is a feeling that I have been blessed and privileged to experience!

With Eternal Gratitude & Respect
With Love Always

DISCLOSURE

The characters and events depicted in this book are real. My interpretation of them can be considered as imaginary.

Any perceived discomfort, embarrassment, pain or hurt is completely unintentional. If so, then the author expresses his regret and tenders an apology to any of the characters portrayed.

The first entry in this personal diary of sorts was on January 3, 2013, and the last entry was on April 9, 2013 in Mumbai, India. The book's title flashed in my mind at the stroke of its last entry. There are two more brief additions to it, made on my return to Canada, just prior to resuming my work there. The diary then sat in my handbag for eight months, when I brought it back to India on December 7, 2013. I read this diary for the first time ever in January 2014. After reading it, I felt an urgent need to share it with as many people as possible, albeit given that it is in English language and will not be accessible to all. Given that my penmanship was also influenced later in life on account of my profession and the urgency of its demands, my writing is considered by most as beautiful a script as Sanskrit, but unreadable. Hence I began re-transcribing it in a legible, readable form.

The original had no chapters or even paragraphs. Certainly its construction required rules and framework, which I have attempted to do. The jacket design, motifs, statements, preface and introduction were all done by me after I read my diary for the first time. I wish that this be published if possible in my own words, barring the welcome assistance of an Editor to help create the final form.

PREFACE

This is utterly original. It is maybe quite different from anything you have previously read. The content of this book reflects a journey into the "insanity that is mind" and explores the depths of a spirited, romantic, loving heart.

With gratitude to the original writer, whose name, I am sorry to say, I do not remember, I quote the following:

"When sifting rice, watch for the grain of sand

When tossing sand, look carefully for the grain of rice"

Is this all fiction with a few kernels of Truth?

OR

Is this all true with a few husks of fiction?

If such a doubt arises in the reader's mind about the reality of the story that follows in this book, then the writer's work is accomplished. Given what has transpired on these pages is as much a mystery to the writer as it can be for you.

But, can you find any diamonds in this pile of burning coal?

I possess very few of them and have given this my all, so there are some hidden diamonds in here waiting to be found!

Introduction

This is the first unintentional attempt at such a treatise for this writer, who has previously never written pieces over 15 pages long. It has been somewhat traumatising, more so for its writer than any of its readers. Its apparent wound was deep but a soothing balm from within has prevailed to temper the perceived trauma. Today, almost a year later, the surprise and the lessons from it continue to reverberate in my life. Maybe I am now a good person from this experience. I won't say a good human being because, just being human is good enough! (If the great actor Om Puri ever reads this, he will remember this reply of mine to his complimenting me more than fifteen years ago in his home) Yet, look at the 'insanity' of this physician. Instead of trying to live up to the dictum of the Physician that states 'heal thyself', I am picking at my wounds, re-transcribing it on this trip, almost in its totality to make it legible enough to be published.

Sheer madness it may seem, I know. But man enjoys misery that is constant, more than any joys or moments of happiness that are evanescent. Forget for the time being any moments of bliss. The only creative piece in any of this may be the title given after finishing the book, and the design of its cover and its words after I finished reading it for the first time this year. Maybe, it is all that you need to read of it.

Partake of it at a glance, browse through it; maybe it will provoke some of you to take the gamble and walk out with it from a bookstore or as an eBook from an online store. Any writer wishes his or her work to be read as widely as possible. And this one, I believe, is worth more than a passing glance of curiosity.

If necessary, this will be published at my own cost at a budget I can afford. A few requests from family and friends will necessitate gifting some, including one copy, apart from my handwritten manuscript and electronic format, for myself as a memoir of a time well spent. But when they read this introduction they may all wish to gift something to make life a bit easier for the main characters, all of whom richly deserve some additional financial help. Ah! Surely a copy as a priceless gift is rightfully deserved by the person who is at the source of all this writing, and it's unfolding drama and minor tragedy for the writer. But, the English language maybe being alien to her repertoire of skills, I am at a loss as to how to make it accessible to her.

I cannot translate this myself into the languages she can read and understand. So, the help of a translator will be needed. My computer skills are bare minimum, so, I cannot use that medium myself. I am largely handicapped when it comes to computer use, as I do not possess a computer, and my abilities with it are related only to professional use, medical literature and official email communications.

On advice of friends and the exorbitant cost of putting the written words into a digital format, I have chosen to do it myself on just a spreadsheet, with my brother then teaching me about transferring it into word format. I must be boring you to death with these details, but just like in my profession, this is equally honest writing on my part. This is a spur of the moment, spontaneous outburst almost on a daily basis. Originally, it must have had multiple errors of both prose construction and grammar, which I hope the computer will take care of.

The jacket cover is designed and ready in the author's heart, broken into pieces, each of the shattered pieces reflecting the image chosen in its totality.

This is above all, a gift to me that I would also like to share with you, the reader: The first, and likely the last, unless 'sanity' returns in my future attempts at this art!

Take the risk; I can almost guarantee that it will leave you feeling richer for having read it!

A NOTE OF CLARIFICATION AND SIGNIFICANCE

The beginning of this book is in no way an indicator of what finally took place. Yet, Chapter One is the essential foundation to understand how this narrative proceeded to its apparent conclusion. All proceeds from the sale of this book in any form will be divided amongst the main characters in this book and NGOs of the author's choice.

Chapter 1

3/1/13

Reading and writing were the glorious passions of my childhood, along with the joyful innocence of play and pranks that every growing boy indulged in those days, which seem lost to the current generation, seemingly better off than the so-called good old days of my growing up.

Today, on the verge of freedom at 55, I feel an urgent need to re-examine the message that I learnt from the latter half of my life in Canada, in a rewarding and fruitful career in medicine, as well as the life ahead of me; although that message has much more to do with accumulating material needs enough to generate a comfortable retirement, from having to keep working for a living after age 55.

Five months and two days from now, I will find myself at that mark, if alive. So 'Am I Ready?' is a nagging question. Being comfortable is not necessarily being content. Given my few vices, retirement for me is a tricky balance. Obviously it is not my intent to retire from my chosen profession of medicine. Having taken baby steps with more than 15 years of honorary volunteer work in areas of my skills at Surya Children's Hospital in Mumbai, India, the desire to continue doing it almost full-time without the benefit of an income from my vocation is a luring proposition.

A question looms in front of me today: Being single with no immediate dependants of mine, except my extended family comprising of my two brothers, a *bhabhi* (sister-in-law) a niece, a nephew and my aging housekeeper now unable to come from his village, is the kind of retirement I desire, feasible? The prospect of living half a year in Mumbai in my deceased parents' apartment in Sion, the other half in a jointly owned cottage on Georgina Island, Ontario, Canada, enjoying the benefits of the dollar to rupee exchange anomaly, prompts the wish for a courageous decision to stop working for a living soon. In Canada I own just my car, one fifth of a cottage but not the land it stands on, and hopefully plenty of goodwill from my profession and almost 28 years in McMaster, my most cherished place in Canada.

For over 15 years, I have been fortunate enough to provide honorary voluntary services at Dr. Bhupendra Avasthi's Surya Children's Hospital. I do this twice a week for 10 to 12 weeks during each of my yearly visits. In addition to this, I have been privileged to work twice a week with Dr. Armida Fernandes and the SNEHA group at Dharavi, Sion Hospital's Urban Health Centre for three years. It is fitting to put in a brief mention of my attempts to be equally productive here even during my holiday time with family, friends and personal growth. Two years trying to work with the bureaucracy in order to revamp an almost defunct primary health centre system of the Mumbai Municipal Corporation did not materialise, in spite of some very sensible ideas from me that were disregarded. I did try what I could with the help of Dr Armida Fernandes and her very talented selfless team of assistants, but frustration crept in and I parted ways as I was unable to make much headway with the powers to be. The work at Surya happened as an accident. A fortuitous meeting with Dr Bhupendra Avasthi way back in the mid-90s led to the blossoming of a friendship that has survived the test of time. He is a dedicated, courageous, visionary person who has single-handedly transformed step-by-step, and brick-by-brick, the face of Surya Children's Hospital. He has allowed me a free hand, adopted my suggestions and ideas, provided for all possible material resources to allow my skills as a newborn intensive care specialist to continue in a similar vein as at McMaster. He has been instrumental in fulfilling some of my dreams of bringing the model of Universal Healthcare to sick newborns of indigenous families by waiving off almost all their fees no matter the amount. A large proportion of such newborns from poor families are being treated free thanks to his acceding to my request, it being my main condition of serving in an honorary capacity there and teaching the young generation in this field. In a way it is my selfish motive also, a way to give something back to the country and the institutions that trained me. Surya allows the possibility of being the biggest charitable private medical hospital for sick newborns with the largest neonatal intensive care unit in the whole state, and possibly the country. Alongside him are his wonderful team members, his sister, Dr Shobha Sharma, my protégé from McMaster, Dr Nandkishor Kabra, a very talented pool of postgraduates in pediatrics and neonatology, and a dedicated nursing staff under the brilliant leadership of Sister Shameen, who is a role model and leads by example the nurses. Without her this unit wouldn't be anywhere it is currently.

Right now, to me, the paramount question of importance is "Do I have enough for my simple needs to guarantee that I do not outlive my material resources?" OR, more likely, "Would my wealth in all probability outlive my life?" A tantalising dilemma that I know many would love to find themselves in! My friends repeatedly tell me that I will outlive them all, be there to give a shoulder to their funeral pyre. By giving myself over to long walks, a diet of raw veggies, nuts and fruits, and rarely ever eating throughout the day except in the evenings, as well as doing without cooked food for almost 7 months of the year, I have set myself up for a long life. In spite of the habit of smoking six cigarettes a day for more than 30 years but neither at work nor on my long walks; and a couple of drinks of alcohol a day for the last 15 years - never on night calls - I remain healthy and will live to more than a 100 years is their estimate. It reminds me of the Japanese fellow who was asked the secret to his surviving up to 117 years in good health. His answer was that it was due to his cups of Sake, and his penchant for loving young women. I have no idea how far that is true, but if so then he is speaking from his own lived experience and maybe that is why his heart is alive and his mind sharp!

But I digress, as is my nature. The thoughts jump ahead of the story I hope to write. So, to come back to the opening line of this book, reading remains, but writing for some long years had disappeared. Just having read a passage from 'Of Human Bondage' by Somerset Maugham, I am left wondering whether what I understood to be my passion may just have been no more than a habit, a hobby. And, like some others such as music, sports, movies, television, newspapers, magazines, idle conversations, etc. that have left my life almost totally, I worry that reading too may fall off the radar, leaving me with only the passion of enjoying aimless, purposeless walks for hours on end almost daily, except when I am on call at nights in the Neonatal-Perinatal Medicine Unit at McMaster. The walks have become the defining moments of my existence, apart from my profession for the past 21 years.

Something good after all did come out of the tragedy of my divorce that has left me single today. But it is an aloneness that has grown; now, I love to enjoy it with an acute sense of protecting it at every cost. It has brought in its wake a silence of the outer. An attempt to gain the silence of the inner though is proving difficult, my mind still the monkey on my back. I hope I can shed it before life takes leave of me.

Could I survive if I were to become blind or crippled and wheel chair bound, is something that haunts me often. Now, my living will declares that the world to me in such a state would be an anathema to my existence. So my advance directive makes my choice clear in the event of such a calamity in my life. My elder brother here in Sion, and my dearest friend abroad, BabuMoshai in Canada are the appointed trustees to carry out my living will. As I ponder now, having seen innumerable instances of courageous men, women and children in my imagined calamitous situation continuing to overcome such adversity, I feel humbled, ashamed to be so selfish to express a desire of having my life ended if such a tragedy were to befall me. Then came a thought; an acute sense of keenness to discover and recreate the lost passion of writing. They were often letters to family, friends, loved ones, some random thoughts as essays, at times abstract, but often tainted by the unwitting introspection of what it may finally become - an autobiographical sketch of my life.

Writing, I hope, comes back to me again like the seasons of nature. I realise that if I were to become blind and lame, it will not be a barrier to my ability to write, but very much so to my ability to practice my profession. Much of my earlier pieces came both from my thoughts and feelings. If I try today to still my thoughts and stimulate my cherished endeavour again, I hope to have kept the feelings alive, to be able to have at least one crutch as a stimulant, a catalyst to resurrect that lost ability.

So, let's assume it to be true. Being a sentimental fool, ruled by my emotions as my family and friends remind me often, and known as a no-touch verbal flirt, with many romances / loves in his life from a distance in the early years of my youth, today, I am left alone. My wife's choice to leave me despite absolute fidelity of the body, mind and heart during our seven years of marriage has left many wounds on both sides. Neither have there been any affairs after my divorce, and none of my previous harmless romantic interludes have ever been at the place of my work, the temple that is my professional life in McMaster and also at Surya. Anyway, I suddenly feel that the prospect of an unattainable, unachievable eternal romance with a person or nature or more likely my own mind can become the ultimate reason for my heart to be able to dictate over my mind.

This book is barely a glimpse of what I have the potential to write, the story of my life; the germ for this idea having arisen from the fact that I have now lived half of my life in two countries each, India and Canada.

So, if you have read this far, I cannot give an indication of what may unfold and how many feathers may be ruffled. And if you haven't, then it might just serve as an obituary to me, written by me, too long to call it an epitaph, too short to call it my story...

Each life has its own story. The telling and retelling of it adds myth and imagination, so as not to make the facts too boring or repetitive. For, barring a few rare exceptions, most lives remain indistinguishably ordinary in their living, which then is the most extraordinary thing about it!

Each day is a subtle reminder of a humdrum existence, untold despair amidst a few evanescent dewdrops of pleasure, joy, happiness, contentment, etc. The vast multitude of humanity struggles to live, yet wants to hold on to life dearly, fearful and unwilling to accept death as the only certainty of life. To many, I say to almost all, life must seem purposeless, meaninglessly mired in the habitual routines of daily living. Yes, there are few more sophisticated toys and gadgets to add novelty. However, they soon become a powerful tool towards a sedentary lifestyle, overloaded sensory existence replacing the carefree unstructured joys of a childhood that I can't see ever being reclaimed by the new generation, during the remaining moments of my life.

Beyond childhood, adolescence, adult working life and raising a family with all its ramifications and stressors that make life cumbersome (though of course there are also fleeting moments of pleasure and happiness), suddenly, old age descends and retirement looms, leaving one to wonder, whatever did really happen to my life, and what next?

Each life is full of many vignettes - some very defining, if lucky then at most one or two seminal events that define an opportunity seized or lost. Yet, how many of us continue to tilt the balance more towards regrets of 'ifs' and 'buts', rather than an acknowledgement and gratitude of having made it so far? To be able to have the memory to recount a tale that may well be ordinary yet quite unique, given no two lives can ever be similar, may be considered as a gift!

So the idea of a book like this must begin by deconstructing it into a multitude of pieces, in which the reader also can find something familiar. It can be comic or tragic and it may create the feeling of 'I know this, I have seen this, I too have experienced similar such events and more, this is my story too, so why couldn't I write it?!'

If any reader finds this to be true, then they too can and must find the time, the freedom, the luxury that comes from the fulfilment of needs and elimination of wants in life, to be able to embark on such an endeavour. Fruitful or otherwise, the unburdening of memory, putting words to paper may just serve as an accomplishment in itself without any expectation of a reward, financial or otherwise.

But in a way, a so-called autobiography is inherently an egoistic exercise, not unlike a daily diary perhaps. It is coloured with some degree of judgement, praise or criticism of actions and experiences, either of oneself or others, or of circumstances and events that have touched one's life. It is also the dredging up of memories, and for someone like me, renowned to possess almost a photographic memory, that can become either a blessing or a curse.

Inherent then, is the tendency to embellish, exaggerate, twist the facts and mould the truth. The retelling from a memory years later is often coloured by subsequent events that have shaped the contours of a fragmented memory. In trying to create a pattern that is more coherent, smoothened and assembled, a half-truth or lie may emerge. This, because none of the other players involved have in themselves the ability to correct it, either possessing a lesser memory than mine, or have since departed from this earth.

The true worth of such an autobiography is debatable, unless one defines it only from the perspective of the other. This in itself is a flawed argument, for how can anyone presuppose to know others' mind in its totality, when one can barely fathom the true depth of one's own mind?

I realise having written so far that in spite of a deep love of reading, barring a few exceptions, the novels, books and other literary works which I thoroughly enjoy are those with down-to-earth snippets of conversational pieces within the work. They help in providing a balance to long drawn out passages, allowing a seamless transition to the flow. This form of interruption triggers my continued interest in the reading of such literary works. My previous pieces (unpublished), written over many years, though appreciated by others who have read them, are all singularly lacking this crucial ingredient. It has always been the style of my writing. So, an autobiography that stretches endlessly without such episodes of relief, even though it's mine, will make it somewhat taxing for even me to read it, though of course, I will have no problems in the writing of it.

So, there's the first nail driven into my coffin. But I have already begun this process and my close friends are desperately waiting for it to be written, gifted to them, and to claim royalties from its publication after my demise. (Wishful thinking!)

How then is one to write an autobiography? I am singularly handicapped by having read just six and a half of them - Gandhi, Paramahansa Yogananda, Thoreau, Teddy Roosevelt, Franklin, Lincoln and half of Ho Chi Minh. A few biographies too, via the lens of the author's eye. A gimmick that may have been employed by some already, like going back and forth without any logical sequence of time and events, may make it more readable or more confusing. Given my nature of rambling around in the dead end alleys of my mind, tracing and retracing events that have shaped my life, it may scarcely make for a coherent narrative. So by now if I find myself at a loss on how to approach this exercise, faltering already in trying to proceed with it, then there is hardly any incentive or excuse for anyone else to consume what might soon become a tedious affair.

One way to get around it is to discipline my thoughts. Begin by looking forward from the time my memory crystallised or by looking back from the present moment and liquefy that solid memory. But writing, like any other art form, should rarely be subjected to rigid discipline, rules, or a framework. It should come naturally, spontaneously from the perception of a vision alone. For it to be a work of beauty is solely the prerogative of its creator - whether it be a writer, painter, sculptor, dancer, composer, and so on - but not in any manner the business of the spectator. At the same time a true work of beauty is its own reward. But how can one forget the masters of renowned arts having died in abject penury only to find their works priceless, appreciated and sought after by collectors after the demise of its originator. Such is the insanity of any genius, the creative vision uplifting its own spirit and soul far superior to any other rewards for him or her.

So then, can a daily humdrum living not create the vision of joy? Where, why, when and how has a human being lost the original unparalleled source of exhilaration, bliss and peace of living life itself?! Most are mired in petty, trivial matters, losing equanimity and balance in each act of daily living. For, life in itself is the supreme masterpiece, the glory of it realised in its culmination at death.

Living life on its edge is then the surest way of achieving perfect balance.

Chapter 2

I lost my train of thought. Writing on hold. Now at a loss of how and with what to continue or begin anew as I dread reading what has already been written. Having somewhat demolished the idea of an autobiography, maybe I ought to begin with the experiences of this visit and allow my heart and mind to roam freely. Start with what comes naturally in the present moment and see where it takes this narrative.

Sitting on the sliding window sill's granite platform ledge of my living room, above the row of plants my *bhabhi* has arranged and provided with tender care, I am tempted to reminisce again, negating what I just wrote a little while ago. This is the first time ever that I have been able to sit like this in my home, thanks to the second instalment of renovations started the year before last and completed last year.

With the diary on my lap, my feet stretched out and my pen lightly resting on the page, I am suddenly captivated, seized by the vision of a pair of hands reaching to fill water from a copper pot into a water bottle steel flask; I watched transfixed. The sight directly across from me encompasses part of the whole scene I see of my surroundings every time I lift my eyes, when having either stopped reading or writing.

As my gaze traced upwards, I recognised the forearms and then the face. It brought forth an indescribable feeling from the heart and to the mind a memory worth expressing.

I first saw her on my walks last year, on my route that includes the Kikabhai Hospital lane also. Ordinarily, I am oblivious to the umpteen faces I may come across - humans, animals, objects such as motorized vehicles, and the noises too. I focus mostly on the ground beneath my feet or a few paces ahead of me. My attention at times is arrested by the delight of laughing children, their shrieks of joy at play. At times I am diverted by the songs of the birds and the fragrance released from flowering trees when a sudden burst of wind gushes through. No music from my Walkman or iPod for the last three years on my walks here or abroad; I take unadulterated delight in the unfolding of unexpected scenes on the street, though not purposely searching for them. But this is not about me - maybe it is though!

An ordinary face, earthen complexion, slim and tall, the first quality I sensed and appreciated about her was an exuding simplicity and grace. No one gives me or her a second look, but I was left then with an inexplicable need to see her again. Contrary to my purposeless walking for hours on end, a secret desire and hope to cross her path again made a home within me. I just saw her, I guess, twice later during the whole trip the previous year. Now, as fortune (misfortune it seems) would have it, she happens to be the housekeeper in my neighbour's home diagonally across from mine. It soon became apparent that she lives with them. Lost is the dream and wish of running into her on my daily walks, having earlier presumed that she was either coming or going from her place of work to her own home.

It had never occurred to me that she may be a college student and not a working woman. Why that thought never came in the previous year is difficult to explain. Maybe I did not see her with a knapsack or purse when I first ran into her, and so developed

23

my own conclusions without a thought. Not knowing her name or background, I surmised by her appearance, to be barely half my age, somewhere in her mid-20's or less. I am struck while seeing her today, by the unknown dimensions of her life negating my previous assumption. So ultimately, to write about her is to let my imagination run wild, yet at the same time, to be in the present moment with her, taking some clues from observing glimpses of her daily life, when chance presents with such an opportunity. Given the surprising intimacy of her physical presence right across from me, there is yet an insurmountable gap in my knowledge of her.

I observe, unable to take my eyes away from the briefest of glimpses afforded to me as she goes about her work. She is rarely seen to step out much except to water her plants and tend to a garden cultivated by her similar to the one my *bhabhi* has done beneath and around our living space. An occasional small errand must have been the moment when I first saw her last year. There has sprung an urgent need, unexplained as yet within me, to know her.

Once seen at the vegetable vendor's, I dared to exchange a few words with her, asking of her wellbeing. She answered in one word as we crossed each other. Since that meeting at close quarters, barely for an instant, I have not stopped thinking about her. I cannot truly find the reasons for it yet but the thought may have risen from a feeling buried in me since the previous year. Now I have created and invented scenarios of a conversation that I would like to have with her, should there be another meeting by chance again. Currently the language of our conversation is muted, one sided mostly, limited to some gestures of greetings on my part, a wave of my hand, a stolen contact of the eyes, unsure if there is any reciprocation of it, but it does not seem to bother her much, for she has once returned my wave with one of her own.

I notice the patience, the attention she gives to the tasks of her day. The sight of her bare hands and wrist, her full forearms and elbows seen every other day is quite magical to me. She wears two outfits alternating with one another; the top of one has sleeves that end mid upper arm, and the other, mid forearm. Tantalizing is that sight. She seems to possess a gentility, a devotion, as her eyes are locked unwaveringly on the task at hand, one of the countless many during the day. I see her entering and exiting her kitchen, collecting milk bags left on her window grills, making morning tea and possibly breakfast. Then she ventures into the courtyard with a bucket of water to tend to her garden in front of the living room, and plants by the other door leading onto her balcony, which is sealed off leaving only the main door for access. Sometime later the whistle of a pressure cooker is heard, and a *patla* (a wooden board used to flatten dough) left to dry on the grill platform outside the kitchen window. A few hours later, I see washed clothes hanging on the strings of her living and bedroom area balconies. I notice her in a new outfit around 1.30 pm or so as she enters the kitchen for lunch and the cleaning up of the afternoon utensils. I get only an occasional glimpse of her till about 3 pm, when she shuts the kitchen windows. I leave for my walk usually around 3.15 pm during the pleasant cool days of Mumbai's winter. From the street an hour or so into my walk, I notice the windows reopened. I hope for that hour, she has had a well deserved afternoon rest or a short nap. I walk many hours, running small errands and chores alongside for the family's needs or mine, but my mind is often occupied by her thoughts, the purpose of stilling my mind's chatter on my walks becoming fruitless as I am unable to keep her from entering my realm. Soon, I no longer even try.

Last night, I dreamt that I couldn't figure out her face and woke up wondering where I was; then it floated up, as if a veil had been uncovered, and a smile materialised. A serene face, a voice barely heard yet, a smile once seen at close quarters revealed a discoloured upper tooth and visible gums. Her eyes not yet locked into my embrace. A walk, neither hurried nor slow, a natural ease to her, as she seems to go on, seemingly unaware of the adoration that her very being has stimulated in me. I find no logic or reason, nor substance to this sudden obsession of mine, attempting to translate these fleeting moments of her sights into the vision of a conversation that I somehow know cannot lead anywhere. This unknown is appealing, its outcome undefined. There is both pleasure and pain in this waiting, the meeting, if any, will likely be disappointing given that there is no future to this silent 'romance' of mine.

When the word 'romance' hits the page, the line shifted and I took a deep breath in surprise. As I feel this word, I come to the conclusion that maybe this was the real, unrecognised subconscious stimulus for my attempt to begin writing again. An imagined romance, likely from a much real source rather than an abstract idea, but at the same time I dread the ending of this illusion and resultant cessation of this superfluous writing.

Her two outfits are elegant in their bare simplicity, and are colour coordinated quite well. A coincidence, given that I too, wear just two outfits on a weekly basis, a pair of shorts and a simple white *peran* (Thin, short cotton *kurti*), washed daily, ironing them with my palms, wearing them on alternate days. However on two consecutive evenings, Wednesday with Dk *mama* and family, and Thursday with my Seth G.S. Medical College buddies at clubs, necessitate the wearing of trousers and T-shirts, at times socks and shoes, which I hate doing here or abroad. Just like a neck tie is an abomination for me, so are socks. I do not wish to ever strangulate myself in a tie or a coat that adds unnecessary burden to my clothing, so too I need my feet to breathe. As my colleagues know, if my feet cannot breathe, I cannot feel or think! Not even at work, as I wear Birkenstocks daily at the hospital and similar inexpensive imitation Bata sandals on walks. Unfortunately, they have stopped making them for the last ten years or so, and I am on my last pair of a lot that I kept buying and storing over the years. Yes, must be some patent lawsuit filed by Birkenstock that has put an end to my affordable Bata sandals. I cannot afford the Birkenstocks for regular walking since my sandals run out from wear and tear every three months. Anyway, that aside, shoes seem needed sometimes on these outings to cover the cracks in my soles and the ulcers on my feet from the prolonged activity of walking. This a common experience in the first fortnight of each visit and then it settles down a fair bit.

Accustomed as I am now to the pain and burning, the absence of it may make my visit less real, less rewarding. As the famous Zen saying goes, and I quote from its master: "If the shoe fits, the foot is forgotten". You may think that my wish to experience the trials of such discomfort is some sort of masochism.

Also, weekly on Tuesdays, and Thursdays, I don a different pair of shorts, T-shirt and sandals for a full day of teaching and management rounds in the NICU at Surya Children's Hospital, a part of my continuing honorary volunteer work there since the last 15 years and more. There is so much more to say about all the good work done by the charitable doctors that I work with, but it will require many chapters in a separate book, when I write my memoirs before I forget it all. My mind a veritable warehouse of memories both rich and troubling is also an instrument for projecting and imagining the future. Moving constantly between the past and the future, it however does occasionally catapult me back into the present moment, albeit momentarily, and then drags me away from that precious experience. However, the heart is grateful for being in the here and now for those fleeting moments.

So, a lady likely in her 20's, a fulltime live-in housekeeper, has captured me in what is beginning to feel and is dangerously developing into a prison of my own making. I wonder why she seems so content, so comfortable in what she does, going by what her day and life appear to me from a distance. Oh! How I wish to know of her! Does she hope or dream of college, a marriage, a home of her own, to begin a family and so on, factors that make up most human lives?

What does she fancy, what are her desires, her joys, regrets, means of entertainment, leisure time, holidays, vacations, festivals, days off, movies, shopping, eating out, treats, etc., that many of us partake in so regularly without due gratitude or any lasting joy from them?

Maybe I hope and pray that she is like my visualisation of her, a living embodiment of an ideal that few ever achieve in life. I wonder if she ever examines the monotony of her days, which I still have not completely enumerated, doing the same tasks day after day, only to recur with unerring similarity the next day. In her I see a seeming acceptance; a surrender to her ordinary existence, yet finding meaning and satisfaction in it. Or better still, having no thoughts about it and living each day as it comes. On this visit, my last three weeks have had the same habitual monotony that makes my day too disappear without the semblance of any so-called productivity or creativity as may be the opinion of others. I, so formally educated, with the benefits of a rewarding profession and career, my expressed desire and passion of wanting to become a doctor from an age of nine or ten years old, as known to my family, having come true. Yet, this morning I feel it would be a blessing should this monotony of mine ever match my imagined monotony of her days.

I have a sinking suspicion that this is turning out not to be about me but my unreciprocated - as yet - admiration of her. The apparent sizzle and heat of my feelings and my emotions are fanned by a perceived coolness on her part as of now. She likely has complete disregard of what may have over the past few days become obvious to her after many very brief moments of courtesy to me on her part. Now, my stolen furtive glances thrown her way repeatedly when I stop writing to gather a thought causes an unavoidable appearance of her in my sights, and my solicitation for a greeting from her may have become quite apparent. My attempts to look for her in the window as I clean and dry the utensils at night, the last act of her filling two flasks of water and capping them off gently, no other

28

sounds, no voices heard then the careful, almost silent shutting of the kitchen windows by 9.30 or latest 10 pm, the lights immediately turning off; in that moment her day ends and in that ending my dreams begin while I am still awake.

This is fast becoming some sort of a nightmare, the stimulus not very clear to me yet. Our paths so different, our separation evidently irreparable; no matter which yardstick one chooses to measure this by - social class, cultural, educational, language, geographical, material or any other such domain - and most importantly, the generational aspect to this slowly evolving drama of mine.

Yet this hand refuses to stop, the mind refusing to discard this looming obsession, maybe in some manner recognising and giving support to this longing of the heart.

I missed her watering her plants; maybe she hasn't watered them yet. More likely is the fact that I missed it, having been absorbed in writing this soliloquy at a furious pace for the past hour or so. She must be doing the laundry now, having remade the beds, cleaned the rooms, and removed the last two pieces of dried clothes from the balcony which I am not privy to seeing from here. I have to understand her routine as best as I can, for there is no other possible way for me to know yet. My vision of her is restricted because very little of her space is visible to me, but somehow she is slowly beginning to occupy all of mine.

When you know something in totality, its charm is over, the mystery is lost and the story comes to an end. In the retelling of some of her activities, some repetitive, it is the guesswork that keeps it alive and feeds fuel to the fire lit. How often it may be true in many other facets of life that the pleasure becomes meaningless once the object of desire is attained. The mind then hankers for a new desire, which by its very nature is insatiable. Maybe she knows this too, and has never looked for anything more than her basic needs in life. If such is the case, and I hope that's true, then all the philosophy of life is already her practice. She may have achieved what all of us, in spite of our so-called glories, struggle in vain to find.

Almost noon, and I have finished my breakfast with a second round of tea and a cigarette. I have hardly seen her, barring a few shadowy appearances in the darkness of the areas visible. My selfish motives made me wander out to our courtyard gate twice in search of her in the balcony with no particular pretext to justify it. The overnight clothes have been removed except for her black leggings, her half sleeve *kurti* is missing, and a couple of towels are hanging on the line – a busy morning for her with probably extra chores. How her duties to others seem to delay her obligations to herself. A bath pending, then a change of her outfit, soon enough the last bit of cooking and lunch after having done the laundry. Where and when is she due for some rest? I hope she has an undisturbed afternoon nap and I pray that her sleep at night is dreamless and peaceful. Oh My! How much have I begun to envy her real existence? In some manner, I crave her lifestyle but I have no energy, nor the ability to do the tasks she sets out to do each and every day.

Most of my young adult life was spent on education and then working at my profession; now the advancing years make me nostalgic about my past events. The number of times I may have hurt others and in the process, myself, my affairs of the heart, the romances and delicate flirtations of the mind coexisting with the joys and laughter of my childhood and adolescent days. Some lingering vices, my predictable days here and abroad, yet a sense of calm is beginning to pervade. Some anxiety though, often surfaces during the daily disappearing days without having done much of substance, but then she takes over and I feel the calm of utter rest enjoyable once again.

I saw her at the window; she did too, having no choice, given our kitchen windows face each other and I was standing facing the platform, directly in her line of vision. No smile was forthcoming today; a stern look imagined or real, a quick retreat on her part, a sign maybe that searching for her is totally unwelcome. How much I crave for her wave, a half smile from her, a locking of our gaze, an understanding of language and words amidst the silent gestures. Bit surprised and disappointed was I, surely, for she has more often than not responded without any trace of irritation. A conversation to make the conclusion of this longing being futile, an end to this self-absorbed inspiration derived from her, a search for another tangible reason to keep writing is the feeling I am left with this instant. The end of this vignette, the recollection of another or possibly the dawn of a fresh new one!

After years of procrastination, this time the writing has been much more sustained, prolonged, and spontaneous.

The only material aspect I have noticed of her is her mobile phone. An absolute necessity, I understand, in this city and land, I refuse to possess or own one myself. Yes, there is one provided by my university, given my nights on call and need to use in case of an emergency. I do not know its number - it's a Blackberry, and it is kept shut all the time barring maybe five occasions when I had to use it to answer a page while still on the road, held up in traffic. It is an uncomfortable instrument for me, and talking on it or to anyone else on their mobile phone is as if I am talking to someone on the moon. So I remain the exception in this matter as in many others, not to ever claim that this is the right option for everyone else. Maybe she listens to music on it, in addition to conversing with family, friends, a loved one in her life or getting instructions from her employers. She might watch some television as well, my own evenings occupied by a couple of short serials, which are popular today, watched by my brother. She probably doesn't watch them, as at that time she is often working in her kitchen.

Houston! We have a problem. Just like Apollo 13, as the day unfolded, my reverie was subject to a free fall, on the verge of a crash burn! You don't understand, neither do I, so let's proceed and try to make some sense of it. From the writing so far, if you have read it, you must be somewhat certain that common sense is a quality I do not possess in any abundance, super sense is what my family, relatives and friends think that I do have in plenty - their opinion not mine.

Her kitchen window shut an hour earlier and opened an hour later, a departure from her ritual. Returning from my walk at 7 pm, I found it shut again, lights on the inside, very faint shadows imagined by me, given that the frosted windows do not give any such glimpses, so just an illusion prompted by the faint sounds of cooking heard; a surprise to me, given Indian cooking with shut windows is not what I have seen in mine and her home. But they do have a chimney hood over their cooking range. Obviously my first reaction was to feel that she has become wise to my persistent glances, now probably unwelcome. I consoled myself that as the temperature had taken a sudden jump; maybe it was to protect her from the mosquitoes out in full fervour. Later at night it opened again for a brief period and we saw each other when respectively doing the dishes. Her cleaning area facing the kitchen wall, mine facing our and her kitchen window, so the glance and look was limited. She saw me, refused to look further, no smile, did not acknowledge my customary greeting, backed away from view. I lingered on, stunned at this reversal of fortune, drenched in a silent storm of my own making for a while, before resuming my kitchen duties with a vacant look in my eyes, seeing my star disappear into a deep darkness. She shut her windows as if she had banged them in anger, turned her lights out on me, as if sharply, which is at odds with her gentle nature.

This is now a wakeup call for me, a reminder of the futility of my unbridled passion, the embers now dying, nothing is left but the ashes of my fancied imagination. The abruptness of this cold dowsing on a seemingly hot day was completely unanticipated, for she has often engaged in reciprocal greetings and exchanges of looks with smiles in the past during our respective night time rituals. She hasn't shied away before, knowing she is in full view of me and continuing on with her tasks, unmindful of being seen. This departure from her routine seemed purposeful enough to put a halt to my aspirations which had been gathering some weight, forcing me to remove my blinkers. Tough to digest this change in attitude, yet there is simultaneously a solace that the inspiration was enough in itself and the time may have come to move on to another story and see how the rest of my second month here unfolds.

But before that, if I were to dare read what I have written of this childish fantasy, I will likely trash and burn it all. But given that this is a diary of bound pages, ripping them out is not an easy task without damaging the unwritten pages of the rest. It may take a while to pick up the pen again, but there is a story lurking in the background over the last three years, different and tragic, seemingly coming to terms over time.

And if you are still with me, I hope I will be able to create something good, something touching out of this one at least. If not, I continue to beg your pardon. My joy and sorrow continue to stem from just this process itself, and to me that is quite enough, but there go your royalties, my friend! The previous saga obviously not over for me, just like the survival of Apollo 13's scary return back, safely enough, this too will surface time and again like the waves of the oceans do under the influence of the moon and the wind, then returning to its original stillness, the state my original story is currently hibernating in.

Chapter 3

Akhilesh, eight years old, the light of his parents lives. A bright articulate student, a calm face with clear radiant eyes, innocent and possessing an intelligence and eagerness to shine forth. He, the only child of Masterji and Missus, as I call them, not having ever asked their names, nor do they know my name. Both with barely functional lower limbs, probably affected by polio in childhood. They carve out their living via the means of running an artisan gifts workshop a kilometre away from their humble first floor apartment, about half a kilometre from my home. They get around in a hand driven tricycle wheelchair, their future hopes resting on their able bodied son. Taking pains to ensure his productive schooling, a decent education along with English language skills, leading to a career that could provide solace, comfort and material support in their ongoing years.

Often in the top three in his class, their aspirations are justifiable. Well mannered, often smiling, fresh and clean, taking delight in rides with his father on his way back from school, gleefully stopping at the corner variety store for a treat of his favourite cookie, candy or popsicle. I first saw them three years ago on my walks. They return from work at different times - Missus around 4.45 pm, Masterji, being the Manager, later around 6 pm. They pass through my lane just behind the main road of Sion. The lane is a stretch of 300 metres or so, quiet, serene, shaded with multiple trees on both sides, comprising of nine buildings each on either side. It begins at one garden and ends at another.

The first is the Mata Lachmi Trust Hospital's sponsored garden. The second one was a concrete triangle which, in my childhood, saw cricket games and tournaments played almost every weekend and during holidays or school vacations. Now, since 2001, it has metamorphosed into a very colourful garden with trees, bushes, hedges and blooming flowers almost perennially. It is nicely kept and well maintained by a paid gardener. Around its boundary is an iron railing which does not disturb the senses as it is lavishly covered with creepers and vines and bougainvillea flowers. The boundary is to prevent stray dogs and human miscreants from defiling or ransacking it. So, it has to be felt and admired from a slight distance, which is a bit sad; reminds me that a thing of beauty has to be kept imprisoned for any lasting value, while I always believed that freedom of anything is its own beauty.

I recognise though, now having seen multiple gardens and open spaces in this city, dying from neglect or littered with refuse and garbage, ransacked, vandalised and abused often in multiple ways and means, the protection that this garden has is worth it, even if it is caged. The entry and exit is a single gate locked with key access only to the gardener. This is sponsored and maintained by the "Onward" group as a commemoration to the dawn of the new millennium. The sponsor - an ex-resident of our lane - his generosity adding new lungs to this locality and city. It is also aptly titled the "Securi-tie Garden".

The lane of my childhood memory was a quiet peaceful enclave, a sought after place to make your home. On top it was a one way street with heavy vehicles being prohibited from using it except for school buses and emergency vehicles. This, given there were two hospitals across from each other, the Mata Lachmi Trust Hospital with the offices also of the National Association for the Blind in its premises, and the Sitalaxmi Hospital, a private maternity home now no longer in existence, replaced by a Karnataka Bank branch; a metaphor for health being replaced by wealth.

Today, this lane can become quite noisy, thanks to an ever increasing number of motorised vehicles plying through it, the building of two multi-storied towers, increased population density with exponentially growing car ownership numbers adding to its woes. A shortage of parking spaces on the streets, non-residents often parking early in the day before heading off to the station to catch their trains, can lead to unsavoury altercations and a minor fracas when tempers boil. This happens partly because not only have heavy vehicles started using this lane with impunity, but it is being used as a two way street by many, including even a few residents of the lane. With cars parked on either side, this can often lead to traffic jams, especially during the morning and evening rush hours, creating a cacophony of noise and incessant impatient honking. This just adds to the growing disturbance of the silently noisy human mind of today.

There are traffic constables on duty near the first garden and a police *chowky* along with officers on duty by the corner of the second garden; yet, in spite of this presence of law on both ends of the lane, there seems to be no fear, and an utter disregard for this law with no punitive action taken by the police, often turning a blind eye to this repeated violation. So, I miss the calm obviously, but I continue to ignore and keep walking this lane and beyond as part of my route repeatedly each and every day, at times being accidentally hit on my shoulders by the side-view mirrors of big SUVs, no matter how hard I try to avoid this occurrence by stepping aside. I bear such physical pain silently as I have now often done with both psychological and emotional ones in my life as best as possible.

The Mata Lachmi Garden too has now been beautified by a local Corporator. It is busy with children in the mini playground, young adults using its gymnasium, the elderly using its circular 50 metre walking path for an evening stroll, as well as benches for them to rest on, and the long standing non-functional fountain in the centre. It is open to the public for a few hours every morning and evening. It sees congregations of young and old, servants, maids and cooks from the houses in this lane. A place to unburden their problems and woes, seek sympathy from each other, give voice to their complaints, discuss delicate issues, exchange gossip and happenings of the private homes they work in and other relevant conversations, as well as organisation of labour class unions and their meetings. A new phenomenon has occurred over the past few years. I see a rapid increase in the amorous meetings of teenagers and adolescents, not only in this garden but at the bus stop just outside its gate, on parked motorcycles on either side of the street, shielded from their parents' eyes, as none of those I see are residents of our lane.

It is a sea change of scenery in all its aspects from the time of my growing up here. Gone forever it seems is the unadulterated pure joy of street cricket, *gilli-danda*, cycling, skating, and pedal scooters without a care or worry for injuries during evenings, weekends, holidays and vacations. Gone too are the simple street vendors of food items, candies, musical instruments like the *Ektara* and flutes, the merry-go-rounds, the horse rides and the multitude of minor yet real joys of growing up in this lane, which are now just part of a dream and a memory. At least there is one saving grace - the two gardens provide for a breath of fresh air in this increasingly polluted exhaust fume lane of today.

I feel as if the essence of my lane has been lost, or is it that I refuse to move on with the changing times? Then why does it feel as if that essence is released as a fragrance every time the young lady living across from me steps out into the lane?!

Anyway the lane begins at the first garden and ascends quite steeply up to the hospital some 75 metres in, then steadily rises, reaching its peak just before my building. It then flattens out and carries on up to the second garden at a level gradient.

I first noticed the Missus struggling, using all her strength to negotiate this incline. I started to help push her wheelchair and giving her arms a well-deserved rest till the corner grocery store across from two temples. This was repeated often on my walks, even helping Masterji whenever I had the opportunity. Over time, I began to look forward to this exercise of mine, often signalling them from a distance to stop and wait till I reached them. They too, in turn, it seemed, liked meeting me in the lane.

And as is often the case in many such situations and scenarios, conversation begins between strangers with an exchange of basic information and a mild curiosity at play; it becomes a means to listen to each other's work, hobbies, interests, habits, family life, members and so on and so forth. Often I used to help them up to their home when in the midst of a conversation, detouring from my usual route and then returning to it. It would be rude and impolite to leave the thread of an unfinished conversation hanging. They would often express regret for making me come all the way and ask me to carry on and not complete the journey for them. I always declined unless we had become silent before reaching the turn to their home or if they had to stop at the vegetable vendor or the grocery store for shopping. That is how I found out where they live; their first floor dwelling was in a building with no elevator. I learnt how they tackle the staircase where they store their wheelchairs and other aspects of it. In the past, they lived on the fourth floor of the same building! I cannot imagine how they managed to live so far up with no elevators or any other facilities for the disabled; not that living on the first floor is much easier, but it has to be somewhat better than living on the fourth floor.

This year I see them later than usual, my walks beginning much earlier and their daily timings not certain. I had, however, not seen

Missus for many days in December 2011, when there were fewer times that I ran into them. It was only later that I learnt of the reasons. Masterji has an assistant, Ganesh, who works with him, is ably bodied and now helps him all the way, the exceptions being when he is unwell, away in his village or running a stall for them at exhibitions.

As if their struggles were not enough, life dealt them another crushing blow - in June 2011, Akhilesh the light of their lives, the feet for their physically challenged condition, and the shoulders for their old age, was tragically snuffed out within a few hours of an unfolding nightmare out of the blue.

It was an ordinary day. Having finished his homework, eaten dinner and watched some television, Akhilesh felt a bit uneasy and went to sleep. He had been otherwise well, a completely uneventful day with no indicators or warnings of the disastrous events to follow. He woke up around midnight with fever, a bit disoriented and started having fits; seizures in medical terminology. Unable to fathom this sudden change, and limited by their being differently abled than most of us, scared and obviously worried too, his parents called upon the help of neighbours. A taxi was arranged and he was rushed to a private nursing home a kilometre away in Sardar Nagar. He continued to have seizures for what must have seemed like an eternity to his parents. Despite many efforts there, his fits continued unabated for over an hour or so. An ambulance was summoned and he was taken to the emergency room of Sion Hospital, also just a kilometre away at most. There, they succeeded in finally stopping what is called a refractory status epilepticus - in common language, an unrelenting prolonged state of fits. Akhilesh was now unconscious, almost comatose, was put on artificial means of breathing support, a ventilator and multiple medications. In addition to the precipitating cause triggering this episode, the aftermath of it led to most of his systems failing, leaving him in a critical situation with many complications. In spite of all efforts, he never recovered, remained unconscious, did not breathe adequately on his own and all attempts to revive him were in vain and now futile. Akhilesh died within a few days, his light extinguished forever from their lives.

A harrowing experience, a tragedy of enormous proportions, no matter which way you look at it. A dazed couple - their grief and anger shaking every aspect of faith, belief, trust, and hope. An utter sense of despair, helplessness that took a toll on their health, especially Missus' in all dimensions. Masterji bravely tried to carry on living, supporting the precarious condition of his wife, putting aside his own sorrow and dejection. With stoic acceptance he found refuge in his work and his memories of good times with his son and as a family, even though troubled by the deafening silence engulfing his home, his evenings and his sleepless nights.

Can one ever imagine the quiet horror of their lives? An only child, the delight and joy of their lives, the vibrant evenings of togetherness, all shattered into pieces. Each shard of his memory piercing their hearts, each wound more telling than the original one.

Missus was almost catatonic. Her mother came to share in their grief and help them in any manner possible, though herself elderly and not in the best of health. Missus began to lose interest in every activity of daily living; she lost weight, barely ate, was almost imprisoned in her home, unable to go back to work inside or outside her home. She carried the burden of this tragedy on her body and soul, from which recovery seemed distant and precarious, her husband and her mother trying everything possible to nurse her back both physically and emotionally.

Masterji, steadfast as ever, burst into tears when on my yearly visit in December 2011, I naively asked him about Akhilesh on my first meeting with him in the lane, completely unaware of the tragedy that had consumed their lives. He broke into painful sobs, saying, "Sir, I have lost everything, I lost my son!" He recounted the horrifying tale of their experience, still crying, his pain palpable as if it had just happened. I, at a loss for words, was completely stunned to hear of it. A gamut of emotions paralysing my speech, the deep feelings leaving me shell shocked. Anger and despair at the failure of my profession or a realisation of the helplessness and humility at this senseless act of destiny or nature - it hardly matters which one! I just managed to gently touch his hands, and bent over to hug him, all else left unsaid, except for the tears that ran from my eyes to mingle with the never ending ones of Masterji. Ganesh was with him, his pain, his efforts to hold back his own tears, that sight and the meeting and its words often flash in my waking hours and sleep time as vividly as the first time I experienced that moment.

Over time, each and every day I waited for them and helped them reach their home. I would offer words and gestures of solace and comfort, and medical explanations as best as I could to ease their hearts and minds. I kept the one sided conversation going so as not to trouble them in having to respond and relive that event again. Each of them lost in his or her own thoughts and feelings, I, slowly uncovering their silence with bits and pieces of Akhilesh's memories. I hope with such meetings, recollection of their past joys and events shared together with the gentle touch of tenderness, it may have made their tragedy bearable, if one can ever bear such a loss and carry on with life. I guess, though I cannot know for sure, not being a parent myself, and with no desire to be one. But I think and feel as one to all the new born babies under my professional care, as is often remarked by their parents. The grief of a parent in losing a child must be insurmountable and one of the greatest tragedies in life.

As if this were not enough, Missus' mother took ill and died, adding to the trauma, loneliness and grief she was already trying to come to terms with. Masterji's family came to help tide over this second tragedy and help regain some balance. They too, then had to return to their respective lives. Missus started going to *satsangs* (prayer meetings) every Sunday afternoon inside a home in our lane just two buildings away from mine. It is host to a number of women, young and old, either having had a loss or other problems of life. Masterji, often accompanying her, then strolling the streets for a few hours before escorting her home. She slowly regained her poise, accepting the dual losses, and began working again half time, recovering a semblance of a so-called normal routine of life. Her health started to recover, she gained some much needed weight and now on this trip I see her working full time again. Her smiles, a few of them at least, have returned when I run into her and help her across as before. But behind every smile there doesn't lurk pleasure or happiness, just like behind every tear there isn't always anguish or sadness.

What is the courage and determination that drives such a recovery, or is it mere resignation, helplessness and the understanding of having had no choice, nor ability to control and change the circumstances and the resulting tragic event? A deep surrender and an abiding belief or faith must be at the core of what appears on the surface, at least to be a re-established life amidst the ruins and routines of daily living. Surely, there were lingering doubts about the circumstantial and medical events that I tried to explain, help dispel, emphasising the severity of Akhilesh's illness and the likelihood of significant impairments should he have survived the catastrophe. That has, to some extent, brought a sense of closure, if ever there is such a thing. Closure is a word bereft of much meaning, designed to provide relief and comfort, easy to utter, much harder if not impossible to personally experience and accept. A compassionate demeanour with tenderness, love and affection is the only soothing balm I could provide to a pain deeply embedded in their hearts. The scars both visible and invisible, for which there exists no definitive cure for this couple.

In this country, human life seems to have very little value. Yes, in war and riot afflicted countries the same truth applies, but this country is not engaged in war with another one, and is presumably at peace. As someone has said, too often peace is just the preparation for another war. And so too, in India, there continues an internal strife, akin to being at war with itself.

An overburdened public and exorbitant private health care system often bankrupts families unfortunate enough to seek its attention and help. On top of that, there are untold incidents of various social and political ills, physical and emotional abuses, the absence of any safety nets - all of it you are well aware of and no point in my repeating them. All of this collective tragedy touches us only momentarily because it is far removed from our conscious selves, unless it is an individual tragedy striking close to home, then the shock and trauma lingers for a whole lifetime. Their tragedy unique in its own right is unfortunately a tragedy occurring far too frequently in many families known and unknown across this land.

Compounding their heart-wrenching losses is also the multiple challenges they face on a daily basis from being differently abled. Mumbai, the premier metropolis of this country pays lip service to many similar families. They remain just as numbers in the census if lucky to be counted, their reality defined by a piece of paper or a card such as a Unique Identifier or Aadhaar card, the latter being a lofty ideal, its promises remain to be revealed or to unravel.

I wait to gather another story. Maybe looming in the near future on my walks, bus or train journeys or farm visits with Murli, my dearest friend in India, or from my exploration of the multiple tribal villages in its surrounding areas. I have been on such journeys, staying alone for just about a week at the most at a time for the last three years. I have seen from close quarters enough issues, some of them I hope to make a little difference to in the times to come, having voiced my intentions and broadcasted them to the Universe. Many events remain engraved in my memory, waiting to see the light of day, and for the reader, a cause to turn off the lights as this dreary monologue lulls you to sleep.

A couple of days break, hibernating thoughts. A stimulus gave shape with this old saga resurfacing as I knew it would. Like the churning of my memory, the bubbles rising from the depths of my turbulent ocean, leaving just froth on the surface, a calm and still mind proving to be ever so elusive.

Chapter 4

Yesterday, I was with Murli at his farm, my morning spent reading, when I had the longest glimpse of her. I noticed her graceful long neck, possibly adorned with a simple delicate chain, but I am unsure of it. She was spending time with her potted plants, waiting as I found the arrival of a couple of gardeners. They whisked a sizeable amount of her plants away in a cart, presumably for pruning, cleaning, replenishing the soil, decorating, and otherwise embellishing the pots and plants, and lo and behold, half her garden was emptied while fresh thoughts kept leaping into my overflowing mind! I could gather from a distance, a few snippets of her instructions and discussions with them in her native language, Marathi. I was a bit surprised at the tone of her voice - it seemed shrill for such a delicate, graceful attitude of hers; the sweetness imagined by me was missing, or was it just the case of sour grapes on my part? Her complete indifference to my attention is palpably clear to me, but this story continues to take leaps and flights of my fancy without reaching anywhere. My disappointment is beginning to provoke a re-examination and with almost 90 days left of my visit, this saga seems to be heading towards a sorry and dismal ending.

Young, somewhat dark-skinned, almost cocooned within the walls of her employer's home, I have barely seen her outside enough. I wonder about the deficiencies of fresh air and sunlight taking its toll on her as she continues on in her years. Too early for her to realise the impact, she may be a bit ignorant of this basic preventive measure for her health and wellbeing, agreed though that fresh air outside her home in this city is a debatable and contentious point. She works long hours, as do a lot of people I guess, probably sleeps quite well most days and nights. Each of her days not much different from any other: aptly too, as I suddenly realise that my days have been identical as well. My life is habitual, possibly monotonous but never dreary, and I find a sense of lazy comfort and contentment in the passing of each day.

Anxiety is likely to surface once the threshold of March 10 dawns, and it will create a sinking feeling like on many of my past trips, that April 10 night will no longer be spent at my home. This idyllic, blissful holiday will then rapidly progress towards its inevitable termination. Suddenly this 'doing nothing' phase will end and a multitude of other duties, obligations, and pending tasks will descend like vultures, pecking at me, beckoning me to revisit my list of 'To Do Things' before time runs out on me, and then a mad last minute scramble will ensue. The final renovations on my home, and with it, my aspirations of searching for a retreat away from this mad city for myself and family and friends pending, and many other chores trivial and meaningful leftover to be accomplished will leave me with a sinking feeling, wondering what really happened to my holiday!

With each passing year, this burden of feelings is accumulating slowly and steadily, goading, maybe guiding me towards the fancied goal of an extended, never-ending sabbatical from working for a living. Welcoming it feels, a phase in life filled with such seeming joys without much worries of the world. Maybe this trip is beginning to look like a prelude to achieving that state and a test of how long I can go on like this without any boredom. Either restlessness or searching for ways and means to occupy my time productively as it is called or expected by others needs to be eliminated first, before I can truly find my way through this fantasy of mine.

My farm visit over with, I returned late at night, and after a quick small dinner, I retired. On days of such visits, her windows are invariably shut when I return, barring an occasional exception. The next day was the Maharashtrian traditional Makar Sankranti day, also associated with the Gujaratis' Kite Flying festival every year, and symbolised by a greeting of '*til gud ghyah, gode gode bola*', ('take this sesame and jaggery offering; speak sweet and sweeter words') when you meet any Maharashtrian. I was on my way back from my brother's home across the lane, after my ritual of spending some twenty-odd minutes talking to my nephew while he took a break from studying to eat his lunch. I sit on their swing and scan the three newspapers in ten minutes or less while he prepares to chat with me. He regularly without fail comments on the moot point of my asking him for the papers if all I do is just keep flipping the pages without reading much of any news. It is like the flipping of my memories, hoping that by my inattention, none of them will register, stick to the present moment, carrying me off on a tangent. Wishful thinking though, it will likely take years to do that, if not this whole lifetime. But I have been trying deliberately to forget my memories for the past two years and slowly, steadily a change is becoming barely perceptible. I was late returning by fifteen minutes, as we both watched a tennis match at the Australian Open while he ate, finishing the sports pages of the Times of India.

Crossing the lane, I noticed her at 1.30 pm in the courtyard; she seemed to be heading out. Their second gate was open but a pile of *reti* (black sand) and cement may have prevented her from exiting through that gate. She turned around, came out of the main gate and ran into me returning home. A golden opportunity presenting itself as I wished her greetings for the occasion in Marathi, she wished me back with a radiant beaming smile in Hindi and carried on. A coincidence, my delay, her exiting the main gate, the heart vainly wishing that she had done so on purpose after having seen me crossing the lane, retraced her steps, for only through the main gate could she have met me, and I her. I do doubt the veracity of this conclusion, just my imagination wanting this gesture on her part. The day moved ahead; I went for my usual walk, but now carrying three miniature Swiss chocolates in my pocket, knowing for certain they would begin melting. I so desperately wanted to cross her path again, greet her again, this time with something sweeter than mere words. Not being a cook, *til ladoo* (traditional sweet) was not on the menu of my offering!

I walked for a while, but there was no sign of her returning. But then, around 5.30 pm or so, as I don't wear a watch, I saw her at the second garden on the opposite side of the lane when earlier she had gone towards the first garden of the lane. Seeing her from a distance, I crossed over, just had a moment as we were about to pass each other, with she giving no indication of wishing to halt. For me, it was an opportunity to engage in a conversation with her that was rehearsed multiple times in my mind, if she could ever spare a few minutes of her valuable time. I bowed with a '*Namaste*' and offered her the three miniatures, having myself stopped in front of her. She smiled sweetly, said only one, and took it from my hand without touching my palm. I barely had time to apologise for it being melted, but she was already past me. In addition, I had no chance to reveal the meaning behind the gifting of the three chocolates either. It is an old ingrained habit from the days of courting my future wife, now ex-wife, trying to imply either that, 'I like you, I miss you or I love you' depending on the situation. Well, the interlude over, I continued on wondering when did she return home to step out again in the opposite direction, and how did I miss her coming back, knowing I had prepared myself as best as possible not to miss that moment.

I finished my walk and returned home for my Monday evening market visit with my *bhabhi*. As I left with the cloth carry bags, I saw her in the kitchen window, her face turned towards me. I apologised profusely for the melted chocolate. She said that she knew, and had put it in the fridge immediately. I too had forlornly put the remaining two in my fridge. So ended the mirage, the evening progressed as usual. I saw her a few more times during the respective tasks in our kitchens, mine less onerous, obviously. I completed them leisurely with interruptions, gazing across for her look, this obsession of watching her ordinary appearance unfathomable to me, having given reason and rational thinking the solemn, proverbial heave-ho!

If you aren't, I remain quite curious, anxious too, to find out how this unfolds and where it ends - the ending, likely not pleasant to my liking, but the thrill of this unexpected apparently one-sided romance enough to last a very long time for me.

I also saw both Missus and Masterji, wished them too, and to complete the Pandora's box, ran into Pooja and Jinal, my so-called adopted nieces of sorts, whom I first met three years ago in the Kikabhai Hospital lane, and had exchanged a few bits of soothing words when I had found Pooja crying incessantly. We have since exchanged minor pleasantries on many brief occasions. They know of me as an uncle from USA, having forgotten that I am from Canada, but do remember my profession. Pooja has requested and taken my number and email address on multiple occasions, promising to call or write, but hasn't done so. I haven't asked for hers though. Pooja and Kunal, a young teenage love affair, may have now ended as I saw Kunal just a few days ago with a new flame by his side. Well, multiple stories coming home to roost, yet this visit going by far too fast for my liking, given the fact that I have basically been doing nothing.

It is, after all, a sabbatical from my sabbatical! After what seemed to have been a reconciliation of sorts, we have now again exchanged the bare minimum of looks unaccompanied by some smiles or meeting of the eyes from her side. Except when I was standing at our gate waiting for my nephew to come down so as to wish him for his exams, I found her hanging her spotless white leggings. So, I naturally greeted her and asked her about her wellbeing. She smiled, but said nothing. This is the same about all our encounters during various moments of the day - far too similar, non-progressive, beginning and ending in an identical manner, stuck somewhere without any indication of either a progress or a retreat.

By and by, I notice a bit more about her. Like this morning: a small stud in her left nostril. I barely get a chance of a wordless gesture, a wave, a smile, a lowering of my head and closing of my eyes in respect, before the meeting of our eyes finishes in a bare flicker without allowing even time to blink. My imagined hesitancy of her and my own, a few minutes of conversation are desperately needed to tell her of my adoration, my writing, my use of such innocuous encounters and their real purpose. Maybe also clarify if she feels I am staring at her and prompting her to return the look, her sixth sense seems to be well developed, but more likely may be the fact that no one wishes to be stared at. I need to refute such a perception, if that's the case in her mind. This incomprehensible longing for a young unmarried woman, though starting as a catalyst for my writing, I am glad to know myself, that it has completely and absolutely honourable intentions. I can't emphasise that any more forcefully. Yes, I have other longings, and someday, when this reverie rudely ends, a storehouse of my likings will keep this writing going. Not using up all my bullets at once, as the saying goes. And given my elephantine memory, not likely to be forgotten or lost over time, so long as I remain healthy. But they are from the past or maybe a future source; she is very much my present, she makes me feel alive each moment of every day!

Chapter 5

Like many housekeepers of her nature, and unlike a majority of us, her mornings appear extremely busy, maybe just like any lady in the house with a family. That work continues to be unrecognised, barely rewarded in most places around this world. But that is not the point I wish to argue about; many others have done so in vain. She doesn't get around to her own bath and change of attire till 1 pm at the earliest, having begun her day at 7 am except on Sundays when she begins it around 7.30 am, the household mostly asleep, given a holiday from outside work. I keep wondering if there is contentment in what she does, or is it because of lack of choices. At times, I have seen her look quite happy talking on her mobile; hopefully she has an equally charming suitor pursuing her and I hope he has the eye to see what I have seen, and a similar longing for her effervescence. Sometimes, she may be talking to family or friends or taking instructions from her employers. Suffice to say, I have not seen her go out on any prolonged outings of her own, or spending time for herself on eating out, entertainment, or just an aimless walk. Is it really a life of never ending drudgery, of working for others, or is it that she has found the real essence of life in its ordinariness? Serving, often with a smile, I have never seen her angry or talk with irritation or a loud manner suggesting any displeasure. How different she seems to me, from most of the educated and well-to-do people, whom I have to meet and deal with regularly amongst family and friends alike.

Each day of mine experienced in its similarity, hers imagined by me to be the same also. Yet it is different from one day to the next. The barometer of my gauge is unable to understand the play of light and shadow, the fullness and absence of her glimpses. Yesterday, the accidental vision of her twice on my walk, brief errands for her, for me, an opportunity of interrupting her, lost as I had to come home and open the door for our cook. I had no time to follow her and arrange my imagined conversation as she was soon back in her kitchen. I was left wondering about this coincidental miss, a warning maybe of it not being the right moment. My hesitancy pronounced, yet umpteen times rehearsed in my mind. I dread that such a meeting on a street so close to our homes may lead me to stutter and scramble, my feelings may take over the carefully imagined words of my mind and it would all come out horribly wrong.

It may all be one-sided, so this delay may be a blessing. Subtle nuances of her appearances every day, her occasional acknowledgement of my gestures allowing me the opportunity to unburden both the heart and mind, yet scared to examine the true nature, the motives behind this imaginary life of two completely diverse people. Separate in all aspects and likely to ever remain so, that is the only intelligent conclusion of this relating, a relation-free relationship, as the Holy Geeta suggests.

Distance is the key, though thoughts of her are quite near, her absence is the real presence. This craving insatiable, seven weeks into this story, neither moving forwards nor backwards, just oscillating in the middle. Time ticking away, the joy of my mornings remaining constant. However, in the evenings, I am unable to occupy myself sitting on my ledge, the night dawns for me, and I go to sleep with the vision of her window opening by the time I wake up and prepare for the first cigarette of the day.

It appears a quieter day today. It is a day our plants are not watered and it seems like a rest day for hers too. She has not followed a proscribed routine as yet, surprising me occasionally by sneaking out in the evenings, given her almost regular routine of the mornings. This perceived unpredictability adds mystery to her being. Saw her briefly, her back towards me, going towards my school in the evening. I had finished my walk, and was waiting for the market visit. I followed her, hoping to overtake her and request an exchange of words. I noticed her on the mobile, suddenly a peal of laughter with gay abandon, I chose not to disturb her and watched fascinated, was there also a touch of envy? Perhaps! Although by now most of you may feel that I have disturbed her enough.

Everything about her seems stunning, long strides, slim tall appearance with dignity. I realise even though short, her hair is abundant, thick and rich, anchored by a simple round band. For a moment I forgot that I have always been enchanted by long luscious flowing hair, enamoured too by a traditional Indian *saree* on a lady - both make my heart melt away. I cannot suppress the longing of running my palms through such hair from the crown to the tail; the feeling is extraordinary, at least in my imagination.

I circled back and await another opportune moment. I doubt that she ever thinks about me. I often wonder, what about friends her age, someone special in her life even, but have never seen her meet such a person or share intimacies with them. Living her dreams in apparent aloneness, catering to her employers' family each day with few exceptions ever. Time is running away; she is as patient as ever, demanding nothing, seemingly happy every moment. I have never seen in my limited glimpses of her any signs of despair, sadness, dejection, anger or tears. Her sleep, a short afternoon nap and a long one at night is likely very calm and peaceful. Where does she find the time for herself in her waking hours, for I have yet to see her doing nothing!

I had a fairly busy evening in the kitchen, three instalments of cleaning and drying. I refrained from lifting my eyes, forced myself not to. But just for the tiniest fraction of a moment my eyes met hers looking across and it was over in an instant. By the time I sat for dinner, windows shut, lights out. How quickly she ends her day, or so, it seems to me, a ghastly reminder too, of how my day has ended. Just daydreaming, fortunately not dreaming much at night, making an effort to drop her from my mind each night and beginning with her afresh in my heart each morning.

January 31, a prolonged break from my writing, as work once again commenced in my home, allowing scant opportunity to indulge in the continuation of this desire. Not to say that there haven't been further encounters, initial ones unfavourable. A chance meeting in the evening, my attempt nullified as she had to go back home to cook dinner. I could have accompanied her, something prevented me from suggesting it and the moment for decisiveness was missed. I am unsure if her response was a snub given politely in the face of a genuine reason but it felt like a sudden brake to my runaway feelings. Yet the friction resulting from that encounter could not steal away nor still my thoughts. For a few days now, sitting on the balcony entrance steps, I try avoiding the look, deciding instead to see where it would lead. Either the train would get off the tracks or begin to move forward again. Either me waving a goodbye to this fantasy or hoping to see her reach out with her hand towards mine and climb aboard towards a destination that is distant, uncertain, maybe unreal also. A journey leading nowhere but to a heartache when reality clashes with this illusion of mine!

I started walking again looking to the earth, leaves, or sky, avoiding meeting anyone's eyes, trying my best to not let my flirting heart rest on another face, except when I see the wheelchair tricycles on my path. I time as best as possible to be near the first garden close to 4.40 pm using the clock in the lobby of the multi-storeyed tower.

By the way, I saw Masterji on Sunday in the Kikabhai Hospital lane beaming with joy. He had won the first prize in a local carrom tournament, though he himself doesn't possess a carrom board, just a nice tournament striker made by Ashwin, weighing 15 grams, protected carefully from any damage within a case. I was happy, proud of his achievement, and congratulated him effusively. It brought back memories of my childhood summers playing carrom in our courtyard during holidays and weekends and during vacations, from morning to late night. I was accustomed to winning more than 95% of the games I played, singles or doubles. The teas, breakfast, lunch, evening coffee all a part of the losers' treats to the winner. It's been ages since I played it, though our cottage in Georgina has the necessary equipment.

He went home thanking me for my interest and wishes. Later I ran into Missus returning from her *satsang*. While helping her I informed her of her husband's win, maybe giving her an opportunity to get a treat for a well-deserved celebration, such moments now likely few in their lives having lost someone so near and dear. I now wish I hadn't told her. But it had come out spontaneously as an expressive feeling of my own joy from it. I realise it would have meant much more to her, the news coming from her husband. His delight in surprising his wife with this piece of good tidings, I unintentionally might have soured, stolen from the rightful bearer of it. My deepest apologies, it was an utterance out of sheer pleasure, part and parcel of having become somewhat close to them to share in their joys and pains alike. They are now busy preparing for their sports day in mid-February, the National Wheelchair Games. I can see their enthusiasm for simple pleasures that the educated elite may have well forgotten. Masterji, being the manager, has lots of tasks and extra work resulting from hosting this event on top of his already busy schedule. Yet, I see no trace of any complaint or sign of the pressures involved. Cheerful he is - full of energy, like a child enjoying a new toy.

Since that event, it seems that I have been seeing less of her inside and more outside as she has been going out on errands almost twice every day. At an odd time I was going somewhere, saw her hanging clothes, she smiled of her own accord and my heart skipped a beat! I was thrilled, but wondered whether my distancing myself a bit had prompted a conciliatory gesture on her part giving a glimpse of her interest in me. Two days in a row we seem to be more in tune with each other. Today, I asked about her plants when I found her in the balcony hanging clothes, taking the initiative soon after that smile of hers. I asked about her watering frequency, her knowledge and care of them, her hobby, her home in a village near Ratnagiri and plants from there. Surprisingly she then sweetly pointed out a plant of *patra* leaves from her village - *Patra* being my most favourite Gujarati *farsan*. My *bhabhi* takes enough pains to make them often on my visits each year. *Patra* leaves initially used to come from Murli's farm, but of late no such luck, so *bhabhi* buys them from Matunga market. She kept answering my inane questions with utmost patience as I wished for our conversation in her courtyard to never end. I introduced myself. She replied she knew my name having heard it many times from Arham's greeting me loudly and often from his home upstairs, above her flat. She is also aware of my profession. I too was correct in recollecting her name having heard it just once by chance when her employer had called upon her. It had registered in my mind and now stuck like glue in my heart.

I then stupidly asked for her mobile number. She replied why? Stumped at her answer, with no prior rehearsal for it, unable to tell her the real reason in everyone's viewing, I lamely attempted an excuse. I might want to talk to her about plants or ask her if possible to bring some seeds when she was visiting her home in the village. She got back to her work. I retreated slowly ruing at what could have come to pass if I had carried on with my real intention and let her know of it right away.

Things seem to be picking up the pace, fools rush in where the wise fear to tread. I can sense a bit of the former in myself. Leading this along, unsure if her responses are out of mere courtesy, deference to my status, aware of my being much older, keenly aware I am a visitor, a migratory bird for a short time here, only to fly away abroad for the better part of each year. With time running out on me, I wish that she too has some similar feelings. I wait to see how the events will unfold, a confrontation with her being the major dilemma in my life. I am relishing that prospect in some manner and dreading the implications of it also. She in her simplicity is beginning to attract me more and evermore; the heart is now gathering strength to fight with the mind!

This isn't my typical verbal flirting. It seems to be the beginning of an ominous occurrence. Maybe the less I am in touch with her presence, the farther she will recede from my heart. What do I have to offer, except to bring in her life an adventurous romance, a courtship? Having observed her daily routine, with very little time for herself, I hope I can bring to her an entirely new experience in life. I assume that she has no other secret admirer like me but I sincerely do wish that presence for her. But I am never going to ever remarry, nor ever have a child. So, she is already being denied the due status of a wife and the fulfilment a woman achieves from becoming a mother.

However, logic doesn't know nor can it understand love. This may just be an infatuation, but there is no intention to touch her physically except to watch her in her simplicity, gaze from a distance and if opportunity presents then look into the depth of her eyes. Maybe she has just become a vehicle to indulge in a romance after decades for me. A surrogate, a substitute. Given that her close proximity is accidental and a play of chance, plus the fact that I get to see her almost every day.

This morning saw her return from her garden, her smile half hearted. Yesterday's conversation had revealed that her voice like her is gentle and sweet. Why I thought of it as shrill or harsh before is not true. Or is it that my listening to it directly addressed to me, strikes like the musical notes of a melody in my being? I crave the sight of her constantly again, a sense of peace pervades within and around me. I long for a conversation again, having made a hash of the unexpected gift of the previous one. The more I wish for it, the less certain I am of any good reason, but the feeling envelops me and seems to create a faint glimpse, a vision of the words I would like to convey if she ever agrees to my request for a dialogue. I will likely remain dumbstruck in that event, hoping the silence or a meaningless conversation conveys the message of the meaningful.

Two months remaining, this story hanging on by a slim thread. The more the weight assumed in this one sided reverie, the sooner the thread will snap. In spite of all this, there lurks a desire to know the outcome sooner rather than later. And at the same time, my procrastinating nature and obfuscation is paramount in letting this drift slowly, allowing no hiccups, no jump starts or sudden halts. The gentility of its progression carrying a fragrance via a soft breeze constantly blowing, caressing my hands and letting the words appear on their own and fall onto these empty pages.

A deep anxiety probably lurks in my subconscious self, that a culmination of this affair, satisfactorily or otherwise, is best delayed, any outcome promising nothing good in it at all. It may only serve to put a full stop to this writing that has resurfaced after some years now, a crutch to unscramble yet support my romance along.

Today's glimpse suggests the possibility of letting this image develop slowly with care, with some distance being kept. A step back from this craving of a conversation lest I end up smothering this genuine flowering plant. A woman working at her chores with few breaks for herself, in complete awareness, lost deeply in her tasks, each day identical to the previous and the next, no trace of anger or sorrow. At the same time having seen and heard her occasionally talking to others in her courtyard or in the lane, her smile develops spontaneously. I am touched with a bit of envy, trying to gauge whether half smiles, full smiles are different for me or just a habit and part of her friendly nature. Not having seen her close at hand for more than three occasions, I find it difficult to know if along with the smile, are the eyes and gestures similarly habitual, or are they suggestive of some indifference towards me. There is an urge to know this soon and at the same time a fear that I will lose it all.

Never having had the courage of a gambler, risks of such nature are alien to me; the throw of the dice futile knowing already the ultimate outcome. This is mere indulgence, yet I allow it to run its course. Events will happen, deeds will be done, and I hope I can remain just a witness to her charm, her beauty, and her presence, and cherish this unforeseen happening in my life.

Maybe she is one of the pegs that I hang on the clothesline of my romance. A change is happening. The utter naturalness of this lady is far more appealing than the artificially decorated women I have been seeing until now. Unfortunately, some of them remain oblivious to the fact that they possess an inner beauty that shines forth in the absence of makeup and similar such cosmetic usage, choosing to paint it over just because society expects that to be the norm. She, without any of these props, is quite comfortable in her own skin. This then is just the furthering of my romance, more like romancing my own mind with my heart, hoping to achieve mastery over my monkey mind, changing the centre of my existence, my day-to-day living.

This trip is different in many ways, patience rewarded with the third stage of my home renovation being undertaken, just like my own self or no self: to move upwards from the mundane, esoteric routine towards a state of fresh calm, the peace of silently doing nothing much. Anyway, the past two days since that meeting haven't been good in the sense that I imagine some reluctance on her part to engage with me. The glimpses no longer frequent, a refusal to observe, the quick disappearance of her face, while her hands linger unhurried at tasks. The vision of a new outfit when she came home late last night but the tasks in the kitchen over much sooner than I had imagined, windows shut by 9 pm. I rarely venture out beyond that time. But around 11 pm, I had to go for some emergency medicines and noticed lights on in the front, possibly the television also on. Maybe I have been mistaken all along regarding her nights and sleep times. Early to bed and early to rise may be a half truth. Maybe, because it was a Sunday evening, she may like watching a television movie or just my imagination going bonkers. For, in fact I had not actually seen her face, only shadows, maybe part of her employer's family only. No vision of her this morning as her window opened late. Just now our own hired help has come to water our plants in a new blue and pink outfit and a black sleeved top. I assumed I would see her again in her new outfit but she came out in her three-fourth sleeves top, and never glanced across, with her hair dishevelled, a tired slow walk to water the plants. I missed her returning to see if this story has further legs or if it has crawled to a full stop, period!

No matter how hard I try to avoid her thoughts, my mind comes back to chewing on the same thing over and over again. Maybe she is there as a lesson for me to search for a glimpse of my other half within myself!

If so, it is a rude and improper approach to give any more hints of my attraction, maybe infatuation, or lead her on only to leave her halfway. An unsubstantiated assumption, given that she hardly harbours any feelings similar to mine. The pull and push of this affair, if it can ever be called that, making my days go by even faster, which is then the last thing I want. Savouring every moment, realising that not doing much has suited me just fine, never bored with my activities, rather inactivity or time simply spent, the promise of a new unknown journey beckoning.

Yesterday I introduced myself to her employer, spent a few minutes talking at his balcony window, his wife listening also. She came out to water her plants at the usual time, though I wish it were because she wished for me to see her. I was going out, looked at her, murmured a gentle '*Namaste*', I carried on and there were no looks the whole day. I realised much to my chagrin that she had been away all day. I went for my seventeenth day ritual of a brush haircut after my walk, showered, watched television, had two fresh lime soda drinks and a few snacks and later felt a burning in my stomach. An aftermath of eating multiple chilly 'bhajias' (Jalapeno pepper fritters) along with cashews the previous night. Both are my favourites, but I probably overdid them. Then, empty stomach all day, a late afternoon tea which does not suit me anymore, may have triggered the episode. Antacids and Pan 40 tablets twice, relief took a long time coming, tossing and turning, finally asleep late after 1.00 am. Woke up at 6.30 am, a call to Brooklyn's family - a precious pre-term patient of mine who was discharged from the NICU on this date a year ago – to wish her for her homecoming anniversary, the household renovation workers not coming because of a social function in their community, so it is a routine Sunday with my usual activities.

Each day like in nature, hot and cool, sunrise and sunset, waxing and waning of the moon, wake and sleep cycles is how this romance is moving. But, like the moods of nature her responses are always fresh and unpredictable. The barest of acknowledgements, then out of the blue, a full smile and return gesture to my greeting, a reply to my asking where she was off to. This bud has seen the sunrise, yet hangs around refusing to blossom and open its petals, no fragrance released yet, biding its time patiently, uncaring that the appreciative person's time is at a premium now. Yesterday, her hands appeared like a dance *mudra* (gesture). When I see her hands now, I often can't see her face, and vice versa. Subtleties about her so appealing, her vision and her thoughts come to me unannounced on my walks, even when reading, yet not so in my sleep or in my minimal dreaming. The day finished, a new beginning to the story each morning, ending with the closing of her windows and switching off of her lights. Nothing lingers around to trouble my sleep.

This is a friendship worth having, for other than that there is no other relationship possible. This connection is enough for now. Building layer by layer and crumbling into bits and pieces each day, only to resurface again, wounded. Whether stronger or weaker is difficult to say until the structure takes shape or becomes just a castle in the sand. Maybe this phase of mine is like that of a child gleefully absorbed in play at the beach: Building figures out of sand that disappear as the tide rushes in, the child taking eternal delight, both in its creation and dissolution, fulfilled in the activity itself, returning home without any regrets or memory of its unstructured, fully attentive play awaiting with innocence another outlet for its unbound energy. The next day it remains uncertain as to where its mind, heart and being will find an unexpected joy.

So precious must be this feeling of not carrying a burden or regret of how its play was over the previous day, a new fancy waiting in its wings to grab its attention and leisure time. I find it difficult to absorb myself in another activity. As this game, if it can be called that, remains incomplete, no winner or loser yet, unequal contestants, my weakness is in her strengths. Both of us unlikely to gain much except misery one way or another; even if this ends in a fruitful manner, the taste may remain bitter for both.

This mystery is self-created, a simple rational exercise will cut it into pieces, unravel it like the peeling of an onion with nothing left within. I know it, yet refuse to do it. So is it that the mind is suddenly cooperating with the heart till it builds up its own latent energy to overwhelm, overpower and crush this bud, leaving only the thorns intact? Either way, a wound will remain, a scar indelibly etched, imagined or real, but worth having. This pain is a lot sweeter than any of my so-called pleasures.

She returned, a tired look; I was writing standing up. Few people lingering in her courtyard, the raising of her eyebrows. But a good sign at least, that she engaged in whatever manner she did. I doubt that she has the time or inclination to nurture such soft feelings similar to mine. This, my own indulgence, but I am grateful to her for allowing this interaction; some indifference during the in-between times covered up. Nothing much lost, nothing much gained - the scale often balancing, but without any hints, tipping one way or the other. Good that it still has some life in it otherwise it would be dead if static. A half stride forward, a multitude of steps back, yet there seems to be enough to create some substance for my next two months here.

I suddenly realise that her tired look could be one of resignation or a tiresome acknowledgement of the fact that there is no escaping my attention as we both aren't going anywhere anytime soon. There is a glimmer of hope knowing she had quite a busy weekend of work and her look may just be a reflection of her exhaustion or the so-called Monday morning blues. Page 61, and 61 days left to my departure, a mere coincidence or the harbinger of an unsavoury exit from her life!

I can feel the ending looming, yet it has been wonderful while it lasted. Since the morning look, the whole day spent thirsty in search but all seeking in vain; resting alone in acceptance, with denial as its shadow. I find today a double whammy staring at me. I just found out that our hired help will be moving with her family to another place away from our building and so, will no longer be able to tend to our plants. This decision stems from a termination agreement along with a generous financial compensatory package between her family and our society. She has been kind, bubbly, articulate and recovering from the tragedy of an unexpected stillbirth at term about three months ago. She loves our plants and takes care of their watering with tenderness. She offers suggestions to enhance further my *bhabhi's* already aesthetic and beautiful landscaping and the variety of them. She wishes to make watering and cleaning around them easier and more accessible. I pray that her life in new surroundings is better and her story also will surface and get expressed in words at some time or another. But, I forget, you may have not read this at all or left it halfway and unlikely to do so again. So remote then is the possibility of your knowing what I have written so far or what is to come about the stories lurking around me.

Each affair of the heart ends with a disturbance, true, yet there is a feeling that I am learning to live with it, absorbed in the moment as best as I can be, allowing things to be as they are, more or less of their own volition.

Each episode arising, staying with me, biding its time, occupying my mind and heart, not immersing itself totally within, running parallel to each other, never reaching its goal, it remains as a distant, unattainable horizon. But the journey occupies me, allowing the ability to enjoy my aloneness. My conversations are dropping off, trivial day-to-day events losing their hold. My walking and reading is increasing over time alongside with this writing, though without much substance for the reader, yet thoroughly enjoyable for me. The heartache is real, the story imaginary and elusive, a fiction created by me, and its ending determined by circumstances.

No look today from her but I saw her. The same morose look and slow walk back, eyes downcast. Wish there was a way to go running to her, give her a hug, and express my feelings in silence close to her. She has no idea as yet I guess, maybe just a hint of my increasing obsession as per her thinking, but to me it is pure adulation of her. Letting this drift, a period of absence away from her when I go stay at Murli's farm and travel the villages around on foot in a few weeks' time, away from her, amidst nature, in solitude, it may bring a clarity of its own and confusion no more. I care deeply for her as is quite obvious. Why? That's a stupid question to ask of myself, for it seems to be stupidity par excellence! What if she gets to hear of this from me? Her responses, if any, are likely to be sharp and reactionary. Doubt she will ever have the time to listen, and even if she does, very unlikely that she would be patient enough to listen to my continued inner talk. So it would end there and then, this heart will look for another romance to amuse the mind.

While so many of my previous wants and desires have fallen off the radar, this unrequited love is deeply seated in the state of desire. This one seems to be more masochistic, but there is an aura of thrill and excitement, without the burning generally associated with passion, for there is no lust and no heat in it. A distant companionship, a long-distance friendship is the only likely possibility if any. Whether this feeling remains a year from now I wait to see, or will it disappear like one wave into the other? Even if it is a figment of my imagination, she is acutely aware of some of this, and her on and off moods either imagined or real, may backfire, a game of testing my affection or resolve, or waiting for a crucial encounter for me to finally lay it bare on her plate. I doubt that this feeling will ever be lost over the time that remains of my stay here, most of my day revolving around some of her movements, my expectations enormous, and her attitudes unclear, ambiguous in the totality of her response.

An attempt at choiceless awareness is failing, stuck on the rungs of a ladder that I should never have started climbing in the first place. A push or pull is the only option, to either crash or realise and reach the happening desired. A monotony of her days, a reflection of mine too - different yet identical in many ways. Come to think of it, monotony is the bane of human existence, with few scattered moments of unexpected events making one day different from any other. Very few would have the experiences of newness every day, they do happen but we are never there to take notice of them. Fewer still take delight in nature's basket of freshness, creativity, dissolution and renewal every second of every day. A lesson visible yet unseen, the sounds heard yet not listened to, the mad rush evident even in my life of cultivated patience, though it seems on hold on this trip. The more the craving, the less peaceful is my sleep; each day, spilling over into the next, nothing significant occurring.

Somehow, I too do not possess it in enough measure, and am unable to develop my sensitivity to any reasonable extent to enjoy nature's bounty recurrently. Yet, there have been moments of pure joy, albeit fleeting, that leave no indelible memory of why and when. But after many years, this is my most untroubled visit, with few anxieties, fewer cares, basking in the state of doing nothing much of substance. There is the beginning of an acceptance that this leisurely state will likely crumble the moment I go back to resume my real work abroad. How in tune I have been with my two separate lives that it leaves me questioning which one of them will flow into the other and overwhelm it! There isn't an iota of boredom - small household tasks accomplished with gaiety and patience, contributing what I can to family life here, easing burdens in the small measures that I am capable of.

Chapter 6

The lady watering our plants seems buoyant today in contrast to yesterday when she was feeling dejected. On the surface, an easy acceptance of some life altering event, a change in residence and lifestyle, hopefully for the better it seems, as her mood reflects, carrying on as if nothing were amiss, a light conversation with me, as is her habitual routine.

Today is a day when just a few of the plants need watering. This enforced feasting and fasting decided by us for them makes me think about it: Isn't it better to water all of them daily in small amounts, instead of alternate days? Agreed the weather is cool and pleasant, evaporative losses at a minimum. But like humans and most animals too who drink water daily barring camels in the desert, why are plants cultivated indoors treated differently? Yes, in the wild, in villages and towns and streets in the city, no one waters them daily. They depend on seasonal rain or dew, or sink their roots deep down to draw upon the earth's aquifers to quench their thirst and survive. How do they tell us when they are thirsty? Either from their withering away, when it might prove too late to resurrect them, or in their drowning from excess, when also it is far too late to salvage them? What is the right balance of catering to their needs? The lesson probably is that, when we humans decide for a part of nature, we will probably be more wrong than right in our judgements. Equanimity is never achieved by us. How can a part decide what is necessary for the whole of nature? Maybe just one of us among millions lives a balanced life, so how can our acts ever be? Doing less or overdoing is the realm in which we move constantly, basking in the glory of the flowers and fruits arriving or in the regret that in spite of our care and attention, the plant failed to blossom.

So too, is this relationship. How best to nurture it along, a delicate treading of the waters, sink or swim or just let it float? Then resistance will be eliminated, the story will move forward, guided by an unseen force, the will of the universe acting depending on whether this meeting is pure or base in its desiring. But desire by its very nature is of the mind/ body and as such 'impure'. So is this a desire or something else? Is it a need or a want? Even if it is a figment or rather a total creation of the imagination, an incurable fantasy, a fruitless occupation, or unrealistic indulgence, I find it productive. Maybe just a consolation that while doing nothing, this makes it all worthwhile: a rational explanation for the irrational.

I just missed seeing her as the painters arrived. Nothing with her has yet been gained so the loss does not appear tangible. The timing, odd for any greetings, even if I had seen her, given there were so many members of the morning staff around. Is there then a fear of decorum, courtesy or the fear of being judged foolish, should my inclinations become evident to everyone? She will soon be on her way back, the miss being repeated as my brother is standing by my shoulder. I will refrain from my customary greeting. It hardly matters, for she barely shows any interest now. She hardly ever looks my way, unless my gaze sends the vibration of a perceived stare that immediately makes her look towards me from the subconscious discomfort generated. But when I got her noticing for sure without any fuss, her brief smile sure began. I lowered my eyes and smiled in reverence, and she smiled some more. Today her walk is a bit brisk; just a hint of something that now surely occupies a bit of her mind while it occupies most of mine. When I say this, it assumes my mind, its occupation of debating pros and cons of this, the heart I know has no such room for debate or division. This cheers me up. There is no sadness, there is nothing much I know of her, and this is as pure a feeling as I can ever have. I just love seeing her. Distance makes the heart grow fonder – a saying of much repute, but here there has never been a meeting of that sort at all.

In two months' time, the distance will be almost infinite, so a taxing time lies ahead; let me enjoy it while it lasts, for no relationship is eternal amongst humans, barring maybe friendship. But relating with her... Ah! That's a different matter altogether. This writing of course is as monotonous as is most human life, but from an ordinary mortal like me, how could you expect anything different?

This is just the projection of my mind. I perceive what I myself have chosen to create: an illusion, deceiving nobody but myself, the futility of which is evident but not understood. In this 'lack of desire' hides a desire, the efforts to still my thoughts now in vain. But a time will arrive when it will reach a crescendo, a peak, and the writing will end, reach a valley, an abyss, for a new seed of thought or a feeling to take hold, and a different kind of writing will emerge. Maybe of short pieces again, like in my previous years, a sigh from the heart that may occasionally deserve a gasp of appreciation!

Does it matter? I indulge my thoughts; most of the writing is for me. But having shown some of my earlier ones to others, there must be a deep seated desire for it to be acknowledged, commented upon, praised or criticised. So there is already an impurity behind this, a motive, yet the writing has often been purposeless this time, but then so is life!

If everyone eventually does leave everything behind, the old, wise, and experienced person replaced by a new, absolutely blank slate, a *tabula rasa*, it is unfathomable that we still do not understand or accept the beauty and essence of both life and death. Just a clear look at nature is enough to reinforce this lesson, but we have lost our eyes, ears and touch to penetrate this reality. Anyway, there have been many others who have said this often before: this isn't an attempt at plagiarism. My hand runs freely, the gap in translating my thoughts and feelings into words imperceptible, just like the gap in between our breathing in and out. This writing is unable to still my mind, so in a way it is an equally unproductive exercise. Since I seem to have plenty of time on this visit, maybe this is just a pastime, someday for me to read again. To edit, chew and eat up some of the words, create a different form, maybe more readable, less verbose, repetitive or monotonous, but equally without much substance. It may emerge and time will continue to march on quite indifferent to my attempts. Time is the greatest enemy: it hardly cares what I do with this anyway.

At least this writing is fluid, spontaneously melting, for that the heart is grateful to just a pair of hands in a window! That seminal vision allowed this to surface during a month of otherwise aimless activity, continuing, eagerly awaiting the next chapter of disappointment and disillusionment. Something will happen as it always does, unpredictable in its time and content which will discard this activity from the periphery out or sink it into my centre of which as of yet I know nothing much about. This is still very much a doing on my part, an unrealistic expectation of enjoyment, a titillation of the mind, yet there is the whiff of an elusive fragrance that only I can sense as yet!

A busy day running errands, medical issues in family, patient consult, long walks and a routine that got disturbed. Plants and pots issue, a bane of conflict between family and members of the society, stemming either from jealousy or envy, using the guise of rules and majority opinions. Ridiculous it seems when the world is in desperate need to make it greener as the conscience of humanity is seemingly poised to take a radical turn thanks to the commitment of the young generation. Our garden, so carefully planted and nurtured by my *bhabhi*, is a beautiful sight to behold - soothing, and generating a calm that disappears as soon as one steps out to our lane. Dressed in the garb of regulations passed by majority, they want us to remove a sizeable number of them and keep a bare minimum in the courtyard. They are carefully arranged so as not to impede the activities of children playing or any movement of people. It is a classic scenario of a situation where those who have only thorns in their lives want to create trouble for those with flowers.

How do you tell my *bhabhi*, who lives across from my place and has cultivated a similar garden in her home environment, to remove a lot of her carefully tended plants from our courtyard? The pain of separating them from their brethren and from herself is like a mother being told that the children she carefully nurtured with love, affection and utmost care have now got to be removed from her sight, given away to others or to be destroyed if there are no takers for them! That pain is bound to create an anger that is unmatched. Ask any mother about such an option and you are likely to face the ire and fire of a woman enraged. Given the pressures we have faced from some neighbours, this circumstance is now of sufficient alarm to create a rift within an overall happy family life. Misery then takes hold, builds up in small doses, old hurts resurface and can lead to the manufacture and escalation of a rift, the source of the problem though originating outside of us. I am becoming more and more removed from it, hoping for an easy resolution, yet my irritation can also erupt unawares, though in smaller doses than before.

The roots of these conflicts are shallow and easy to uproot. But if done during moments of anger, there is the real danger of damaging the precious roots that have allowed the family's tree to bloom with both flowers and fruits. Then the plant carefully tended to, could be lost. With that comes a feeling of despair and frustration, a sense of futility takes control, preventing the ability to plant a new seed, given its outcome will be tragic like the previous ones, thus allowing weeds to take over.

Who am I to give advice or propose a solution, when all my talk at times is labelled as philosophical argument? The art of listening is lost on both sides thanks to an indifferent framework of regulations. I try to rise above from these very meaningful conflicts for the one whose work is about to be forced into submission from the pettiness of others. So my cultivated aloneness and patience gets disturbed, selfish now of my moods and time, I then react inappropriately. The ripples of such disturbance now much smaller, and not far reaching as I bring myself back to my balancing point of equanimity momentarily, only to find another disturbance lurking in the wings to serve as a trigger. Such is the life of any family subjected to minor incidents from within, and major ones from the outside. To paraphrase something read long ago and I may not even have it rightly, from Tolstoy, I believe it originated: "Happy families are all alike, unhappy families too; just the ways and means differ superficially." I may have got it somewhat wrong, but it doesn't matter as long as you get the underlying meaning better than I have been able to put into words.

I am learning to live in this milieu, just like I have been doing abroad, though this home is far more preferable, yet my work is much more of value abroad I believe, though I may be wrong about that too. My escapes here are my own, in my solitary activities, but some skirmishes and apparent conflicts can surface and lead to easy viewing and listening of others in the neighbourhood and by the hired help in this house. I am, at times the culprit, suddenly it brings home to me the message that "I am the world and this world is me".

Human nature being what it is, there is obviously a vicarious delight in any neighbouring family's verbal spats. I too have experienced it, hearing a lot of those happenings from neighbours all around. They soon become a source of gossip and amusement, an entertainment of sorts, a vulgar pleasure in seeing other families struggle through moments of unhappiness with a search for an elusive truce and peace.

Anyway, this morning I am met with cool, rather almost total unresponsiveness on her part, when just yesterday I had the benefit of her smiles. Maybe she too has heard the minor commotion of last evening, though it was resolved quite amicably in a very short time. In her simplicity, yet each day arduously hard for her, she must be left wondering as to why people, who have so many materialistic pleasures and loved ones around them, can on occasions have so little good of themselves to give to each other during moments of inevitable upheavals in any family.

More and more I feel myself distancing from the so-called educated, civilized middle and upper class people and find her down-to-earth existence charming and elusive. An urgent need to know her, spend time with her (not that I haven't already, whether it be in my imagination or in my words) seems presently impossible, unless a magical change in our relation occurs. If I was to profess my feelings to her, I can only assume that she will be surprised, more likely shocked. But it will have to be done in some way or another. Though I don't see any real opportunity for it emerging soon enough, given the constraints to her apparent freedom, and limited occasions presenting themselves to me till now. Like many times in the past, I will be left ruing on the day I leave, of having left this unresolved. I can never find her alone long enough to bring matters to a head, cannot find a boat to travel from my shore to hers. This river of my imaginary flight is a barren desert which no boat can ever hope to cross. It is not from lack of trying. My intentions are now becoming clearer to her, my searching her out quite obvious by now. But I can understand her aloofness, her distancing. She has no real clue about what is churning in my heart, what a drastic choice I am on the verge of making... I doubt I will ever find her within time to tell her.

So I suffer a sweet sorrow, this writing giving me the joy I can't yet share with her. No two days with her are similar now, her responses dropping a hint and taking it away the next time. This game of hide and seek appealing I guess, for I have no other choice but to play by her rules. My cards mostly open for her to see, but my hidden Ace she probably has no knowledge of, or of what I may try to reveal through it.

Why do I feel a sense of loss at losing, or the feeling of gain with just half a smile of hers, when in reality I don't have anything from her except my own troubling imagination? Dreams and flights of fancy seem more real, even when awake, knowing it was and is a dream; still I cling for its continuance. A peace pervades every moment I see her and gets disturbed when she doesn't reciprocate.

The more I write the more it is reaching alarming proportions, the delay in reaching a finale not in my hands. The outcome, if successful, will subject me to enormous ridicule from one and all.

Do I fear the consequences of either her denial or her acceptance? Either way, there is going to be "a trembling heart on the line!" Will I stand the test that looms in front of me to take this to its finality? Is this writing a surrogate marker of a seed of courage trying to break open in its own time and season? Will it bring forth a plant, for I have watered it enough with the juice of love and care? Allowed it the space to manifest its destiny, neither smothering it nor allowing it to wilt from lack of attention? OR will it die rotting?

Where is the guarantee of any of such outcomes? All I can say and hope is that I have given almost all of me to it. Effort, attention when opportunity arose or was manufactured by me, part naturally, part accidentally, but none of the circumstances have been with either deceit or cunning.

This is as pure as any of my romances can get. A reminder of a past one: that too did not come to pass. So I dread repeating the same story again. This time however, there looms a large handicap of untold reasons staring accusatorily from my mind and its logic, but the heart waits trembling. The beating of its wings waiting to take flight only to realise it still remains imprisoned. She hasn't allowed any space for it to reach her with the message. To take a bit from Marshall McLuhan, and paraphrase it, if the medium is the message, its life is doomed from the very beginning. This bird, except for its own mother has no other support to fly. It knows nurturing from just that one source. Also a deep trust that existence will have its way with it, the decision rests in its ways, in its law, it will reach either nowhere or everywhere. It is no longer unconscious of what awaits, now aware enough to understand that it has achieved some and the rest will unfold as per the will of existence.

Is there anger looming from the destination? Is the suffocating absence of space, the freedom to fly for this message, deliberate, chosen, on purpose or from ignorance of there being a message waiting to reach her? Why can't I accept the fact that the destination's response too is the act of existence itself? Shall I find comfort from that knowing or do I want to explicitly hear of it? Is it an opening or a closure that I am seeking, is there a solution to this problem or none? I am reminded of a wonderful saying and I quote from memory: "If there is no solution there isn't a problem." How comforting it seems - some words on paper. In reality and experience those words time and again are just empty, purely philosophical, neither existential nor experiential.

The problem is "ME", not an event outside of me, the solution too resides within me. Yet it is one that will need, if not support then at least not even a semblance of hindrance on her part.

Chapter 7

How often does life take an unexpected turn, a pleasant or a painful surprise, or a seminal event from which there is no turning back? February 8th was once such day for me. It happens to be my cousin sister Bena's birthday in San Francisco, but that is beside the point anyway.

Two months of constant chatter of my mind, the churning of emotions in my heart all reduced to a silent gesture, condensed into a single atomic *sutra*!

All the meaninglessness reduced to the bare essential message expressing a finale. Just three words expressed in sign language using my fingers and palms.

It was an odd unexpected moment of running an errand for family when I saw her hanging up clothes for drying. She smiled of her own volition, I stopped in my tracks. I conveyed a silent message without a moment's hesitation or any thought or regard for the consequences or complications that might come in its wake. It all happened so spontaneously and instantaneously, the only doubt being whether she received and understood it or not, the delivery taking a few seconds only. I did not wait to see her response or reaction; can't explain why I chose to carry on and not wait for it. Now that I think of it, the coward in me must have surfaced. She will need as much time as I have to deliberate upon, but there was finally a sense of relief within me.

Two months of uncertainty reduced in an instant to a certain uncertainty!

Twenty hours since that fateful moment, I have not seen her. Busy with my renovations, then my usual silent greeting while going to a function in the evening, but unsure if she saw it. The torment over, the torture now begins. I will be away all day at the farm, so the story and its suspense will linger on. Weekends do not provide much possibility of finding her alone, so next week might bring some evidence of her judgement. My silence has conveyed all it possibly can. Whether her receptiveness is astute, insensitive or ignorant remains to be seen. She can give me some hints if she chooses to do so, for I am available right across from her at least this morning.

SHE SMILED! Oh My! On her own, coming out to her garden looking at me or for me it seemed. I would have missed her as I had gone inside for a second but had arrived back on my perch in time. My world now suddenly brighter, heart skipping a beat, delight and joy emanating, I can feel my face relax and take on a glow. A deep breath, for this may just be the beginning of an unknown, troublesome and arduous journey. She will return soon. Do I keep writing or wait to solemnly greet her? I just wish I could rush out to her and say, to hell with the world and its judgement or condemnation or acceptance. A sentimental fool and now a confirmed idiot too! Suspense is killing me, the next minute or so is *make or break!*

It has all come *crashing down!* She never looked at me again while returning. I just stared shocked in disbelief. These ups and downs are now a suffering impossible to bear. The day ruined, not much time today to question her as I leave for the farm. The minutes and hours will be interminable, time will stretch in agony. This affair is very, very different from any of my previous ones - so much sweeter in the pain being generated within me. Will this heart break finally or will it be left empty of any feeling of romance forever? Is this the necessary culmination to the hurts I may have caused others, now returning back to me in more than adequate measure with compounded interest? In this loss there may still lie an unexpected gain, but I do not see any of it at the moment.

I have to learn to live with this loss too. The totality of her beauty and simplicity has sunk deep into my recesses. What began as just a play of her hands has engulfed me in the flames of her spirit, in which the only offering will have to be my love, unrealised but reached and rejected.

A solace has to be found; there is no balm to soothe my wound except by her grace. So many metaphors, allegories, and old sayings come gurgling up, but you have heard or read them often before.

So silence remains the epitaph, an obituary of sorts, for the one who has risen in love and fallen to dust! Her shadow lurks across this imaginary ending at the moment. I was chasing a rainbow of my own creation, but now I am left with just a mirage in the desert. The greenery just outside my window, hers now barren, then why have I been continuing to reach out?

This longing is impossible to evade, and a stern refusal within me of coming to terms with her hesitations. Her denial neither absolute, her acceptance minimal, if any, her limitations obviously many towards my flattering advances. A much demanded sacrifice of her youth and her dreams.

How to convince her that this love is deeper, purer, unblemished by any passion of degradation, this caring more than I have ever felt! She has no clue, nor have I given any reasons for her to believe in me, plenty of doubts naturally for her. This is an unchartered territory for both of us. A prayer is the only answer, or rather a sense of prayerfulness towards existence. Let the decision, the destiny rest in its bowels; so easy for me to say, yet so difficult to accept it in totality.

How her momentary presences and absences bring turmoil into my life. A small boat constantly tossed by minor waves. Will it leak, take on water and capsize, drowning me or will it take me ashore? In either event, I remain mired in sorrow or in exultation, the joy, happiness, peace and any such other buzz-words unlikely to come, for the many hurdles that would have to be crossed if this journey takes me home.

Never have I written like this, and it is unlikely that it will ever happen again. Most, if not all will be considered trash and burnt along with me, exit unceremoniously as will I.

This one desire, still very much a desire, may be an impediment to my future growth, if any, or bring in its wake a state of mind in which there is no longer any desire left! I place a big onus on her; she is young, but in my estimation, growing in maturity everyday by leaps and bounds. Never have I come across anyone like her.

Is she for real, could she be the source to recognise the inner woman within me?! And if so, then I can become a complete human all by myself!

A sinking feeling takes hold of me as I ruminate upon the first half of the last sentence.

IS SHE JUST THE CONCEPT OR THE IDEA OF WHAT I SO DESPERATELY LOVE IN A WOMAN, OR IS IT THAT I JUST TRULY LOVE HER?

IS SHE THE SOURCE FOR THE ROMANCE OF MY MIND TO BECOME A DEEP LOVING OF THE HEART, LEADING TO MEDITATION OF MY BEING, AND A PRAYER TOWARDS EXISTENCE?

This sombre mood lingers on. Suddenly I feel more alone in my aloneness, which has often previously generated the peace I have felt in my solitude of many years. Then why does it hurt so much? Why is something dying within me? Why is someone else the source of my loving, living or dying? Unless, of course, I have imbibed her to such an extent, that I now call her my very own being.

No scope of a meeting of the eyes now as she goes to do the washing, leaving me drenched in the rain of my silent tears. My well will never be able to dry up, and sorrow overpowers it more than any joys. The source of its crying is inexhaustible, hopefully eternal. Sweet is this drenching, refreshing is its feel, a birth each moment to the here and now. This writing though - an absolute contradiction of the above-mentioned words. Moving in this duality back and forth in my imagination without a tangible source from my memory, how long do I have to nurture it before I can say, 'Why is the pen in my hand like the feelings of my heart, not silent enough to stop?!'

Just one morning after, this story is on its last legs. I stand crippled, unable to fathom this turnaround of events. *But haven't they been manufactured by myself?*

These pages over many mornings can be summarized into no more than a few bullet points, then *why all this fuss?!*

The conclusion is easy to read, and impossible to digest; yet I will have to swallow this bitter sugar-coated pill.

So here is what may be considered the sum and substance of my days:

1 – I am on a sabbatical from my sabbatical

2 – Walking, reading, writing, doing household chores and running errands, basically amounting to "*doing nothing*"

3 – I may have begun to reclaim my golden childhood again!

4 – Time spent in the final renovation of my home that commenced three years ago.

5 – *A subtle vision of a pair of hands captured my heart and gave birth to a plethora of stars, yet left the sky of my heart empty!*

6 – A final *sutra* in silent gestures gave voice to this emptiness.

7 – *No echo returning, the language of silence absorbed into the void.*

8 – *Yet, I feel richer than I have ever felt before!*

So this, then, is the goodbye. The 58 days now left for me add up to the unlucky number '13'. And that is the paramount feeling coming home to roost.

Chapter 8

February 9, an early morning walk having woken up at 3 am, sort of making up for the missed walk the previous day, having been away to the farm. The body was missing its routine three to four hour walk, so the mind awakened it. I missed seeing a bud open into a blue and white bluebell flower, but noticed it after my shower. The opening may have stirred dormant longings and given voice to it, as she was unexpectedly found trimming plants in her garden on Sunday evening.

The meeting never materialised. Yet the words passed from my lips, the message conveyed in all sincerity and compassion for her, and maybe a bit for myself too. My words only ended up dying in mid-air. Certain I am, very certain that there is no lust in my loving, yet summarily rejected was my declaration to her. A day's flower that withers as evening comes. Words always make a mess of expressing love – neither the silence behind the words, nor were the words understood by her. In her rejection I still find this relating more enduring.

Romance finished, replaced with caring and a sense of friendliness towards her, even if it is now one-sided. Her simplicity and delicate grace with just a hint of rudeness, rather, an abruptness in her tone may have ordinarily registered as an insult, but it did not feel that way to me. Her life is presently far more precious; there are no desires for an aging man's wealth. Once again, it affirms my faith in her day-to-day existence, a trust in the humanity of the labouring class.

In the so-called dying of my own flower, I can feel its fragrance lasting forever. The flower wilting but alive this morning as I went out for another walk. Maybe the lessons are being learnt, but the distancing from her makes her feel even more near and dear to me. I have carefully avoided looking for her or at her window. I haven't troubled or caused her any harm, but the silent looks and gestures have stopped from my side. Some moment, I will bow down to her again with folded hands in an apology of sorts and also with deep gratitude for the one sided entry of her into my heart. She will remain a presence, a reminder of a fertile imagination, a declaration of the truth that this heart is still alive and throbbing, not dry, still overflowing with feelings, able to laugh and silently weep its tears!

This writing, having begun in a large part thanks to her, it will have to continue in its free flow. Either it will take inspiration from other events or from raking up the past and the reopening of my memories. I know full well, she will surface again in unguarded moments, drowning and salvaging me; a reminder of the continuance of a glorious loving phase, untouched by the heat of passion or desires of the body and mind. She became a need and source for my writing to emerge again. She is left knowing that I had been loving towards her but has no idea of the ways and means, except that the ending has been of her choosing aptly made clear to me by her.

She has jumped from the so-called beginning if any, straight to its ending, the middle having remained a path unknown to her, nor does she seem to care about its loss. No regrets, no blame, no guilt really. She remains alive as a spark in a field of embers that has left much ash in its wake, the smoke drifting up, fogging the mirror of my heart. But those dying embers will continue to keep the fire alive. In spite of her denial, I have offered her blessings for her life ahead. I haven't had the chance to offer a hand of friendship, but in my obvious caring I hope she has understood another message too. If ever, unfortunately because of circumstances or otherwise she needs any help in life, I hope she will seek out a friend like me who deeply cares for her, and I hope that friend will be me.

Love exists with form and without, the unsaid part of it I hope she has felt and if so, given any image to it of her own choosing.

Five and a half hours of aimless walking, looking down at the earth, in the calm of the dawn, the blazing heat of the afternoon, attempting to still my runaway mind and a stuck heart, avoiding all attempts to look at her - but she kept popping up on and off giving rise to waves again of an imaginary explanation should I run into her accidentally. She would never stop to listen though, it is a tough ask that seems so remote in its occurrence.

This morning, an interlude again. She refused to look, though I am sure she noticed me looking. My earlier decision not to do so, swept away as I knew it would be the moment I saw her again accidentally. It would be natural, instinctive for her also to look and surrender to that feeling, unless she has exercised restraint and control over her gaze. In her rejection of me, she refuses to go away, the next eight weeks a trial of my love, a test of my ability to forget and keep praying with blessings for her future life wherever it takes her.

Her brief words dripping with irritation will ring in my ears, yet there is no noise in them. I can remember much more of her silence from that fateful encounter than her harsh words.

If this love is true, then it must and will keep flowing towards her. If existence gives a breeze to carry any vibration either of my thought or feeling then it must attempt to reach her time and again, because no energy is ever lost when released into existence. Yes, given that she will refuse it, it will return back to me in full measure and more, for anything that touches her, touches me too now. Not knowing much about her, if she has so firmly settled within me, it is now impossible to know myself either!

But she exists as a block, a layer difficult to unravel, in that missing will rest the domain of an unfulfilled life.

She hasn't understood the gestures of my overflowing heart, nor the clarity and transparency of my gaze. Maybe words are what she needs. To hear, that I love the totality of her simplicity without any thoughts of her physical body. Given my age, that kind of longing has been slowly and surely disappearing over many years from my repertoire of needs or wants. Surprisingly the flower in our garden has stopped its wilting, and in its demise might be the ending of this rapturous affair. Or is it being sustained for a while longer as my love continues to shower into the atmosphere surrounding it? I dread knowing myself to be a romantic that when this ends (and it surely has, hasn't it) or after I leave, am I going to substitute this with some other? My heart says no, this time it won't, at most it will settle into a romance with Nature. This is just the preparation for the ultimate love and remembrance of the kind of writing with which I indulged myself on Georgina Island or at Murli's farm some years ago.

February 13, two days after my late uncle Ck *mama's* birthday, new air conditioners and roller blinds being fitted at home, only a short walk possible. It is the wedding anniversary of Arham's parents, Hetal and Kunal, and I have Dairy Milk chocolates for them. My wishes are not for their marriage but for living a loving life together for almost a decade, with a child who has become the apple of my eye. His loving voice greeting me, always with joy and delight on his face, most people remark how much love he has for me and me for him too.

Digression is my nature; so to come back to what I was saying, writing except for poetry is often an exercise of raking up the past either from memory, knowledge, and experience, or from the projection of the mind into the future. Though both my memories and feelings of this illusory romance are heartfelt, however much I argue otherwise, both past and future are of the mind and not the heart, which should know only the present moment and act from it. It is genuinely only from there that each feeling is eternal and timeless and often compassionate like this one now. I wish I could convince you and also myself that what is being written is mostly from the heart and each moment overlaps into the next. Either moving forward or back, but very much anchored in the axle of the here and now. It is like a spider's web, a continuous process of weaving, stretching, pulling together, reaching to create a semblance of poetic imagination in this laboured prose.

Well, February 13, my romance is definitely over, but one sided love remains, dissolving itself and I am left wondering, what next?

Chapter 9

If I were to start looking again while walking, this fickle imagination of mine will find another simple woman to adore and feel for, now that I am completely uneasy about the artificial, painted and decorated women I occasionally end up seeing on my walks. Is she so much more appealing because of her monotonous hard work all day, a constant reminder of my monotonous lazy day, or is it because she is close enough and yet distant from any more experiencing of her? Avoiding the look, hoping to see her hands and face fade away from my memory, will I be able to picture her again similarly in my waking hours?

Can't remember any dream of her barring a rare exception and one more time when my sleep was delayed. If so, then that would be a thought that came to me when I was awake and not a dream come up from my subconscious mind. So awareness in sleep is missing, as also in my dreaming which by definition is a lack of awareness anyway. But am I dreaming less or am I completely unconscious and in a deep sleep? Which of these is better for me in the long run is rather impossible to say at present. Also, I have to learn to leave things to any chance encounter, not solicit a meeting and see if this story has a final nail left to slam into my coffin. If so, hopefully it will happen before my time here is up!

This morning is now day five and my flower has a companion close to it - a bit smaller, yet similar. So though I remain alone, my flower is enjoying its coupling. A smaller bud too is seen as if a potential child is yet to be born. She can't see them all with a car parked in our courtyard but may be able to see the couple if she looks. But she has consciously avoided looking in our direction since some time now. If that is so, then off and on she must think of me, it must occupy her mind though not her heart. Given in case she finds me still looking at her, she will have to glance away abruptly. All of this likely makes for more nonsense from me.

This is the meaning of a fertile imagination - a ground laid to waste, no seeds left to bring the greenery, flowers or fruits, only weeds mushrooming, pulling them and watering them at the same time...

Written on Feb. 14: I saw her in a once previously worn new black top again, as if meaning to say, your Valentine's Day is dark, though I am still glad even with this negative connotation. An early evening with Dk *mama* and family at Bombay Gymkhana, work at home completed. Arham and parents visited to wish me on this occasion, and I returned the wishes with three Dairy Milk chocolates. A sense of joy is released within and around me when I see young children playing, occupied totally in their activities, all purposeless and in the moment. Three days in a row these visions keep visiting me and I suddenly recall reading about the practice of meditating at a cremation ground. Meditating upon death to give value and meaning to life. Why choose only that?!

Here is meditation upon life, watching a young child of three years or so, in its purity and innocence, unburdened by worldly knowledge, with the very essence of life unsullied and unpolluted. Virgin and fresh, encompassing all the moods of nature as it's very own. Why not meditate on the beginning of such a life, forget the middle years and take a quantum leap into the meditation on death or dying instead?

These two polarities are all that is real, eternal in meditation, but transient in its appearance of a continuing cycle of birth and death. Choose one or the other and you will miss both! A choiceless awareness of both is the only wisdom that leads to the understanding of the essential and the meaningless, and the futility of the rest will then drop off on its own. A desire for it will still be a hindrance, accept and surrender to this essential reality and one can be nowhere and everywhere. This piece of writing is rushing at me from my mind, truly speaking, not from my being; for I have yet to practise doing meditation at all, but it is the answer I am knowingly looking for and missing eternally.

I take utmost care to not look up while cleaning utensils unless I am certain intuitively that she isn't in the line of direct vision. As I struggle with this, my fight is slowly petering out, less and less are her thoughts as I force my mind away. But how can the mind control the constant fleeting thoughts within itself? Either it is trying to dominate the heart or the heart is slowing down on its own accord, knowing its feelings now have to be kept buried inside. Either it is due to a state of resigned helplessness or the realisation that this was doomed from the very beginning. The ending written inexorably in its very origin, yet the middle has been a painful beauty to behold.

Time is rushing by quickly, less than eight weeks remain. A multitude of tasks and nitty gritty piling up. Soon will come the urgency to stop this madness and regain enthusiasm to finish both the essential and trivial jobs pending. Yes, there isn't yet the anxiety or worry; somehow I have managed to reach a state of mind where such matters don't bother me much. If it gets done, it's okay, if it doesn't then who cares! An oxymoron, as it is me who has to do or not do them. In this decision is a sense of peace in a way, as events unfold of their own bidding. Looking now for just one event that is fresh and new each day more often than not suffices for the rest of my day's sustenance, which is damn right monotonous when viewed by you.

The two flowers remain in close proximity, exchanging the gentlest of touches when the breeze stirs them up from their state of rest. The coupling momentary, but each basking in its own and the other's fragrance, delightfully serene as the first ray of sunshine settles on them. In their separateness is a visible union, two more buds close by waiting to blossom - sheltered in a veil of perfection, a pregnant pause, time standing still for them, but not for the observer. Each of their nuances a poignant lesson of life, how blind, deaf and insensitive we have become not to learn anything from them. The butterflies and birds have often come to them, sharing sweet murmurings with their brethren, the breeze picking up not to miss out on this silent communion of nature's glory and abundance. Its joys momentary, living and dying simultaneously every moment, yet so very *alive*! No desire to rush, content in their laziness, uncaring of what I feel or write of it, but likely aware and non-attached to the other, only attached to its own root and being.

Suddenly, at the same time flashes a memory of a very recent event of two days ago, of a mother and daughter at a clinic where I go to await my friend Tuks to finish his work for the one hour meeting of good old friends, Seth G. S. Medical College and K.E.M. Hospital buddies of mine including Professor Bvd and Pabi. The episode was of their already waiting for two and half hours for the doctor to see them. Then they were to travel back to their home in Airoli in the peak hour of late evening traffic. But they were not being tended to. They had come without an appointment, an emergency it seemed, left unattended by the bastions of medicine. Six to seven hours of their time lost without any result for what they had come. Yet no anger displayed, a disappointment and frustration held in check and a silent departure without having their problem looked at. I was left aghast witnessing this incident. The elderly mother was clutching a file from Seven Hills hospital, the daughter probably at least having taken a half day off work if not the whole day. They had come to see a vitro retinal specialist!

How blind was the specialist himself or herself, is a metaphor that struck my heart! An inability to make an exception in these circumstances - if it is not cold hearted and bordering on callousness, then I don't know what it is. But who am I to judge, (having already done so) especially having observed just one half of the story, and why judge?! That is a theoretical point which I myself am finding so difficult to put into practice. A spontaneous burst of feelings arose; it was natural and sitting in my subconscious, later manifesting itself here, in my writing. It may probably have struck a nerve, given that I am in a similar profession, albeit in a country with universal healthcare, but I felt aghast and apologetic at the same time. Yes, indeed I have miles to travel to reach that equanimity but the realisation of my error today will go a long way in making such episodes occur less and less frequently as I stop reacting and respond instead. I hope to generate a continuity of remembrance, and though artificially practised for now, it may become constantly natural over the remainder of my life.

I have been writing for an hour now, she hasn't come out to the best of my knowledge or vision. Decorations and preparations for a wedding in the courtyard, (for a family living upstairs) may not have allowed her the luxury of her daily love affair with her garden in the morning. She will likely do so in the evening, whereas the night of my affair has ended in her life. Having disappeared into her next chore, she will be back in one of her two regular outfits. Yes, her black top will hang in the balcony to dry. I will get to see it reduced to a thing only, something essential of her being will have gone missing from it, detracting from its totality and its beauty.

See how she surfaces without warning, without hints, catching my attention unawares. This seems as difficult as anything else in my life that I may wish to forget. No semblance of activity there, no shadows seen, yet yesterday her windows were open all day until 9.15 pm. As soon as I looked up, I saw her walking within, the glimpse as fleeting as the blink of an eye. My writing continues - she knows, yet rejects it, her responses now colder than Arctic ice. Her response to my declaration is a death sentence to this affair. Yet, it is the very source of my writing. It begins with her, meanders around, skirting its borders, partaking the events surrounding her, transcribing into words, moving away, exploring other avenues, vignettes, then circling back to return to the original source, when the mind and the heart have exhausted the other experiences.

Yes, this one lives on. In its very absence is its real presence. There is a feeling that I can keep up with this for a long, long time - the words infinite, its substance zero! A fruitless boring monologue, tiresome, excruciatingly cumbersome that even I dare not read what has transpired on these pages, till it gets a new direction, till it is able to convey the essence of this search in a meaningful *sutra*!

A break for my breakfast, and I saw her while sitting in my dad's chair. The breeze picked up and died down suddenly. She is sweeping the floors while I drench myself in the fiction of my own creation. On February 12, five hours at Surya, a three-hour teaching round and a mock exam, she never entered my thoughts then. But she often does on my trips to Murli's farm or when sitting silently amidst nature and of course on my walks too. So, is my empty mind the devil?! But isn't an empty mind the death I am waiting for? It will be shocking to realise that all of these have just been my thoughts taking on the guise of feelings, the mind lulling me into a belief that it all originated in the heart. This doubt is now germinating, and reconciling with it is difficult to accept. Maybe it is a likely truth, as my ongoing experience reflects. Do I see it and accept it as the truth? If so, THIS WRITING OF FICTION WILL HAVE TO STOP!

Break free from this bondage. The freedom of knowing this unpalatable truth is a must, if I have to evolve further without the support and aid of any such crutches. Presently it feels like Mulla Nasruddin holding onto his crutches, even when he has the ability to walk unaided; a self-hypnosis overcoming and overpowering any attempt at self-remembrance. The misery of this delusion attractive, the alternative unknown - so I hang on to it for lack of a better potential outcome. Isn't such the state of most humans, or is it just my belief that it is so?!

The *sutra*, the final straw is missing, or am I just delaying, postponing what I very much know, refusing to accept the inevitable conclusion of this painful but never a sordid saga.

WAKE UP JAY!!

Chapter 10

There seems to be that possibility!

In eighteen hours I have been privileged to witness two events, one can say at complete odds with each other or one can surmise that it is an indicator of duality in human endeavours.

At an exclusive location in South Bombay, amidst plush surroundings of the Bombay Gymkhana, one Friday evening, I heard a remarkably eloquent and spellbinding presentation by Dr Radhakrishnan Pillai. He is the author of the book "Corporate Chanakya". He has a PhD. in Sanskrit and Chanakya's *Arthashastra*. For an hour he provided brief insights into the history, career and strategies of Kautilya's (Chanakya's) life and wisdom encompassing human and social responsibilities, lessons in leadership and management and the role of corporate social responsibility. Obviously, in the limited time possible there were nuggets and principles distilled from his major treatise, impossible it was to cover all aspects, nor was there an intention to do so. An interaction session with questions and answers followed his presentation.

I listened carefully to the exchange, congratulated him and summoned up courage to ask what I thought to be a simple question at the end. His presentation had talked in one breath the exciting and optimistic next twenty years in store for India and in the next breath bemoaned the lack of mentors for today's young generation compared to those in the recent past who challenged British authority and rule. I asked him if he has an "Atomic *Sutra*" similar to "Quit India" or other slogans to instil passion, and ignite the young minds and conscience of the new generation, similar to how the latter slogan had done. The "Quit India" slogan had created a spontaneous feeling of self-sacrifice in the nation's collective populace to create a movement that finally led to the end of British Raj in India.

The answer was long, dwelling on past history and leaders, but with an honest acceptance, acknowledging that I had posed him a challenging question. The answer wasn't direct enough, circumambulatory and in my perception a bit evasive, though what he said may have been true. Better to have said "No! I don't have such a defining *sutra* now!" I was probably asking too much of him and in hindsight, the *sutra* I wrote for myself just at the end of the previous chapter could have been the answer I was looking for from him.

Isn't it paradoxical that we seek and search what is already within us?!

This morning as promised to my dear Masterji and Missus, I spent three hours at the National Wheelchair Games at the Sion Hospital barracks, amidst their workshop and dwellings for the "differently abled". I saw an amazing enthusiasm, joy and acceptance by those less fortunate. The challenges of a sporting activity undertaken in the spirit of friendliness and gaiety – they patiently awaited their turn, helped each other participate and cheered on everyone's attempts at the various games organised. There was delight in just competing without it reeking of any negative aspects generated routinely from competitiveness. The way they encouraged each other was an eye opener for me.

Many young volunteers equally happy to be there to supervise, help, and record the events in the early hours of the morning on a

Saturday was nice to see. I was speechless, my mind still for many moments, a sense of peace within my heart prompting yet another look at life in its totality. I applauded heartily, congratulated them, this, my first, first-hand experience of such a live event, having only watched it before on television.

The opening ceremonies by school kids, their music band and parade, the discipline with camaraderie, their smiles, inviting everyone for breakfast and lunch, all very simple words and gestures but my experience unforgettable. It left me with a sense that people with so little materially on top of so many challenges in their lives, can live joyfully in the moment, without a trace of sorrow or despair showing. I did my bit, helping the participants and spectators in their wheelchairs as some recognised me and welcomed me, it all felt like a happy family and friends' get together.

All this I will remember - the contrasts of an evening past and the morning's arrival. Different scenes, dissimilar events in every manner you can think of, left impressions hard to erase; wouldn't want to anyway. It was a privilege to have witnessed and become a part of it. Yes, I couldn't stay for the late afternoon events, chief guests and other dignitaries' arrival as I had the Saturday visit to Murli's farm, he graciously delaying our departure to allow me this opportunity.

I found that the chief guest was Dr Deepak Kachalia, a buddy of my close friend Matthews (Balan) in Canada. Both were physiotherapists having studied together, and quite good friends also. I had last seen Deepak many years ago at Balan's wife Susamma's father Mr Abraham's 80th birthday celebration at their home, and terrace of Bethania building near Portuguese church in Mumbai. A family and friends get together attended by relatives from different parts of the world to celebrate a life well lived. He was terminally ill but alert and articulate, unfortunately he died a few months later while I was still in Mumbai. Sorry to move so far away from the event, just the coincidence and memory prompting this digression, but it's an indicator of how this writing has been continuing for some time now. Then my phone call to Balan to inform him of the events I was lucky to be a part of.

I saw in the glimpses of that morning, both the glory and tragedy of this country. A game that unfolds each and every day in innumerable lives across this land of prosperity for a chosen few and varying degrees of poverty for many. Yet, whether there are winners or losers, the message is powerful from both of them.

"PARTICIPATE IN THIS GAME CALLED LIFE". And when the show is over, be grateful you had the chance to do so. The curtain rises and falls, so live life as if acting in a play and retire having given whatever you could to this celebration; music, song, dance, misery, suffering, happiness, joy etc., knowing you will or maybe you won't get a chance to play another day.

Without economic prosperity and elimination of poverty, hunger, illiteracy, homelessness, there can never be the fire of a spiritual realm of existence in us as a society. Yes, occasionally there is someone poor in eons of generations who reaches the state of a mystic like Kabir, every aura being that of religiousness in such a person, but a poor society can never be religious. Fortunate are the few who have made it and remain silent having known the unknown, the absolute truth, so as to never return to play again. And if they do, it is with the sole intention of helping and guiding others to achieve similarly. Many mired in hand to mouth existence, trying to forget their misery, remain however drowned in tears for what they have known to be their daily life.

A beautiful visit to the farm, later than usual. As I returned from the morning festivities, a cool breeze came and it felt that the temperature dropped by 3 to 4 degrees in Mumbai, on the farm a difference of almost 10 degrees lower than our previous weekend there. A pleasant day and a late start to return but arriving earlier than usual. A first-hand experience for my friends, my having told them before many times of this based on my understanding of traffic density, but previously ignored by them. Now they too have seen the validity of my opinion. As Buddha and Mahavira did, repeating the same message at least thrice so as to register with their followers. Easy for me to say, but I have read and heard messages multiple times from my dead master Osho through his books and voice, yet deep seated indolence hasn't let me put much of it into practice yet. Nice though it feels to have an insight about missing this, someday it will find a home within my heart and not just remain mere information in my mind. Again it is sheer laziness that postpones the potential ignition of my intellect, transforming the message into feeling in such matters. But, in my profession I am lucky to know that the intellect still shines forth as brilliantly as ever, along with increasing compassion all the time. Sorry to blow my own trumpet but as I said, I have miles yet to travel! But artificial means of enjoyment is slowly disappearing, being replaced by another habit - my writing.

People often complain that I do not keep a personal mobile phone with me. It could help make me reachable, available at home here or abroad in case of an emergency situation for myself or for others amongst my family and friends. My reasons, often reiterated remain the same, but they hear and not listen, though now I see in them an acceptance of it. If on my own solitary travels away, in India, my elder brother has complete knowledge of my journeys and destinations. Abroad, my dearest friend BabuMoshai is fully aware of the times that I am away, either on Georgina island or my once a year visit in June/ July to USA to see extended family. So they both know how to reach me in case of an emergency of their own. In case of an emergency with me, well, if I am in an accident and hurt badly enough to be unable to use a public telephone, I hope for a good samaritan to make the call from the information always carried in my wallet. Of course if my wallet is stolen, then tough luck, I guess! But I am more likely to lose the phone, forget it somewhere or have it stolen. And if I am dead from an accident, then there is no emergency, is there?!

Anyway this is a matter of personal, practical philosophy, so a thought flashes in my mind of a similar take regarding the terminology in use for such a portable device. In most of the West it is called a cellphone, in India it is called a mobile phone. 'Cell' means a jail, yes people are bound to it as if by chains to this gadget, whereas 'Mobile' means mobility of movement, action. So, it is a message of freedom in a democracy. Yet, it seems to me that people in all walks of life here in India are more imprisoned by it than those in the western world, a travesty indeed of the different description used. For, democracy here in India today is just a namesake one, a fiction, a concept, an illusion, yet this country continues to trumpet the hollow sound and noise of being the world's largest democracy.

This morning halfway into my shower, the water slowed and became hotter. I realised that the toilet was being flushed causing this problem, leading to irritation and maybe anger, a corollary of heat that arose within me to match the water's heating up. The moment passed, the toilet tank having refilled itself, the shower returned to normal flow and the mind's oscillation stopped. No longer reactive, but my response came late, as the other source draining the water away stopped its activity. For years the three areas of washroom, bathroom and the sink outside them, were supplied by a single source. The old rusted decades old conduits had clogged up a lot. The experience today must have been a regular occurrence over past many years, but it had never caught my attention until today. The pipes were replaced a few months ago, the connections simplified, this occurrence is less in its severity and discoverability. But today I felt it, maybe my sensitivities have become sharper but more likely that it was a hot day and already the water from the tank upstairs was warmer than usual. But it generated enough discomfort for me to pause and reflect.

It reminded me of a message long read that, the source is one, but the divisions still persist - rusted pipes removed, the mirror changed, yet it has been just a superficial adjustment teaching me a valuable lesson today. In spite of the slower, hotter water, a minor obstacle only, there was still enough of it for an adequate bath with only minimal discomfort. I learnt that I was and had been using more water than I really needed and sharing it with the other did not unduly affect or disturb my bath except momentarily and in that light an understanding dawned...

"*The source is one, receivers many*". In this small incident the nature of greed, possessiveness, need and want seem epitomized. But if we were truly to understand that not only is the source one, the receiver too is one, they are the same, each is in the other and the other is in oneself, that would bring the revolution necessary in individuals. The 'Unity of Oneness' if practised, the passions of all that is negative will disappear immediately and a collective humanity will shine forth.

But these are all words. We have heard read or written them for many lives before and will continue to do so in this life and any future lives to follow. Why then is it so difficult for this message to register and take root in the dormant seed of our consciousness? Is it because we are conditioned to think of ourselves as mere mortals, limited by life span and Nature? Is it blasphemous to think, feel or know ourselves as the Supreme, either full or empty, everywhere and nowhere, reflecting nothing or the entire Universe?

Chapter 11

A very quiet and pleasant Sunday morning. The routines leisurely accomplished, yet seeming as if not much time has officially passed. The clock seems slower than usual. Maybe the unhurried pace of the morning activities on a holiday has made me arrive sooner. The haste on a working day often causing delay, and apparently one finds oneself short of time. The clock moves faster, at least in our perception than what it seems to do so today. These contrasts are meaningful even though a myth of our imagination. But in India, myths are more powerful, more relevant than facts and history. The parables have a deeper lesson to teach, to awaken us from our deep slumber. But we read and re-read repetitively as if while awake still asleep and dreaming for the countless lives passed away.

A Sunday evening, February 17, a family dinner together - *Bhel, sev puri*, nuts and ice-cream. A wonderful complement of items arranged by my *bhabhi*, it also being the family's day long weekend in Canada. Waiting for their serial *Adalat*, I channel surfed and came across *Safar*, my second favourite movie, after *Anand* being the most and first in the category. Both have been watched innumerable times by me. Saw about half hour of three songs and dialogues, having missed the two previous melodies of the first half having been on my walk and preparing for the evening. I showed the children the renovations, they liked them, they left and I retired. The song that still touches me is related to the devastating news that the light of the protagonist's life is rapidly extinguishing from an incurable cancer. She too incidentally had arrived back at her home the moment that song had begun, having gone missing all day since 1.30 pm.

Anyway, these songs remain a constant presence in my life. They bubble up on multiple occasions unrelated to any triggering events, and leave a lingering presence around me, permeating into my ongoing activities. These two films, *Anand* and *Safar* no longer leave me just as a spectator. I imbibe them, become part of them each time I view those films. Incurable cancer is the theme in both, but handled and presented very differently. These movies are a testament, an indicator, a pointer to the journey of life and the destination of death with just the right amount of humour in them. Brilliantly acted by all the cast, they are priceless to me. No need for any books or philosophical arguments or scriptures, dogmas, tenets, rules, rituals etc., they remain the ultimate masters if one can understand their simple and poignant message and teachings.

Maybe I still don't! Otherwise why the need for such repetitive viewing, experiencing them umpteen times! They are firmly lodged into my memory and heart, maybe in my being also. Each scene, each dialogue, every song, every gap, every nuance that is to come next, known to me. They depict the future of any life if lived well, totally, clearly, bluntly and starkly. Any number of adjectives remain superfluous to emphasize the core simplicity of them. Then why is it so difficult to live it? These two and Osho, the masters guiding me, no longer is Osho alive physically, but they have penetrated past the circumference of my life.

It just seems to be taking an eternity for them to touch and change my centre completely. I know of course that change has to begin in the centre and move outwards or else it will take an eternity if tried the other way around.

I know, either a transformation comes suddenly or never at all. That is debatable and has been argued for and against by many teachers and masters. So I accept any alternative to my earlier statement. Suffice it is to say, my efforts are not yet substantial, my surrender incomplete, this waiting an attempt to preserve the status quo. At least moving backwards into my past has become somewhat less of an activity compared to moving forwards, both now in small measures, trying to hang in between on occasions, but still oscillating to and fro. Hoping that the battery runs out and my swinging pendulum of memory and imagination comes to a standstill to throw me in to the present moment instantaneously.

IT WILL OF COURSE DO WHEN I DIE, BUT CAN I MANUFACTURE THAT DEATH-LIKE STATE WHILE STILL ALIVE?!

Unless I give up on my romantic inclinations, become steady with the feeling of romance neither for an object or subject, this effort is destined to fail. With each moment of time unfolding in existence, this pendulum will remain self-charging, not within my control or will power, of which I possess very little, if any.

And she continues to surface again and again, giving the pendulum the push and pull of my own making too. The bucket of water heavy, her balance with the other hand perfect, a grace, a dance. By no means can one regard her as beauty of physical form, yet my eyes notice every subtle and new nuance of hers. As if time has stopped in her tracks and I have all the time in the world to just watch her. She no longer looks but her sixth sense must tell her that I still do.

This look of mine is gentle, head bowed, eyes partly closed, neither violent nor intrusive. Her vision in itself enough for me, a soothing ambience she creates. Whether observed in the light or seen as a faint shadow she leaves impressions on my mirror but not of any lust. It is as if it is allowing the peeling off layer by layer, of my accumulated negative emotions from life's experiences, baring my essential presence to myself.

She obviously doesn't know fully of her effect on me, maybe I am also mistaken, as I too cannot know her deepest or superficial thoughts. Maybe she does think of me as an intruder, somewhat a voyeur of her visible activities. She doesn't have a choice but to continue doing what she has to. Must breathe a sigh of relief when I am not on my ledge. Maybe also when I am deeply immersed in reading, writing, walking, evenings out within and out of town and night times, now that her windows have been closing on me earlier and earlier. She has rejected the essence of my feelings, yet I feel my words are necessary for her to hear before her rejection crystallizes in her mind and solidifies in her heart. That however is a big presumption on my part. She probably no longer thinks about me. Chapter over, move on, must be the quality of her living in the moment that added to my being captivated by her, so now why do I want her to be any different!

But this exercise in futility must have some underlying meaning for me. It will emerge then, if it has to, in its own time and place.

Chapter 12

A song has been humming within me for the past few days. Yesterday I hummed all its three couplets on my walk, always hoping I will someday run into her. But since her emphatic declaration, I have never seen her on errands. This song from the movie, *Blackmail* is *'Pal pal dil ke paas tum rehti ho'*. A year ago on my friend Ba's in-laws' farm near Badlapur, I asked him to play it repeatedly on his iPad from midnight into early hours of the morning! I haven't listened to music in my own home for a good many years now. I suddenly took out my old instrument, cleaned it and switched the radio on. It was still working. There is now a lurking desire to search out a few meaningful songs that could send her a message across our courtyards. That is, if the voice carries that distance to reach her when she is in her kitchen assuming there is no noise of utensils or at a time when she is silently absorbed tending to her garden. The sound loud enough to reach, but not so loud as to disturb her or others. A fine balance needs to be achieved but it will still be impossible for me to be certain of it. However, I know this could amount to a subterfuge, it would negate and become purposeful by design and so be unacceptable maybe to me even.

A chance accidental crossing would give an opportunity for a final rejection if she has no time even to listen for a few minutes. That would be the honourable way to do it. Or if unable, let this saga ride itself out. No deceptions, no falsities, but a direct understanding from words. I find the answers from her gestures clear but not fully acceptable as yet to me. This writing, now very much on the wall. For a man who often lives on the spoken and written word, half the message if not registered, the rest probably known also but awaiting a confirmation, the later it comes on this trip, the better now for me. I continue this way, using her as some would say, a fiction, an imagination derived from a living person as its source. Somewhere there is a pay day or a payoff, the consequences unknown as this play of words continues.

First, do no harm. This is to a large extent really innocent. I have told her the truth, a relative one and wish only for an opportunity to complete it!

Truth liberates. Then why am I still waiting? Maybe a feeling that the substance, the support for my writing will come to an end. These meandering words, criss-crossing fictional alleys of my mind, having sprung from the heart but unable to reside in hers. They have to fall somewhere out of my mind onto this poor piece of paper, that has no choice but to be a party to this senseless exercise of mine. What shall I say of the ink and the pen, its life too will run out from this meaningless jargon over which it has no say of its own.

February 20, my niece's birthday on a Wednesday, my eyes opened at 4.00 am. A two and a half hour walk looking at the stars and the moon, hoping to be a witness to my body walking or to my thoughts. Failed miserably on both counts. This is difficult, it comes and goes, making an effort to keep the mind empty, lasts just a few seconds and then drifts away like a stray dog running hither and thither as she slips back in through my back door. So the walks continue at my pace of six kilometres per hour, three to four hours almost daily, but the mind gallops away at lightning speed. Someday I hope it will tire and exhaust itself out, go to sleep quietly, but it seems to be taking a lifetime.

A haircut this morning, day 18 since my last one. My trip often measured by the number undertaken and the ones remaining. 47 days left, so three more haircuts, the median interval will have to be 15 instead of 17 days. As it is, my hair can barely be held in my fingers and I get it chopped off, prompting many to say where in God's name is there any hair to cut! My niece too is getting her hair groomed, wishes for her, gift of book, cash from family and continuing to write. A busy day ahead, phone calls to air conditioner installers, a patient to see at home, evening with Dk *mama* and family at Bombay Cricket Association Club. The strike call for today not materialising so transport services by bus and train not a problem for me.

Running out of ideas, they will come in their own time. If they stop that would be nice too. For being without thoughts would mean being in the present, the absence of them a welcome gift. The writing will be less cumbersome, less manufactured and more alive out of an ongoing experience of stillness, silence and aloneness. The romance having ended with no signs of revival, yet the heart refuses to acknowledge its demise. Coming back from my walk, I saw her. Earlier returning from my haircut, I saw her looking out, greeted her with a silent *Namaste* and moved towards my door. I no longer wait to see her reaction to my rare greetings, missed her garden visit, saw her on the last step returning, her back to me, so no real contact in the works for today.

Full stop. Period. The journey of this periodic vagrancy of the mind coming to an end. Tired of its imaginary flight, its state of unrest now culminating in an enforced rest. It was good while it lasted. Better still to face the reality that was staring at me all the time. But I had blinkers on, as the heart kept seeing visions of something grand and beautiful. Anyway, I have a multitude of tasks ahead and the end of this indulgence may be a blessing in some ways. It will allow me the time to finish many of my other priorities, none of course of any critical significance except her!

But my gaze often jumps from her captivating hands directly to her often expressionless face that now captures my attention. I find it serene, exotic even, each aspect of it as if finely chiselled by a sculptor who knows what kind of beauty lies in simplicity and can recreate it almost to perfection. If I were to photograph it and present it to you, you will in all likelihood bypass it without much of a glance.

Yet in it I see the flowering of the ultimate essence that the dance of her hands released, to hold a spectator like me spellbound. Caught in that web, I still am on tenterhooks, it brings a calm radiant peace to every fibre of my being and makes me forget my own experiences with a woman.

Yes, women - can't live with one, can't live without one!

But I have somewhat learnt my lessons dearly. In spite of an absolute fidelity on my part during my seven years of marriage, yet ending up with a divorce. Now left alone with my fidelity transformed into celibacy for many, many years, enforced, is what some friends like to tell me! *Majboori ka naam Gandhiji*, is a comment friends pass on my travails and I silently accept their laughter at my expense for I am very comfortable with my celibacy. Now it is an imaginary romance that keeps the heart tender enough to shower love and receive tears!

The end of an affair, but what an affair of the mind to remember! The waking up in its ending, a much prolonged tortuous demise, with all its suffering that was real and happiness that was imaginary!

Chapter 13

I was on my way to the bus stop. Saw her coming from the opposite end on the other side, a distance of just ten metres separating us. This time I did not cross over. I looked, at her and greeted her, she presented complete indifference… or did I perceive a scathing look filled with scorn? I was left with a feeling of complete annihilation, deservedly so. I carried on, occupied with her thoughts, reinforced my decision not to look consciously at her, an effort that has failed repeatedly and miserably so. I hope to stop the apparent disturbance I may be generating, though I am left with the regret that she has misunderstood my attention. Many lessons will remain of this encounter stretching over two and a half months.

A blessing and also a warning from existence to stop this wandering, get out of this romantic *chakravyuh* or labyrinth. Search or discover the deeper waters of my well and having quenched this thirst, move on towards reality.

The mirage of an oasis is over, the desert sandstorm has passed, the dust in my eyes has been removed, and the greenery is not so far in the distance; if only I could learn to walk right!

Given the strike, I reached early for my weekly visit to DK *mama*. February 20, so consciously went to see my *foia* (aunt). It being my *fua's* (Uncle) death anniversary, in addition to it also being the birthday of another nephew in India, and a niece in San Francisco. Dental appointment and BCA cancelled, so spent the evening at home with Dk *mama* and family and returned home. A surprise phone call from Sourabh - Dr Sourabh Dutta, head of Neonatology at PGI, Chandigarh, who spent two years on his sabbatical with us in our department at McMaster in Canada - in Chandigarh and some update on Mac news so passed them on to BabuMoshai who was in Kolkata on a visit.

Read a book titled, *'Prosems'*, the author's name for prose written in poetry format, applauded the writer's efforts but couldn't enjoy all of them, some disappointment too. But that is what many of you may say of this writing, criticise over the pages and pages of fantasy, flights of bullshit, very little in it to penetrate the knowing heart of someone and take root there.

Yet to my eyes and heart, very productive indeed. Rediscovering one of my lost passions, foolish and presumptuous to call it art, the words over time may flow with more meaning and less of memory and imagination. Those two crutches may be discarded but then I will have to be very alert, aware to pick up silent cues from the universal play and create gaps between my words.

I take a deep breath, making an effort to not look across, generating tension within me, for it is time for her to step out into her garden. Hopefully she has finished that task, the eyes wanting to stray, the hands forcing its gaze back onto the page even if the words coming forth are utter nonsense.

So, I have written about an illusory romance in a language encompassing both flowers and thorns. Few besides me may realise there was no root for this plant, a figment of my imagination. A caressing of your senses if you have chosen to read so far, yet very real for me. The pain of its ending, like sap from a tree. To me the metaphor is a living example of its dying, a bleeding heart looking for juice to end its thirst.

It was over before it even began and you call this life, a celebration of birthdays never realising you started dying the very moment you took birth!

So, you expect something better than this fiction, do you? Trust me, you cannot handle the real. Remember the line from the movie, A Few Good Men: "You cannot handle the truth!"

Many have written on such truths many times before, much better than what I will ever write. But we all forget them so easily, including me of course.

I have seen enough on my visits here each year to last a lifetime of accumulated bitter, sad and tragic memories of events witnessed. If I were to pour them all out, you and I both will feel uncomfortable. This will be just a brief glimpse I think as I do not know what all is to follow in my words. It will be the seeing, hearing, reading of events that begin at each of our waking days. We refuse to acknowledge their presence and even if we do, we carry on as if they were absent from our lives. So, for lack of a better fiction, let us get back to a few facts if not part of the whole truth. I will attempt to give you just a small glimpse, for this writing may have been far too serious. A serious life is a diseased life. It is irreligious!

"In the seriousness of this writing is at least the underlying humour and laughter of your judgement that will inevitably follow!"

Do you want me to write of a day that begins and ends in this premier metropolis of India, Mumbai, or do you just wish to wake up, begin and finish your day and sleep it off, mired in the hassles of day to day living? There seems to be no breathing room to spare a bit of oxygen for the many downtrodden eking out a dying existence in this city of dreams.

Shall I begin with the songs of the birds as the sun is about to peep over and announce a fresh morning? Or to the splish-splash of *gurkhas* and servants waking up in the middle of the night, way before dawn to wash your precious cars before you have even woken up to have your own bath? Do I talk about the sweeper of your courtyard, who collects your garbage, maybe even cleans your toilet way too early in the day just so he can go to his productive job by nine am more suited to his skills and education? He needs these two incomes to raise his family reasonably if at all. And lo and behold, as soon as he finishes, you litter your courtyard again with refuse and garbage. At times, it's your leftover chapattis and other items for the birds and stray animals to eat. Living upstairs you forget or choose to do so even though reminded often by people like us living downstairs of the mess you create for us all. Nature's gift of food gets trampled under the wheels of cars moving back and forth, or under the feet of multiple people using it to go about their ways.

Do I talk of the 75-plus-year-old woman, who has been at this kind of a job in her building since I ever began to possess a memory and likely doing this even before I was born in this life? Her measured hunch backed gait, shuffling steps, a bucket and a broom in her hands, unable to reach her job till around ten am. Solitary in her chores, spending a few hours cleaning your mess just to earn some income to support herself and any other family members even at this age. Yes, you have no idea of the mess this country has made of her life!

What about the young children who should be in school, delivering your newspapers, so you can read of the news that transpired without any semblance of feeling that the real news of the day began right in your courtyard, in your toilet, at your window, while you were still asleep?

Yes, we read all that we want of remote events, blind and deaf to the events unfolding in our own very present moment. Forget the misery of your fellow beings that you missed seeing or feeling for, you are not even there to listen to the song of the birds, the opening of a new flower, that plant you have taken great care to nurture but then employed someone else to water it for you. Yes, for years my *bhabhi* has tended to both her gardens herself. But as her kids started growing up and the morning tasks in her household became increasingly onerous, she still managed to find the time to water her plants at some point of time during the day. But the timings of this nurturing no longer remained certain. It was us, the brothers who forcibly asked her to desist from watering the garden in the courtyard, and employed the watchman and his daughter-in-law to do so in the morning. In effect, it supplemented their income, added some relief to the. running of their household and enabled them to partake of tea and some snacks and fruits at times. Such acts in various communities across this city keeps the economy rolling, so all not too bad in the long run, I guess.

You have just lost the thirst to know what the real news is of this city and many other such places, towns, villages, hamlets and so on across this land. It rarely is the topic of your conversation in your journey to work or on your return, in your offices, at the corner *paanwalla* or at swanky clubs in the evening. You may refer on occasion to this in passing, but more often than not the talk is about more important events, can be about politics, corruption, markets, sports etc. Please do not mistake me, I don't mean to say that such conversation is wrong. I do it too and feel knowledgeable, it nourishes each of our egos, and it is a prop for our intellect. That is just fine by me, I am just trying to point towards a balance, towards a need to engage in something far more reaching that benefits a common humanity.

The indulging of discussions no doubt makes us feel and seem caring of faraway or nearby events as well as tragedies, but often it is a headline or a by-line that begins and ends your day.

"What will it ever take for one to realise that to be at a loss for conversation is when the real conversation begins?!"

Chapter 14

An incident occurred in the wee hours of the night. Woke up with a start, feeling an excitement of the body. Suddenly alert, whatever the reverie was, it ended, but surprisingly I have no recollection of it. The excitement subsided and there was no loss of my vitality. Either it must have arisen from my subconscious or it was a mere dream but I am unable to remember. It may be some regret or guilt stemming from an evening with KEM buddies. An unintentional innocent simple question from a dear friend with a very complicated answer may have stirred the memories of both joys and pains lodged deeply in my heart. A recounting of lost loves and the ensuing hurts in lives that may occasionally resound with an echo within me. Luckily I became alert in time to avoid any embarrassing moment. A release of a mess of memories alone and not anything tangible to clean up. One signature drink, as I told my friend is not enough to get dadhi to talk and give an account of the recriminations of his marriage and lost loves. It requires Georgina Island, a cigar and a cognac of Hine or Martell.

Wasn't it Mark Twain who said, and I borrow: "To say that you can love one person all your life is like saying that one candle will continue to burn as long as you live." Or was it Einstein? If I am wrong, I guess my attempts to deliberately forget my memory may be bearing fruit.

A clear sky, a clear conscience! With sex having disappeared from my life for many years, I strive and am hopefully close to succeeding in clearing the sexuality within my mind, just a little bit longer to go and I hope to reach that state. In its wake, will come the utmost purity of a romance that this writing depicts for an astute reader but unfortunately not to the person I am romancing!

A solitary flower and a bud about to break open, halfway into its journey. As I sit watching the slow perceptible opening of its petals, I sense a lesson whose meaning is difficult to put into words, its understanding still to come in this lifetime. Survival and reproduction are the fundamental laws of Nature and sex is its most primordial and creative energy. I may have lost that energy no doubt, hope it is trying to sublimate into another kind, the ever increasing compassion in my profession and an eternal romance with existence.

Two other flowers already plucked by an innocent playful child who had been admiring them for a few days. Waited for my absence to claim them, took great pleasure in showing them to its little friend, and hopefully has presented them to loved ones. The flowers lived for an eternity it seemed. The child was generous enough not to pluck the solitary one earlier. Waited for it to become a couple then a trio, as it left the last one hanging on its stem. Away all weekend, a new coupling may occur, I will be there to see it at the end of the day and one will likely be gone by the time I return.

A lesson, that in my life too, love has come one after another to depart either due to my sins of omission or commission, and the only one left now is that of my imagination, in so far as a woman is concerned.

Somehow I still fail at times to ignore minute triggers that can seemingly bring out the worst in me. Either in words or silent irritation, trivial day-to-day events still provoke a minor reaction.

115

However, towards the whole big picture in my life, I am becoming more responsive and patient most of the time. Though I protect my aloneness, it is not of a negative nature. Avoidance of contact is neither ideal nor something I actively seek, for then it would smack of a cold indifference. But within my large circle of family and friends, opportunities for continued, frequent and recurrent interactions are fewer and fewer, partly given the busyness and mad rush in the lives of those around me. But it can and sometimes does make my day's ending poorer than its beginning, as I fail at times to remain a witness.

Retreating more and more into my aloneness is not the answer as I previously said, and confirmed as you can well see from the mind's chatter emptying onto these pages. Time away this weekend but still in company of dear friend Ba and his wife and her parents. I also do look forward to my week in solitude on Murli's farm. It may help me regroup, rediscover the lost calm. Also help develop the understanding to acknowledge unresolved hurts of those close to me and respond appropriately with help and support. Unfortunately given how close to my return from there the ending of this trip will loom, there will come along with it, as always, anxiety, irritation and impatience as I will keep ruminating on tasks pending with very little time to accomplish them.

I woke up to read the headline of another terrorist attack in a district of Hyderabad.

This and similar such events have been occurring on an almost daily basis somewhere on this earth in alarming proportions. We have now become so insensitive to these distant events happening to others unknown, perpetrated by fanatics known and unknown. Unless it involves a close one, this kind of tragedy fails to touch us for more than the time it takes for that headline to change. Powerless we feel, unable to make any lasting difference, this evil's ghosts cannot be exorcised away, as it occurs daily to keep it alive.

In the death of a few or many is the dying of the real conscience, or rather the consciousness of humanity. The solutions of going after and exterminating them in any form or manner, adds also to a growing list of innocents dead. They are conveniently brushed away in a term called "collateral damage" as part of a greater good. When did we ever forget that each human life has value and that you just can't dismiss or wish it away saying too bad? Or that it is the lesser of two evils. That individual life lost, besides putting moral arguments aside, could have been a Buddha, Mahavira, Christ or Einstein, Tolstoy, Beethoven etc. In that loss is the loss of the oneness that, centuries ago was the vision given by India to the rest of the world.

Books written, movies made, all just another means of tear-jerking, here today gone tomorrow. The grind of daily living not allowing the mind and heart to seek real solutions to the conflict, nor the development of any intelligence to mount a new creative response.

The heart bleeds for a while, replenishes itself only to bleed again, with moments of the pain of surviving far worse than the sudden death thanks to weapons of mass destruction, cluster bombs, drone strikes, missiles and indiscriminate and disproportional use of a response, rather a reaction of a nation, just like the reactionary mode of an individual like me or any other.

Yes, death isn't difficult, it is the living of life that is arduous and often impossible to bear, a saying often repeated by many others.

At a sudden loss for words, numbed by feeling and the spontaneous outpouring, the writing stopped for a moment. Suddenly I see the smiling face of our water lady and I realise that there is still some joy left in this world. Enough reasons to carry on. Each life a miniature world in itself, at times separate, at times colliding. At other times also combining with another but never seeming to manage a balance, moving from one extreme to another. The moments of apparent calm few and far between, often going unnoticed by most of us.

Each with thoughts impenetrable to the other, nor even witnessed by the one in whose mind it originated.

I, myself, a prime example, my efforts to watch the streaming content of my silly mind completely nullified. Not only do they persist, fester and pester me, they insist on taking shape and form, transforming into words of indelible ink on these pages to live forever or die when it is burnt as rubbish along with me.

My time of writing is over, plants to water, now to resume my reading as I defer the task of packing for a very early start tomorrow and a weekend with Ba's family. Also, today is the death anniversary of my father's younger brother. If death of someone or many keeps occurring everyday on this earth, why do we only choose to get attached to those of departed ones who are either family, friends, relatives or someone known to us in some manner or another?

These rituals of remembrance are likely without much meaning, unless in each death we see that at any time, that dead body we saw in the past of someone known to us or otherwise could have been yours or mine! That to me is the key for any real change in an individual consciousness. A revolution of sorts, better learn to do it while alive rather than miss it in your death.

Just as I stopped, the child in that flower is alive, no breeze yet to carry its fragrance to me, but it is there. Yet in the seeing of it, the mind rushed on, the shadow of my romance surfacing, the smoke of it replacing the breeze. The suffering enjoyable, the rehearsed conversation emptying. Now after about 48 hours of careful avoidance, her vision is slowly fading, a good beginning to this purposeful forgetting.

Chapter 15

A visit back to nature early morning, after a late night yesterday. This time, on a visit to my dear friend, Dr Bharat Agarwal's in-laws' farm. His wife Dr Parul and her parents, affectionately referred to as *Nana* and *Nani,* were there as well. Woke up at 05.00 am, made my tea, though my brother had offered to do so, having done it for every day of my trip. The reason for the late night was because of viewing *Saajan* one more time, despite my many viewings before.

It feels as if I am sitting relaxed in my own piece of nature, a soft breeze gently caressing me under the shade of a mango tree sprouting its first flowering. Surrounded by a cashew tree bearing fruits the music of the iPad unable to drown out the silent song of nature. A dog sleeping on the porch, the other stretching, having just woken up. Maybe possibly a white Heron moving silently on the lawn preying on insects and worms. A myriad of colourful butterflies and dragonflies adding charm to this display of the bounty of nature, the sound of water pouring into the reservoir next to me from the Ulhas river. I sat on the rocks dipping my feet in the cool rushing waters on one shore, the other shore with villagers washing clothes. Colourful *sarees* basking in the sunshine, spread out over the rocks like a tapestry of carpets, children bathing under careful supervision of their mothers, a train running on the tracks behind a small hill.

Then in the distance, the hills of Matheran with majestic peaks overlooking the innocuous activities beneath.

Yet, here it seems 'All is at rest', with the rest of human activity continuing at a pace unheard of in a town or city. However there is still the activity of the tradesmen from the city with their hammers and chisels repairing the leaky roof of the pantry store room. The music suddenly switching to an old song of the past. It was an accompaniment on my visits to various discos in Mumbai with family and friends, a lifetime ago. The whistle of a train at a time selectively in the gap between two songs, the sound carrying effortlessly from a distance. The traffic of these sounds, bits and pieces of conversation from within the house and its kitchen drifting across, this is the ongoing present moment as I try to capture it in unnecessary words, transcribe with ink onto paper. To relive this moment again would however be an even greater joy. See how the mind desires still more of something already achieved, always.

Time for lunch already after a big breakfast. A feast for me. *Dal Baati, Mirchi Salan*, a mocktail of ginger, soda and chillies on top of a sumptuous breakfast. A conversation flowing smoothly, eating leisurely, enjoying the smell, feel and taste of every morsel. Nothing forced, a rhythm one spontaneously falls into in harmony with nature, time almost standing still. Our lunch over, we see a pair of herons still engaged in finding their food. One patiently standing, the other continuing its stealthy walk and suddenly a third arriving in mid-air, a flight silent and effortless to land in the distance. The dogs sleeping again, the family retired for a short nap, tables cleared, music turned off, a well-deserved rest for all, mine coming from this exercise of writing, sitting on the swing. The help also having eaten, resting for a bit and then back to their work of earning a livelihood. We are fortunate to have no such practical concerns for ourselves today. *Nana* cooked with Ba's help as well as the ladies', but it was *Nana's* show at lunch. He is now supervising the repair work, his energy abundant; his rest is in his working, he says. The heron snapping at a butterfly in vain, its hunger still evident.

Ba out again to help *Nana*, Parul and *Nani*, who having arranged for two wonderful meals retired for a much deserved rest of their own. Heron flying off, the butterflies merrily continuing their evasive dance. Survival and predatory aspects of nature at play, at such close quarters for me today. The dog stirs, shaking off insects and fleas, scratching itself and rolling around on the lawn. Now up and fully awake, quietly observing the lull in activity and the absence of music and voices. The only sound now is the gurgling of water into the reservoir, all else in nature seemingly at utter rest, continuing a silent activity of regeneration as living beings do so in sleep. The silence shattered suddenly with the whirring noise and deep throated roar of a helicopter arriving and departing overhead. A faint hum from a distance and the horn of a truck by the river responding with a greeting of its own to the beast in the sky.

This farm is about ten acres. An unfortunate event a couple of weeks ago has burnt off one third of the planted trees all just three-year-old mango trees which might have borne their first fruit this year. The charred remains are a heartbreak for the family, caretakers and hired help, and now my experience too. An unintentional aftermath from maybe the burning of leaves and dry twigs in an open area on the farm. I suggested they allow it to naturally compost in a pit and use it as organic fertilizer for current and future plantations, a harvested manure of sorts. The buzzing of a fly near my ear, a sudden gust of wind, the canopy of leaves overhead gently swaying and back soon to its motionless state within a few seconds; as if a gentle caress is reminding them to be awake even when asleep.

The breeze is playing its game of hide and seek, its nuances difficult to comprehend. An airplane flies overhead, life continues its movement in places where motion is barely perceptible. Our conversation all day long are on multiple topics, laughter with some serious talk too.

Rational, philosophical, practical, medicinal, encompassing many facets of what has been until now a pleasant day for us. A lot still remains for further exploration.

I walked through the whole farm when everyone was resting. Walking is the state of rest for me, my most favourite hobby of all. Silence all around, cashew, mango trees, corn stalks, green tea, watermelon, bitter gourd, bottle gourd, coconut, flowering fences and shrubs all around within the farm and its boundaries. Then I walked the scorched earth. Many trees burnt in totality, many others standing and bearing witness without complaints or curses at the raging inferno that devoured its limbs and leaves when alive. The trunks feeling the heat yet unable to run and escape the fires from hell, as they stood mute to the loss of their children. Some dead, some with partial burns of their branches, leaves and flowers, an amputation of sorts, a continued sensation of burning with no soothing balm or medicine to heal.

Do they feel the presence of phantom pain? Does their grief ever end?! I saw in most of the burnt trees, areas that had escaped the torture. The very young branches and leaves not too tall nor proud, survived as the inferno raced across at a height. They have lived, now bearing a few flowers even, some others too showing a remarkable resilience with the birth of new leaves side by side to the dead ones. As if the ones with burns were able to see in their pain and suffering, the birth of something new. Nature seems forgiving of this accidental tragedy, a sense of compassion towards the hard work of humans, not letting it all go to waste, forgetting its own suffering in the process. I am trying to understand its message.

Life is a continuous stream of birth, decay, dying and rebirth. I reached down to the rocks on the banks of the river, a continuous flow of water just yards away from where the tragedy was unfolding. Yet, unable to reach out and help its neighbour in trouble, needing a human hand to stop the harm occurring. Its source of water always ready and willing but missing the crucial ingredient of a witness who could have ended the horror.

I sat in solitude with my few thoughts and many feelings. Hearing the music in the small eddies of the cascading waters, seeing grass and algae amidst rocks. Dowsing my bare feet in its pleasantly rushing cool waters with a blazing sun overhead. No cover for me from the sun, wearing a hat often gives me a headache. But the hot air came as a breeze bringing with it a mist from the gushing fountain of a broken water pipe leading to the neighbour's farm. The spray of mist giving a sense of relief. And I, party to the intelligence of nature, returned to write about it.

Many have written before on the interplay of nature and living beings much more eloquently. The few that immediately come to mind are Jiddu Krishnamurti's 'Commentaries on Living' series, Michael Pollan's book 'Second Nature' and another remarkable favourite of mine is Joan Anderson's 'A Year by the Sea', not only with better words but with simplicity, a much clearer sense of direction, clarity, succinct yet remarkably charming in its details. This, my own, is nothing new or spectacular. You will miss nothing if unread even, but for me, it is my creation. Let it slowly percolate, sink into my centre, become an essential part of my being if and when it ever does.

Then, I can, if I am still there, leave the page empty and disappear without a trace.

I walked across the fallen leaves of the cashew trees. A carpet that squeaked with a crunch at my every step. A music from the strewn dead leaves, now the colour of earth, then barefoot across the thick lush green grass of the front lawn. A silence, an acceptance, a soothing feeling with sensations on the soles of my feet like the caress of a mother's hand massaging gently her child to sleep.

Another round of tea and snacks, one feast merging into another from human to nature's and back to humans again. Woman made food for the body, the ambience food and drink for the soul. And the idiot mind is left to empty its thoughts on paper. Cannot eat them up but can still take some pleasure in revisiting, reading them. A night of starry sky to remember, free flowing conversation amidst a candlelight dinner on the lawn. Music, dance, drinks and food till way past midnight. Then a peaceful sleep as if in oblivion, morning that seemed to come far too quickly; not even a single mosquito bite in the evening or night.

Also the delight of sitting in the evening in the small whirlpools of the Ulhas River, its force like a massage far better than that of an artificial jacuzzi, the feeling quite refreshing. A man made fountain rising 12 feet upwards spraying mist all around and returning the water back down as if drenching in a rain shower. The sounds of the water hitting also the body and rocks like the staccato of machine gun bullets. No one now on the opposite bank, or in the river except *Nana*, Ba and me. The sunset is creating hues of all possible colours. Now a bright moon, almost full, the first appearance of Orion. The evening and night in the company of friends disappearing as time kept moving faster than I experience in my aloneness on Murli's farm.

Returned early afternoon with some produce from the farm, their generosity overwhelming. Thanked every single one of the hired help, Mhatre, Kalavati and her entourage of three other ladies, Ramesh and Maya, the family drivers a part of them for many years. Expressed my gratitude in words as well as in kind which they graciously accepted. And, to Ba and his family my appreciation for a great weekend. They are always welcoming me to join them any weekend I wish, even without any advance notice, just the moment of my wishing for it is enough for them to pick me up every time if I choose.

I slept for an hour, woke up and after a shower got a call informing me that my *bhabhi* is quite ill. I rushed upstairs, checked on her, gave some medicines, fruits and juices and headache relieving balm. She felt some relief for a while. I slept early, no calls at night, checked on her, slightly better, suggested additional medicines. With a multitude of health issues, inability to tolerate allopathic medicines, ongoing anaemia, nagging headaches, stomach disturbances, body pains, menorrhagia a few of her recurring problems. Frequent semi fasts, her spiritual *satsangs, seva* and service at Swaminarayan temple and its various other activities, organizing as well being there for them, stress of household work for her even when ill though with the help of other family members, the burden mostly falls on her shoulders. These constant ongoing activities are done at a cost to her health but that is not fully realised as yet.

Responsibilities enormous, duties multiple, frustration, no doubt quite understandable in her situation. She is the foundation of the family, the exhaustion piling up off and on, taking a heavy toll on body and mind. Her own nuclear family members are of course the supporting pillars, and we the elder brothers doting on them, especially the children who remain at the core of our existence even now. Though time with them is at a premium, given ongoing serious education and a busy career for my nephew and niece respectively.

Chapter 16

I sit at my favourite spot. The day will unfold like many other previous ones, though tempered by illness in the family. A call to BabuMoshai, and an early trip to Karjat tomorrow. A dead battery in Professor Bvd's car at 9.10 pm. My brother rushed to help him out. I ate raw veggies and nuts, had fresh lime soda times two, cleaned up, heard mildly encouraging news of *bhabhi's* recovery, slept early with the memory of the weekend past still lingering. Badlapur seems to have both the ingredients essential to my joys compared to Georgina and Karnala, each of the latter has one missing element. Lake Simcoe waters at Georgina but no hills or plantations. Murli's glorious Vaishnavi farms at Lahuchiwadi near Karnala has abundant plantation and hills, nestled underneath the Karnala fort's peak but no river or lake. Here in Sawragaon farm near Badlapur with the Ulhas River touching its boundary and plenty of plantations, it seems to be able to combine the best of my other two retreats. But Ulhas River is not conducive to swimming, while in the waters of Lake Simcoe, I swim repeatedly, close to the shore.

So, I guess the mind always hankers for a utopian place instead of being content with what is...

But reaching Sawragaon without a vehicle of my own, using public transportation is not very easy, but as I said I am most welcome to go with them anytime. With February coming to a close, my time is dwindling down, and some crucial decisions regarding work and life that were held in abeyance till now seem part of a destiny I surrender to without an iota of my will or effort, and I am waiting to see where it takes me.

Back to reality. Two days of ongoing struggle with *bhabhi's* and now my nephew's illness. Television stand and bookshelves made all day at our home by Harshadbhai but a flaw noted in the work by my astute brother, unfortunately after Harshadbhai's departure, my brother being at his work. The shelves are preventing the bedroom roller blinds from opening, so a frustrating rework of cutting the glass shelves, polishing them and redoing the work the next day. This had escaped everyone's attention in spite of being discussed a week ago about taking care to leave enough space for the blinds. Awareness of the present moment, carefully being alert to the task at hand is a lesson that is often repeated, yet it seems so difficult to learn and practice it when the occasion arises. I am equally at fault. Even after the job was done, I failed to notice the problem because it looked so neat, nice and beautiful. Another lesson that appearances can be deceiving when looking at things just superficially. Isn't that what I have been trying to convey about the hidden beauty of the one who has caught my very being?

After my walk, grocery shopping, and shower, I found my elder brother having returned home, telling me of the problem. He surmised it just from the location of the strings of the blinds, their angle at rest, his observant eye and quick mind had detected a similar fault with the second unit air conditioner's wiring also. His process of observation seems much superior to mine, a simple man with knowledge leading to rapid diagnosis and cure of ailing cars. And I with the human body and of new-borns, now struggling to decide what is the nature of my *bhabhi's* illness, my nephew having already recovered.

Is it viral flu, pneumonitis, malaria, enteric fever given last night's racking cough, chills and fever with an unrelenting headache? Awaiting *bhabhi's* recovery, I cancelled my trip to Karjat with Dk *mama* and Bharat Somani with profuse apologies. It had been organized well in advance. 'Maybe, a part of destiny,' said my brother who was equally worried about her. Next 24 hours being crucial to come to a definitive diagnosis, cure and road to recovery. At home upstairs, my nephew is studying. That is a relief as I do not have keys to their home to check on her frequently and not to call and disturb also if she is asleep. I stayed home all day barring an hour with KEM buddies within close distance of home, this get together was on a Tuesday instead of our weekly Thursday meeting. My trip to Murli's farm and staying there about a week alone now likely to be postponed too. And March will roll around in two days, a mad rush to get my own issues sorted out. I am now resigned to leaving tasks unfinished. Just like my fleeting romance, though finished seemingly, but not yet satisfactorily, as loose threads of it remain tugging at my heart.

My not looking is a suppression, that, out of love and respect for her, I have to undertake. Her thoughts though, are still occupying my days. Her new outfit now worn regularly is quite pretty, yet as simple as she is. I sat without reading or writing for long periods yesterday but was unable to keep my body and mind still. No longer waiting to watch her step out, forcibly avoiding and being careful not to let my eyes stray towards her window. So I have no idea of what looks she may have been giving me as she ventures back and forth in her home completing her chores or running errands. This writing is getting equally tedious, innocuous day to day events of life, which you will hardly have any interest to know or read. As my romance dies, so too, the subject of my hectic writing. At a loss now, my mind occupied with the lingering illnesses in the family, no longer allowing the free flowing gamut of emotions and exaggerations that have drowned these pages in ink, when I had no real worries of my own or my family.

Now I write not knowing why, for what and for whom. The whistle of a pressure cooker, the noise of cooking utensils, the frequent irritating alarms of cars every morning, the routines of life around me no different from one day to the next. So what should I conjure up now? Such is the existence of most lives a million times over, with only a subtle difference in the unfolding of events. Each home no doubt has nuances of superficial change that I am not privy to. Last night my brother did the dishes, I just had to warm the food and serve it. Nothing much new every day, same faces, similar tasks, time disappearing, the wheel constantly moving with few hiccups and creaks. How to bring a continued alertness and awareness to each task is still an impossibility given how deep-rooted are the habits of most of us. Somewhere a jump is needed, a precipitating event or trigger that shakes loose the monotony, apathy and rigidity of this moment.

Just stillness is preferable, a taste of doing nothing becoming the art of non-doing.

Chapter 17

My *bhabhi* is slightly better; I am relieved at exercising patience without resorting to drastic measures. I cut a cantaloupe for her, and she slept after a light lunch. Harshadbhai came and is currently redoing the job, correcting the error with a profuse apology which I said wasn't necessary as I had missed it too. My brother got curtain rods, brackets and plaster of paris to plug the holes where the old studs were removed from. I served Harshadbhai dry fruits and grapes, his favourite fruit, after he had finished his work. I sat on the sofa talking to my brother who was standing at the window. Had no choice but to see her hand reach out for utensils left to dry on the grill outside the kitchen window as she was directly in my line of vision. I couldn't back away in time and our eyes unfortunately did meet momentarily. Her look stone faced. My apologies pending yet, for lack of opportunity, her anger palpable but it has been days since the last meeting of our eyes.

What is it about her that makes it so troublesome for me? Unable to reach out to her, nor able to let her go. Such sweetness I find in her face of anger that it worries me. Makes me wonder whether her feelings of apparent friendliness earlier have left and yet they remain still so real for me. Soon the window will shut, the day will continue to progress, the rhythm of her sleep matching the beginning of my walk.

It has been five days since the viewing of *Saajan*, the songs on the television played with a volume that would reach her by design, as if to make up for all that I couldn't say. She is too smart and well-versed with the ways of the world not to realise my intent, if the music ever reached her. It may create further anger at this audacity of mine disturbing her evening, when there has already been a silent categorical rejection of my advance.

This returning to her, is somewhat like the stuck needle on an old gramophone record, spinning timelessly, creating noise amidst the unsuccessful attempts at silence that I am trying to generate. I realise the turmoil that my activities may be creating for her, yet I persist; such is this ego of mine. Assuming, that she has nothing better to do than think of my fancies. But is it possible for anyone who has heard a declaration openly to never subconsciously reminisce about it once in awhile? I have not left her alone completely since the episode of the music and songs from five days ago. But I refuse to further that embarrassment, so I don't play anything from my large collection of tapes and compact discs of great romantic and sad songs on my player, as I see no reason to hear that music myself. The occurrence of *Saajan* was not of my doing, it was a sheer accident, but the intent of those songs very much those in my heart.

Six weeks to go and after that I will leave. Am I taking her with me? Obviously yes, judging from the writing and my heart!

'THE ROMANCE IS DEAD, LONG LIVE THE ROMANTIC'

An apology again to my uncle, as I may not be able to make it to our weekly meetings in town, *bhabhi* is not recovering as rapidly as I had hoped. I plan to wait one more day otherwise seek a more capable physician than myself. My farm trip appears unlikely now. This morning I find that as soon as the medicines wear off her fever and headaches return. Why should you be interested in such a litany, this interlude is a real mini interval, a lullaby to put you to sleep when the boredom from my romantic inclination becomes too repetitive to convey any edge of excitement. Not to say that you aren't concerned about my *bhabhi's* illness, of course.

The crux of this story is to find what is hidden between the lines, the words are vacillating enough as it is. I hope I have generated enough doubt in you to wonder, is there anything real in some part or is it completely a flight of my imagination? In case you do wonder, then this has served its purpose for the writer too is uncertain of what is the real certainty in all this outpouring!

Best case scenario is that it was a pristine love that germinated but died in a soil that was stony and water that had the salt of my tears.

Worst case scenario is that it is just the flowering of language, usage of words that are generous, exorbitant, extravagantly exaggerative giving voice to long buried feelings. Some of it a distillation of all that I have read, the use and abuse of other people's thoughts and not much of my own, except for the hesitant feel of a romance translated into an imaginary love affair.

Getting back into worldly affairs was not part of my intention, but in this closeness is a distance impossible to bridge. The step ladder was non-existent. So this climb and fall is akin to a dream state. I realise that nothing began, so nothing ever ended. But in the hesitation, in this searching, in this laboured effort, you can, if sharp enough, notice the words are much cleaner and legible enough to read. My hand moving slowly now compared to an earlier time when the words were magically floating, moving fast from my heart and mind and alighting upon the pages of this narrative. That hand was sloppy, yet the feelings and thoughts were pure and pristine.

She has come and she has gone. A face of no expressions now for me. I had put my pen aside. She consciously avoids and I can't anymore, given how limited her sights have become of late. Yet, surprisingly her image now is limitless and timeless within me, as I can conjure up her hands and face and moods anytime I wish. But that is not it seems, what Nature intends.

I suddenly realise that the sparrows that used to wander in my courtyard, playing with straws and twigs, taking sips of water are missing today. The water accumulating on the tiles from the washing of cars or from watering the plants has begun to evaporate rapidly, an indicator that the scorching heat of summer is soon approaching in its full ferocity. The crows awaiting their mid-day meal of grains and chapattis thrown from above are missing today. Wednesday, my weekly visit and evening with Dk *mama* and family on hold today due to the prolonged illness of my *bhabhi*. I hope for an early adequate resolution to the crisis, given a very busy day for the children. Whether the lady of the house is well or ill, the tasks of a household still need to get done with not too many choices left. The day rushes on, the tiring of the body and mind adding to the existing anxiety and tension of the illness amongst the family, despite there being a doctor in the house, her complete recovery is proving elusive. I can understand their impatience and irritation but I don't believe they truly doubt my judgement and my care. Moments of much deserved respite, sharing of burdens, helping every which way we can seem to bring a sense of comfort and calm. *Bhabhi* hasn't ventured out now in over 36 hours, and has missed the new emerging flowers in the pots carefully tended to by her. Even the *tulsi* bearing enough new leaves has survived the past three weeks, two other such pots waiting at Murli's farm for me to bring home. The cycle of nature in constant motion, ever changing, unfortunately though, human life also follows the same pattern, riding this wheel, while existence gives enough hints for it to evolve further.

The time is now to alight, step off from this, take wings and fly into the unknown, the only way to know Oneself!

Chapter 18

A momentary glimpse as I got up to fill a tray of snacks for Muktabai, our part-time maid of twenty years, along with her cup of tea. Took some grapes and went back to my perch. Saw half a profile and the beauty of her taking part in a conversation using animated gestures with her hands that still make my heartbeat stutter and race ahead. Soon she disappears to do the laundry, a heavy duty washing every few days with extra stuff, bed sheets, pillow covers, comforters, towels etc., seemingly a never ending line of them hanging. Those are the days I bet her day must seem longer with her window shutting much later in the afternoon.

If her routines are so precious to me then why are mine so troublesome? Discontent seems to be the reason behind keeping this dead or dying fantasy persistently alive. My leftover days declining at a rapid pace now, the decline and fall unable to be arrested. Time away from her by spending a week alone in Murli's farm, postponed to a later date. Stuck in no man's land. The mirage persisting, hoping still for an oasis of calm and clarity, the breeze continuing to carry her presence that sticks like a grain of sand in my eyes.

A welcome interruption as Arham came from school and visited me with his mother, Hetal and a beautiful book of their spiritual teacher and guide titled "A Life Worth Living", wrapped very neatly and carefully. An opportune moment as I had interrupted my re-reading of Osho's "Kabir – The Great Secret", to write again, having stopped at the message exhorting us to evolve, to search for the life that was destined for one. The date was February 27. I asked Hetal to inscribe the message that was printed on her T-shirt as it seemed both humorous and appropriate, inside the book he gifted. I gave Arham chocolates as a thank you, heard about his dental appointment, his upcoming holidays and trip to the Far East with family, sheer coincidence that it was the same week that I was to be on the farm. But now that I will be in town I will miss his cheerful presence, smiles and daily greetings. Anyway the message inscribed was, ' Please do not interrupt while I ignore you'.

An apt one that comes home to roost given what has been transpiring with me and the lady across.

As I waved goodbye to them, I saw my vision blocked by something, likely a huge bin of flour. I see this every few days, big storage bins washed and left to dry in her grill. Earlier times she would glance across with polite courtesy and so would I with my selfish craving. Now the looks almost absent from both directions as this writing meanders around without any clear direction, continuing to circle around the periphery. Albeit, the circles getting smaller and smaller and it will reach the centre someday where only a pinpoint will remain. My heart not courageous enough yet to take the jump directly to that 'one' letting go the support of the 'other'. Its hopes wilting, its petals dropping off, seemingly taking an eternity to become one with the dust of the earth.

The past two weeks with my stagnant romance, it seems that the butterflies also have deserted this lifeless garden of my own cultivation. Have they sensed it too and come to terms with this illusion, their intelligence much sharper than mine, or have they felt the heat of my now burning heart and taken leave so as not to get singed, burnt or torched by my flaming passion that had just wanted a kind look and a friendly smile at least if not the love and affection I crave?

Better get back to the great secret. It beckons enough to say the 'time is now'. My mum and dad's chair arrived today revamped, with some other items for our home upstairs, one still missing to be delivered later, bills are paid and accounts settled in full. Yet I keep my account open, creating undying karmas of my own with the support of props that are not being burdened anymore by me.

What a waste! This romance could have blossomed in all its purity, added something ephemeral to each of our lives. A perilous unknown adventure with its share of pains, hurts, complications, ridicule etc., but it had the opportunity to climb majestically. From the valleys, echoing the scathing scorn of society to the peaks where only love would have remained. One disappearing into the other without the concern or worry of materialistic survival. An opportunity lost never to be regained. A transformation in the offing with the possibility of bringing about a mutation in both of our lives. I can however argue with myself that she isn't in need of any, for I just love her the way she is!

Oh! So suddenly a butterfly flapping its wings arrives for a split second before flying off to places unknown. It seems that to every coincidence, I give my own meaning. No longer is my approach intuitive, it has now become the ultimate drama of cause and effect.

Bound to the chains of the world, I have chosen to call them the threads of my imprisonment. Delicate and fine, yet possessing the resiliency and strength of a spider's silky web.

Today begins my friend Murli's son, Siddhanth's first day of ICSE exam, maths. This is a calculating mind running off on its own volition to subjects out of the blue. These tangents exercising a mastery over my being that doesn't seem to care much about this tug of war. An endless game of no clear decisive result, never able to exhaust the junk it is holding onto due to a lack of something better.

The last day of February, no leap year is a reminder that I have only 39 days left, each rolling into the next seamlessly. Disappearing like the clouds, leaving today a glorious empty sky. An ongoing still pleasant weather conducive to silence and long walks from early afternoon.

Saw Arham today; no words, just a short wave of greeting. Appears sleepy, tired having had a late night with his cousin and family, a prelude to his vacation from Sunday onwards. I did some chores with *bhabhi* coming down after 36 hours of being cooped up in her home. She made *patra* from the leaves of Ba's family farm, along with the rest of the cooking; it has exhausted her quite a bit. Her health is getting better, my patience hopefully rewarded. Cleaning utensils, my brother flipping television channels in the afternoon came across *Saajan* again. A vignette of two songs today, one having been missed, I stopped my work and fell into a rhythm with its romantic sad melody. I am sure she got to hear a faint murmur of them as her window was open given the large bin preventing its closure. It never occurred to me that she may have already gone in for her afternoon nap. Late evening came, so did *Baazigar* with another favourite song of the heart. Sound of crockery from her kitchen, so I doubt she ever heard it.

My messages are no longer registering with her; the meaning I have been trying to convey is mostly in vain. She has percolated deep within me, beginning to enter daily like a steaming hot cup of tea. A momentary joy of sipping it but leaving in its wake somewhat of a scalding as she keeps pouring cold water on this foggy experience of mine.

An unexpected Wednesday and Thursday evening at home. Did 'Jai Burlington' on phone with Dk *mama*, missing our evening together. BabuMoshai on his way back to Canada, will halt with Rima in Singapore to spend two days with our dear friends Bindu and Ravi, co-cottage owners and their sweet bright toddler daughter Sneha.

Had a humorous ten-minute conversation with him to be continued while in Singapore. Ran into Rashmibhai on my walk, my friend Bawa's brother-in-law. Had a chat regarding books I read and the music I listen to. He was surprised by the changes in my life. He and Aniben, Bawa's cousin, often invite me over, and my response is similar to my response to other relatives' and friends' invitations, a gracious respectful decline as always. He had noticed the absence of Walkman and iPod on my walk. I informed him that now I am a very boring man in social company. He replied, no way, you are a very interesting man. Somehow to me, both are one and the same, two sides of the same coin.

My interests now are quite few. Yes, memory lingers of things that have fallen by the wayside, yet I am able to enjoy them when someone brings them back into my circle of attention. My brother just informed me that *bhabhi* is better, a substantial relief it is to hear the news. My water lady arrived, payday for her too. I have on occasions given her fruits, sweets, chocolates when she has time to have a light conversation with me. Her *dupatta* wrapped around her neck and chest like a scarf, simple and pretty with lightly hued brown eyes reflecting her growing up in the mountainous regions of Nepal (come to think of it, I have no real idea of the colour of the eyes of the lady I fancy). Her exuberance obviously allowing her a survival in this mad city, yet missing the carefree life of her village and the soil of her native place, along with her parents and siblings. She is devoted to her husband; I see them often strolling together in evenings or going for some shopping. She carries on her obligations to his family with a cheerful face, though her eyes mist over when she recalls her family back home in Nepal whom she hasn't visited for almost two years now.

Nostalgia, I had thought was just the realm of the old people. The young are often swayed by the charms of modernity that this city offers, but she reminisces fondly of her simple yet hardworking life on the farm and home after growing up, the work according to her much harder than here. The longing is evident in her voice, gestures and eyes, I can relate to that too. The call of a place that one calls home may or may not be the place of your birth. But for me, the call of death, I hope when it comes is in the place where my umbilical cord was cut, or on Georgina island. That is my hope and prayer, the latter my most loved place and Mumbai the place of my birth. I would consider myself fortunate to have either of those wishes fulfilled.

But my present longing is of a different nature, so close and across from me, able to see almost daily yet so distant from me. That in effect may have kept perpetuating this illusion.

A sudden reminder on my walk yesterday, saw a pair of green butterflies rushing past me, a similar one had come floating into my garden once. A vision of a delicate hand grasping the edge of the balcony grill as she made a graceful turn into the front courtyard carrying a bucket in the other hand. I lifted my gaze on her return, she as usual now not lifting her eyes. I followed her slow walk, a sudden movement it seemed as if she bit her lower lip. I wonder if it is a sign of irritation and is there a different feeling that prompts someone to bite the upper lip instead! Maybe it's just an individual habit with nothing behind it, my constant search for meaning in every act of hers is a fool's enterprise.

I keep the ending prolonged it seems till the time my visit here is over. Yet I know she will never exit my heart, agreed though that she has not entered it of her own choosing!

Chapter 19

I am left amazed thinking about what her response would be if she ever gets to know that a lifetime with me was there for the taking! Security, comfort, and no backbreaking labour to earn a living anymore. Almost like a permanent holiday for her while I am alive.

Abroad I take care of all my needs on my own. I do not eat cooked food at home nor order out unless I have relatives or friends visiting, that too is not that often. Yes, I do go often to BabuMoshai, Balan, Soman, Raja, Hemant, and Sudha's homes, where I partake of many delicacies and culinary delights. At times at BabuMoshai's place I may make my well renowned bread pizzas for the family that his wife Rima and their twin daughters, Nikki and Nina also love. I survive on raw vegetables, fruits, nuts, chips, salsa, cottage cheese, Melba toast, some *chaknas* (savouries), and on occasion a huge platter of *sev puri* and a tin of cashews serves as my main meal. On other days it is always a 7 to 8 topping toasted bagel sandwich. Yes, I indulge in chocolates and ice creams for weeks in a row alternating with each other and then not eat either for many weeks again.

I seldom eat all day until evenings at home, and even at work barring Friday morning breakfast of a croissant during a seminar and pizza at our faculty lunch time meeting to discuss challenging patients in the unit every week. Of course at Georgina I nibble during the day mainly on toasts and dry fruits as snack in between my activities of reading, walking, swimming and biking. I clean my rental condo, bathrooms, sinks, do laundry and ironing, grocery shopping and any such chores myself. A dishwasher takes care of the utensils. So it is not as if I need someone abroad to do any of the household tasks. And if I can't get her to enjoy my tastes in food and she wishes to eat cooked food, I guess I can try to learn and make it or she may wish to do that for herself. Of course, many years ago I have given almost all of the cooking utensils, pantry containers, corning ware and other such needs of a kitchen to relatives and friends. But I do not mind at all investing in them again. I can also make a delicious chick pea salad that all my friends often enjoy at the cottage in addition to my famous 7 toppings toasted Bagel sandwiches. Here in Mumbai too, for the last two years, except for Muktabai who spends an hour in the afternoon doing our laundry, and sweeping and cleaning the floors, my brother, *bhabhi* and I take care of the rest of the chores. Our cook Sharmila comes for an evening cooking of just one item usually our Gujarati *paratha*, *bhakri* or some such item with also the luxury of an off day, at times even twice a week during my stay here. *Bhabhi* takes care of the rest of items for evening meals almost in totality and specialities that she sends for us especially on weekends when the children prefer some different foods. Toast with raw garlic in morning with tea, afternoon fruits, raw veggies and nuts to begin my evening and then the dinner. Indian dessert, or an ice cream or chocolate on some days.

So my needs few and my wants even fewer.

I claim no possessiveness of her, a full freedom of her will and choices guaranteed. All I wish for is just the longing to see her every morning when I wake up, talk to her and observe the elegant etiquette of having her do nothing much around the house if she so wishes, similar to the charm she brings to the most ordinary of her current daily tasks.

I went on some errand for the family and was reading when she too left on one. I sat in silence, saw her returning, she noticed me noticing her, an imperceptible shake of the head, did I also see a frown, but unsure of it. She is resigned to this as I too maybe am about the outcome, it having been decided by her a long-time ago.

Then why did a tear escape from my eye? This longing and attachment is both nectar and poison. She can't see me writing again, as she is off to do the laundry. A 90-minute sojourn before she re-enters her kitchen. An unsustainable calm repeatedly disturbed by the cyclone of her appearance time and again. Why do my eyes stray repeatedly, why do I invite this pain and sorrow? A white butterfly visits, teaching me a lesson to detach from this process as it flits around a few flowers and disappears without any trace of regret, having had its fill.

I was mistaken as I seem to be time and again. She hurried back into the kitchen, then standing at the adjoining door and again went out of sight. The faint shadows of her movement catching my attention even while reading or writing, as if her shadow has fallen on me. So even when not looking or glancing before the event, it triggers a spontaneous involuntary gaze from me catching then the fleeting glimpse of her on many an occasion. She arrived at the window, seeming to have other tasks delaying the chores I had assumed she would be doing.

No song playing, my messages sent across many times now by various means and medium ignored. Uncaring to know its sum and substance, oblivious of the future I imagine for her. Content is she in her present state. An admirable suitor likely in the wings awaiting her attention. And here comes Arham excitedly chattering about a story of his day at school with his father Kunal. Bright, active, bubbling with energy today, he greets me saying he has been a good boy and hasn't eaten a single chocolate today.

A walk, a few errands, a lost bus pass of my nephew necessitating a redo at the depot. *Bhabhi* now 24 hours into a slow recovery, back to her chores and errands in full swing. The weakness generated already will take its toll doing unavoidable necessary activities that are required for the smooth running of the households. Yes, unfortunately, it triggered an unrelenting headache at night, an emergency phone call as I was winding up the kitchen duty.

I went upstairs immediately, anxious and concerned of course, but with a tinge of irritation knowing this was already my intuition, frustrated by the illnesses in young family members, while I have been fortunately healthy for more than 2 decades now. Her constant activity within and outside the home all necessary in fact without the benefit of significant rest, all triggers worrying me about a relapse worse than the previous illness that was seemingly headed for a recovery. Her spiritual work and devotion, tutoring grade 9 and grade 10 children of many friends, her role of a financial advisor to friends and family, her own reading time and multiple tasks that she really enjoys including maintaining and caring for two gardens in both our homes must also bring her some peace and sense of fulfilment in life.

My anger momentarily evident in the tone of my words that immediately halted me right in my tracks. Then an underlying compassion managed to surface and provide some relief with soothing words and medicines too. My advice so easy to give and difficult to practise it in a busy household of four members with multiple needs, that seem to be taking its toll on the foundation and main pillar of our family. This continued certainty of expected setbacks within a short time frame keeps me on tenterhooks. I treated her ailments; she must have slept well I hope as morning dawned with no news being a sign of good news.

March 1, today, another month of aimless and fruitless days over. My work is piling up, will end up doing what I can, the leftover undone jobs will hopefully not be the cause of future regrets. My farm visit is in jeopardy, given the distance. Two more items pending for home, then a reorganisation with disposal of items from the living room. A rearrangement of furniture now creating a feeling of a lengthy openness to the room, a spacious feel about it now. Anyway, a rearrangement of my life also taking shape, but getting lost time and again. The circumstances surrounding me, creating a sense of lethargy and resignation. My visits in search of a retreat for family friends and myself, my week of solitude on Murli's farm unlikely to materialise.

The days will spill over, empty, my cup of continued relaxation, my balance of rest and movement will tilt towards the latter. This ominously continuing yo-yo, coming to a sudden halt as my departure date arrives.

I remain grateful, fortunate to be in the position I am in, seeing the mad rush of everyone's life, the exception being my elder brother's lifestyle. I try my best to make them understand the meaninglessness of trivial pursuits, frivolous activities setting a stage for this fruitless drama to unfold for lives untold. I too in my past have engaged thoroughly in them of course, but realisation dawned, albeit late for me, so I am trying to convey that message from the understanding of my own experience. As I said before, it's always easy to say this but very difficult to convince anyone.

In every sphere of outer activity, be it the kind of education today, career, profession or vocation, trivial matters of toys, gadgets, television, computers, tablets, mobiles etc., you name it, in the end none of these ever matter much in the long run, barring the achieving of the non-doing of the inner. Now, I realise that I could and would never wish to go through another such life again, except the choice of my profession. But I know fairly well that it will happen, a rebirth destined for me till I can ever reach the stage where this cycle ends.

Fortunately though I will have no memories of this life but a wish and a prayer that my next life begins with the sentiments gathered till now and beyond in the remaining moments. The experiences passed through that have allowed me now to just take care of my needs, with very few wants in life remaining. Basically these are related in some manner or another to have rest, relaxation, calm and volunteer work in a professional and social capacity and a reengineering of an inner peace that is somewhat elusive.

The news from upstairs is reassuring, the pillar of the family is holding up, ably supported by other family members. I wait my turn to be of some help again, hopefully not in my professional capacity. This morning, news headlines talk of India's budget, a balance sheet of the nation. Promises galore and as in the past such ones, most will be noticed and understood to have been empty. My balance sheet of this visit often in an equilibrium, give or take moments of pluses and minuses.

At least this writing is the only aspect that has flowers and thorns both in equal measure. And if at the end of this trip, it all amounts to a big fat 'zero' that would be like icing on the cake!

Chapter 20

A glance at the perception of a shadow from the corner of my eye. I see the seminal reason for this writing lingering for a minute doing small cleaning tasks. I look at her, my pen suspended. She will come out soon and so she does in her gorgeous black top embellished with the colours of the rainbow as does my water lady. The mornings still bring serenity and relief at seeing her in spite of what seems to be an overwhelmingly clear rejection, mounting daily from her nuances that seem to ignore vibrations either of my silence or my music that is reaching her. She is reaching back to her home sooner and quicker now, no longer walking at her usual leisurely pace. Hurrying her steps, and limiting the time I get to see her face and her arms. For the rest of the day it is just the play of light and shadow, a profile and then her back towards the window. I console myself, it's likely just the heat of the morning sun making her want to get back to her shelter sooner. More than two weeks now of this drama that keeps repeating, yet never a source of boredom for me.

There seems to be no indication of a twist to this tale.

She is totally absorbed in her role in absolute disregard of the spectator. The one who finds a freshness in the enthralling rapture of every movement of hers, however identical it seems on a daily basis. Maybe I enjoy pain and indifference a lot more than the pleasures that come and go. This melancholy is something that resides deep, is the source of a sweet sorrow. It seems to create some joy, and the more I keep churning it, it surfaces again and again. I continue an easy conversation with my water lady, some of my words may reach her, diluting her opinions about me already, for better or worse.

Attainable or not, she will continue her quiet presence in my life, any other just seems to pale into insignificance in front of her totality. In that she has filtered into and gotten absorbed in the very fibre of my being.

I still wish that she gets to know somehow that my intentions were absolutely honourable. This isn't about cutting her wings off, but giving her my own to take flight to an unknown, unimaginable horizon!

This is an obvious rehash of thoughts already presented, feelings generated out of the blue, being deciphered into words of similar quality but abundant quantity. This is an attempt to delay the inevitable conclusion, a prolongation of my agony!

'I CANNOT LIVE WITH HER AND I CANNOT LIVE WITHOUT HER'

A late breakfast for me, and time spent in getting medicines and a multivitamin with B- Complex injection vial for *bhabhi*. Coincidentally, Arham this morning showed me a toy syringe on his way to school, the first time ever amongst his other such toys he comes down with. And a few hours later I had to use a real syringe and needle; he will come for his chocolate fix this evening. An absolute delight it is to engage with him, will miss him next week for sure when he goes on vacation with his family. She has changed quite early, saw her with her mistress in a *pooja* ceremony and the lighting of a *diya* (lamp). A dragonfly hovers in the courtyard, a tree in front of her building cleared of a beehive, workers selling its honey while I await Muktabai's arrival and I too have an errand to run at the Ganesh provision store.

A long walk, and a delivery of *paneer*, mushrooms, baby corn and bell peppers for the evening stir fry dinner. *Dhoklas* and *chole* from Arham's family, and chocolates from me for a safe journey and a fun-filled holiday for them. A busy evening, cleaned up and came upon an unexpected vision at 10.30 pm of her running across the courtyard with two carry bags. Climbing the steps in leaps, she had a solitary lone evening earlier. Saw her removing the dried wash cloths, I bowed respectfully, she is now totally exasperated with my relentless silent attention.

This morning after a call to Canada and then putting kitchen towels back in the drawer, I opened my windows and as my gaze naturally lifted to turn back, our eyes met. She now takes care and pains to quickly reach for things on the platform and then disappear rapidly out of sight, her hesitancy more pronounced it appears in spite of her lightning speed, which is not her nature. She is probably aware that the longer she stays around her window, the more time and opportunity for me to see her. A phone call from Murli, farm visit postponed to tomorrow, suits me better as I need to be certain of *bhabhi's* recovery. I can complete some work and call the parents of my patients abroad as I do often every year from here.

The last bud has opened, two flowers side by side, likely one will be plucked away in the next 24 to 48 hours. A very quiet neighbourhood this Saturday morning, all seemingly at rest, my rest mingled with echoes of turbulence. I find my sleep broken over the past few days, maybe partly due to the anxiety of *bhabhi's* recurrent illness. Woke up today at 3.00 am, maybe my mind registering that it being a Saturday and the farm visit in the offing, it would not allow my routine afternoon walk. So, exhorting me to go instead in the morning, but the body refused to cooperate, and I decided to stay in bed. But, later I found out that the farm visit is postponed to Sunday, so the walk for Saturday is quite secure now.

All is solemnly quiet, till she exits to her garden and creates chaos in the jungles of my mind. It is getting hotter now with the arrival of March, a sure sign that this prolonged idyllic pleasant Mumbai winter of sorts is on its way out. My sweating will become profuse not just from my walks but from the paraphernalia of pending tasks. The more I delay, the worse it will get. If this writing continues unabated without a solution acceptable to the heart, the pending tasks will continue to be pushed further away. Many of them may be left unaccomplished before my return springs up on me, making me regret the deep procrastination I am showing towards unfinished work.

I spot my water lady returning after delivering car keys to multiple families. The office is closed today so that cleaning job of hers is not needed. Now with the heat, our plants are being watered daily. Still, quite a clear sky, heralding a hot day in store. I run into Missus often, helping her, exchanging polite conversations about nothing much, often may be silent in the three to four minutes it takes to negotiate the lane. I see Masterji also, but with Ganesh tagging along no such physical help is needed from me.

Sometimes, she has a visitor, a woman with one or two kids tagging along on occasion. Tall, dark, always in a single coloured saree, looks to be related but I can't be certain if she is her sister or *bhabhi*. Her brother is at a job in Pune, her sister in the village is what I recollect from our first real conversation. Anyway there is a resemblance in looks, maybe it is because I have begun to SEE HER in most other women housekeepers around her age.

Everything seems to be happening in slow motion today. She is late in getting to her garden. Still in her kitchen, with faint sounds of utensils drifting across to me. I see her at the main door as if on the verge of coming out. But her upright posture, one free hand gesturing, makes me doubt that she has a bucket of water in the other. This constant enumeration of her activities visible or imagined by me, a virtual reality tour mired in fiction. It is in the language of words with no moving video. Makes me wonder, is it still an invasion of her privacy, a breach of ethical and moral law? In a dense crowded urban landscape there is no avoiding seeing her from where I sit or stand, nor is it possible not to hear neighbours' talk. This though may be more purposeful on my part at times but never am I a peeping tom.

An interruption as we rearranged our living room furniture. Dad's chair is back in its rightful place, mum's chair hovering nearby. On dad's chair either I sit or Murli sits when he comes, on mum's chair sits my elder brother. On few occasions, my nephew, when he comes down here, occupies dad's chair. The look of the room is not bad at all, quite open and acceptable in fact with a feeling of spaciousness to it. Haven't seen her again, then I hear Arham calling out to me and my brother. Small moments of joy arrive unexpectedly from the little ones, I am fortunate to experience them amidst the chaos of my writing. A sparrow arrives, sits on my grill, then pecks at stuff on the ground and is gone. These visions now as fleeting as my sights of her. A pale green butterfly comes as I talk to my water lady and see her returning with a small bag in her hands. Folded over, empty maybe, as she kept patting it refusing to look up. Unwillingly occupying herself, a slight tilt of her head staring at nothing in particular. Her boundless energy for multiple tasks on a daily basis is quite amazing to see and imagine. She is obviously very well looked after by her employer's family, more like a member of their nuclear family. Their generosity likely immense to her and in return her attitude towards them is similar also.

A dragon fly in the courtyard, flying back and forth, saying hello and goodbye together, a painful reminder of the one I was subjected to by her silence! This irresistible pull of her, tugging at my heart, laying to naught my resolve of keeping my gaze away. There's something about her that refuses to go away. A magnet pulling at my rusted thoughts and feelings, yet leaving both our freedoms intact. The distance just about enough that any attraction is simultaneously met with a repulsion.

I went to fix my breakfast, waiting for the tea to reheat, looking across vacantly. I suddenly saw her smile and talk to the neighbouring servant, our eyes locked for an instant and her smile vanished. I saw her running back across the steps, her antics as pleasing as a child's without a care in the world. Her artistry an equal match to nature's bounty but now out of view. My tea and cigarette over, the heat overpowering from the overhead sun, an indicator of my own sun on a downward trajectory sinking and setting every day.

A nice evening with family, my favourite meal of *sev puri* and cashews, the serial *Adalat*, my nephew in the chair, a call to BabuMoshai, and an unexpectedly late evening across the house from me. Next morning, a call to Akshay and Bindu, co-owners of my cottage in Georgina Island, preparation for farm visit, broken sleep when for most of the three months it has been quite good. A subtle subconscious mind remaining awake. My feet now with many cracks, a swelling on the dorsum of the right foot, hopefully not a stress hairline fracture of one of its bones, likely stemming from my daily walking of 18 to 20 kilometres and at times even up to 25, if I walk twice in the day. *Bhabhi* is much better, and back to her routine but does tire out quickly. Hope to start iron medication but they have never suited her previously so in a quandary about how to get her back to normal.

A busy week ahead, lots of groceries and miscellaneous items needed, the wallet emptying everyday to be replenished each morning. Just basic things are getting really more and more expensive even for me, in spite of the favourable dollar to rupee exchange. I often now take pause and reflect on the woes of the common man of this runaway exponential inflation with no real wage growth or significant tax relief for them. Forget for the moment the indigenous population, because that will cause another heartbreak.

Not much else coming to mind, the heart given up to her. My life is on hold in a manner of speaking. The superfluous writing has to continue, lest I lose it again.

She will be hurried this morning having started late. She now briefly watched me while cleaning her copper pot. She knows at times I write about her, for I had told her that myself two months ago, when we seemed to be friendly. About my love, she knows it's there. But she may harbour a doubt about its motives or intentions, that is, if she now ever thinks about me. No way to dispel it or make her believe in me. Her silence renders me unable to put any of her fears to rest. The remaining days will disappear as rapidly as the months seem to have gone. And so it shall remain till my next trip back to India, I'll see then if this can continue in case she is still single and across and no longer cross with me!

There's not much I can foresee in the near future to make her understand my love. This sinking deeper and deeper like a stone into a bottomless well, she, not at all thirsty to taste the waters of this well. She floats around in complete indifference or has enough other known sources to quench her thirst, not wishing to explore this unknown old well. However the coincidence of the late night movie *Cheeni Kum* on television, about a 60-year-old man and a 30-year-old woman in love with each other and her own late night yesterday, is not easy to dismiss from my mind.

Chapter 21

Farm visit on Sunday, an exceedingly hot day. Friends, food, St Remy cognac, *tulsi* plants, coconuts and veggies brought back and now preparations to go stay there for a few days. There wasn't a breeze at all that day, a sombre mood of nature, resting in its own intense heat. A message to be comfortable under any circumstances. Sleep though is at a premium on my return. Tossing and turning, the anxieties now weighing and troubling, the attempt at a Buddhist calm unsustainable. A morning call to Susamma, a surprise call from Nandita and I sit here wondering how rapidly, lazily the days have been slipping away like sand through my fingers. A hectic couple of days to prepare for my retreat and solitude, a train, rickshaw and state transport bus ride with baggage, an urgency registered yet ignored for now.

The time will soon arrive to say goodbye to all that is being written.

Monday morning, all is silent, my mind chattering way. An effort is desperately needed to regain an equanimity that has suddenly gone missing. A long phone call to Manisha – who works as a nurse in Pune – last night about her mother, Muktabai. Muktabai's perception of illness, the precipitating and aggravating factors, and the lack of immediate solution in sight except to say that there is no real physical illness of the body. Gave her clues and suggestions to tide over and ameliorate this illusion of her mother, for whom it is obviously quite real. But isn't that the problem with me too? You all may rightly think so!

A desperate attempt is needed to drop my mind and regain sanity. Impossible though it seems to let her go and develop my own awakening. Reading and writing will have to be marginalised to reclaim the early experiences of this visit. The imaginary romance has to die and so it must, so that my real fruitful exercise of doing nothing takes root again. Time away amidst nature will help, though short, it will have to be accepted and utilised to the maximum. For, on return are tasks of such magnitude remaining that it will prove difficult to finish them in time.

Almost always with a few rare exceptions, quite loving and compassionate, this then is the time to find the real source, which is meditation: The real art of doing nothing.

This trip basically has been spent in reading books already read and finding forgotten lessons and newer meanings. Also an abundance of hidden feelings, awaiting a spring that will be delayed with the intense heat prevailing, yes that spring will now have to be enjoyed in Canada.

Yes, I missed the season for sowing the seeds of meditation as I was busy with the seeds of love and romance and now I am struggling with a drought as no harvest is possible.

Farm preparations are in full swing, read Osho's Buddha, slowed my pace on walks, yet time runs ever faster than I imagined. The heat of the day making my every thought simmer on a slow flame. Neither able to evaporate or cool down enough so as not to singe me, the spark for this ongoing fire is of my own making. Water is at hand to end it, but I seem to enjoy this ongoing suffering.

Today I see a kid barely in double digits washing cars while most kids his age are off to school. Destitute beggars, refuse collectors, migrant labourers doing backbreaking work without safety measures, a common everyday occurrence with similar such scenes and many others in every nook and cranny across this country. Daily rapes, accidents, robberies, suicides, murders all as common and routine as the rising sun, sinking India into a morass of apathy and indifference. I am finding it more and more difficult now to engage in conversations that appear to me to be about trivial matters. For others they remain a part of their daily conversation. For many with few hobbies and fewer vices, a gathering at the *paanwalla* shop is a release, a need to engage in the mundane small talk. Meaningless or otherwise, after a long day of commuting and of productive work, it is undoubtedly a necessary activity, just like watching television and shutting the mind off. I too am guilty, as years ago an outer silence was alien to me. I enjoyed talking similarly. Now that the inner talk seems less, the outer routine conversation has begun to annoy me at times. Well from all this writing, the first point is quite open to a debate in which for sure the loser is myself. Anyway my friends used to often remark, dadhi will always have the last word.

This illusory romance is now creating moods that are real. Spontaneous moments of silence are touched with a sense of sadness. My face likely reflecting some anguish, the sense of joy not materialising in my mirror's demeanour. So I wait in a cultivated patience that may over time become as real and evident as the so-called fake and imaginary writing taking shape on these pages.

Another year as more children from my building and neighbouring begin their Secondary School Certificate board exams, an event that every year triggers anxiety, panic, sleeplessness, tensions, illnesses, accidents, suicides, all this in the name of a better curriculum to create PRODUCTIVE CITIZENS of the new India. The CAREFREE days when learning was fun and joyful, are now violent, competitive, and full of jealousy, envy, so-called friends betraying their brethren; I am sorry to say that it is a total butchery of childhood. Ashamed should be the ones sitting in their ministry who themselves never went through any of this and just from their corrupt practices now occupy seats to dictate to the child of today. This is the poisoning of young minds and hearts not to forget the innocent lives lost in this competitive stream now. The great tradition of *gurukuls*, the vision of people like Tagore, Krishnamurti and many others like them are all left to bite the dust. In the so-called Information Technology revolution of which this land is the major outsourcer for the western world, 'I.T.' has forgotten its own culture that was brilliant and often revered by the rest of the world. You have read and seen enough of all this in the news and experienced it in your homes as well, and it will continue to repeat itself, savaging every new generation in the name of progress and the changing economy of the world. I doubt that there is any greater bullshit than my writing but this system does come very close to it!

I have gone through this system in some small measure too. In spite of my declared passion for medicine from very early in childhood, I too succumbed to learning the nonessential. I too had to make my parents fork out their hard-earned money for subjects ultimately irrelevant to my choice of a profession. The only paid tuition I ever took was Sanskrit language, given my memory I aced it, of course without any understanding of it. And, the Agrawal classes for physics, a subject I loathe, just to make sure I do not falter in my goal, and get marks enough to move on towards my real needs. And the early years of my medical college, most of it of no use today and no thanks to it, that I am a fully accomplished physician well regarded by all. But I am sorry to say, not much of what my parents paid for my tuitions nor what I struggled with has had any meaning or bearing on my ultimate outcome. Yet today we are asking young minds to make a choice even one year earlier than I had to do so. There are umpteen examples of children who choose something just to compete with or be on par with their peers, only to realise much later that it is not their true interest or passion.

Just take a moment you so-called well doers of children, sit or walk in their shoes today and you will be ashamed of yourselves for the atrocity you perpetuate repeatedly on these innocent young minds and hearts that are now just fodder for your ministry.

"Shame on you! Your children will inherit all your ill-gotten wealth, you make institutes in your name, capitation colleges, and call yourself educators, yet you have missed the entire education of life!"

Strong words maybe, but remember I write as I see each moment, each day. Many of you in your plush offices, calling yourselves the guardians of education, looking at nature outside your glass windows, ledges with decorated plants, yet smothering the flowering plant that is the child of today, like you were once long before and have forgotten about it.

Suddenly, I had a thought about the so-called doctrine of 'karma', the present situation of anyone being a reflection of past deeds. I have no intention to discuss the metaphysical viewpoint either as a belief or truth nor wish to engage in such a debate. Vedanta and the Geeta aside, karma if a natural law, becomes impossible to prove or recollect it as your own experience most of the time, barring the immediate result of a wrong action bearing ills in the present. Neither knowledgeable nor a scholar I am suddenly struck by an odd question.

If the ills of society, the poverty, the homelessness, destitution, illnesses, hunger, starvation, tragedies so on and so forth in human life are based on previous past karmas of another life, while the materially rich people are enjoying the benefits of previous good deeds, I find myself at loss somehow today? You tell me, whether any person in some of the precarious situations I described above has any hope or chance in hell to make life better and move up on the chain of exhausting his so-called bad karmas. Yes, maybe one in a thousand million will find religiosity a better option than the need for earning a livelihood for himself and his family. The materially well off are the ones whose religiosity or religiousness is ignited as they are finally bored of their luxurious living. And if they do not embark on a real spiritual endeavour having experienced all the material comforts that life has to offer, that then indeed is a shame, especially if they are unable to ask themselves, what better life will be there on top of what they already enjoy living in this life. Do you mean to say then there is no rebirth for them? Or do you mean that if they enjoy this present life with all its comforts and then do bad deeds, they will return to the bottom of the chain of evolution or somewhere a step below? Is this the snake and ladder game of my childhood? If the snake is long or short, and you land on it based on deeds in this life, you end up somewhere halfway or at the bottom, or if lucky throw the dice and you make it home! Then what is that home? So I propose a novel take on karmic philosophy.

The downtrodden, whom we call as suffering today from their previous bad karmas, may in fact be those who had already ascended up to a rich prosperous life and then refused to evolve further. Refused to understand the meaninglessness of that richness being a gateway to a spiritual religious life. Missed the opportunity that was there for the taking, if from prior good deeds they had ascended the ladder to reach the top. Then because of greed or dishonesty to achieve even more, they descended down in their next life either halfway or right to the bottom of the evolutionary chain.

I just shared something that occurred to me but you may not agree with it. No debate, nothing to argue. I concede to whatever is your own take on this doctrine. My deepest apologies, no offense intended, and your criticisms I humbly accept. My take on this subject may not even be lucid enough, just proposing a plausible hypothesis.

Maybe you just have to read the lives of Krishna, Buddha and Mahavira on one side and the lives of Christ, Gorakh and Kabir on the other. Just a few examples of the many; not to forget the devotion of realised souls like Meera, Radha, Sahajo, Daya, and others. If your act is total in of itself, without the expectation of reward but full of love and compassion, and if one can drop the idea, thought, feeling and the action as being that of individual ownership then it will be easy to imbibe the knowledge of the Geeta and other masters, and lead to an understanding of what the doctrine of karma is, and that will be the freedom from the bondage of Karma.

To quote Ramesh Balsekar, in gratitude, from his book 'Confusion No More':

"Events happen, deeds are done; there is no individual doer of any deed."

Some of what I have said on the spur of the moment may trigger a rethinking of the old doctrine and idea of karma. Forgive me if anyone is hurt by it. My idea is just like the finger pointing at the moon - it is not the moon itself.

Chapter 22

Mere Jeevan Saathi – TV, 3.15 pm, Song: *O Mere Dil Ke Chein!*

Murli calls – Her window opens.

This to me has a deep coincidence that only Murli besides me will understand. It's one of his favourite songs. And for many years in the past, 3.15 pm was the time we talked almost every day to each other on the telephone. Now in our friendship such conversations no longer needed and the friendliness remains timeless. Also brings back memories of my late uncle Ck *mama* and my now dead mum, having a phone conversation at 7.30 pm every day. He before leaving his factory to return to his home, and mum just getting ready to cook the evening meal at our home. Then after serving dinner to us brothers, mum would have almost a daily telephone conversation with Rajanimami (Dk *mama's* wife), finishing it before my dad arrived home at 10 pm from his clinic.

March 6 - A Visit to Murli's enclave – Vaishnavi Farms, Lahuchiwadi

Vignette in brief of 5-day stay from March 6 to 10

Following is a very brief synopsis of it, attempts at so-called poetry is titled 'Reflections' at the end.

WRITTEN AT VAISHNAVI FARMS, AND ON THE BANKS OF RANSAI LAKE, WHERE I SPENT HOURS FEELING AND THINKING WHAT I DID IN THAT MOMENT!

6/3 - Forgot to buy cheese and butter. A blessing in disguise. Fridge was out and it would have spoiled.

Train, rickshaw, ST. Barapada, Banbaiwadi, Taragaon, Aptaphata. *Samosa pav* for all. Maaza mango. No water. All three phases of electricity are down, then one resumed working. Sitting near swing. First evening star. Pitch dark. Sky obstructed by huge jackfruit tree but visible over temple. Earth, trees and wind asleep. Stars and moon awake, moving. Fed dogs, cats, myself, and Tukaram and his wife. Conversation and retired for the night.

7/3 - 5.30 am, birds chirping on the *jamun* tree. Hens crowing. Tea, then Ransai Lake and dam. Parrots, seagulls, quicksand. Sandals ruined. Boats, irrigation fields, fishing. Return. Tea and biscuits with Tukaram. Power comes. Relay race to fill water. I began, followed by Somwar and his wife, Sakha, then Tukaram. Binoculars, birds, stars. *Vada pav* for all. Early to bed. Stars galore.

8/3 – Breakfast, tea and toast; Somwar, Tukaram and myself. Karnala climb and back with Somwar. Sights all around, Ransai in the distance, yet dirty water in the perennial *kundh* of the fort with plastic and other litter. Graffiti everywhere. Tea, *neera* and water. Men asleep after lunch.

9/3 - Ransai, Magarwadi, Banglawadi. On both banks, a long stay of 3 hours. Attempt to capture moments in poems and haikus again. Babubhai, Junaid and company. Tea, cookies and chocolates for all. Junaid made onion *poha* and *kokam* sherbet. Murli, Narayan and Baboo visit. Feast for all. Slept at 8.30. Gifts and chocolates for the kids of the hired help.

10/3, Sunday – Mahashivratri, 06.00 am wake up. Tea and toast. 3 hours at Ransai. Tips for all the help, along with expressions of gratitude. Touch their feet for blessings return home. Apologies for any extra work resulting for them. Packed produce from farm. Rickshaw and train. Jam-packed train. Arrived back 6.15 pm.

What a journey and what a stay!

All begins, all ends

Until next year!

Tough it was to depart from this serenity, but everyone has to take leave to come back again someday!

An in-between mood prevails, no breeze today though it is the time for it. Missing it somehow. Am I in tune with nature or is it in tune with me?

I sit, knowing my time here is running out. An ordinary person had an extraordinary experience, found everything appealing. The din and bustle of my other life looming soon. These moments were magical and enough, a rest and peace that will soon be easily disturbed. Am I ready to face it? Do I carry all this with me or will it disappear like a puff of smoke? Stopped writing, began reading again and the breeze too has started rolling in gently, a message probably that my words are like dust for it to carry away without them landing in anyone's eyes.

Everything is present here, yet I remain absent, mired in the dark alleys of my mind.

Conjuring one empty word after another, learning and knowing, still elusive. Baby steps towards it are welcome, but there must be an easier way for them to take roots. Yes, I have read little, written even less the past five to six days, small statements only.

None has any lasting message but somewhere in between the lines is a meaning I wish to decipher and fathom.

Having sat doing nothing for many afternoons now, the silence comes and goes like tricks of my mind. Conversations limited but not missed at all. Nature speaks, I hear but do not listen. Too ready to interfere is this mind, giving the silence a language of words, empty and hollow.

When will I be able to laugh at all of this futile exercise, for I have shed tears already, then only will come the understanding.

Walking endlessly for hours at a stretch, the chattering mind intermittently escapes. Yet somehow it seems as if it's just the mind feeling the absence of mind. A disease that refuses to go away, yet its symptoms seem to be abating. How one is tempted to hold on to this thought and its absence both. If thoughts can stop, so will the pen. But it's foolishly taken up again and the rattle resumes. The crowded memory empties again, the junk discarded yet assuming a recognisable form that will be preserved until my departure. After that, who is to know; not me of course. I wish not to know even when alive. Who am I kidding?!

It will, and it will be just me, who will keep ruminating this cud over and over again!

My heels have cracked badly, their burning just like my heart. Luckily, some cracks are beginning to appear in this rock solid mind, letting thoughts escape without landing on the page. 'A mirror cracks,' that's the moment I await. As it doesn't seem likely, no matter what I do to remove the layers of dust, some more just keeps covering it. The mirror of my mind needs to be completely destroyed. Being inert might be the only possible way to empty it. Done enough, seen enough, a lifetime of experiences have paved deep roads within me. The journey is on those roads, within myself; there is then no other place to go!

If it is mud, a good monsoon is needed to turn it into slush and soil where a new seed sown may manifest its destiny or remain unfulfilled. I, lacking in any willpower or effort, an aimless wanderer and even more purposeless writer, am at least allowing some garbage to be discarded. It has been stinking long enough. There's this worry however that something similar in the guise of the new will germinate again. My mind is an embroidery of the 6 'R's - rethink, refuse, reduce, reuse, recycle and renew. Hope it's not the last 'R', for the old may just come back disguised as the new!

Nothing born, nothing perishes. It's the same stuff all over again. An indolence prevails to break this cycle, now that wants are negligible and most needs are taken care of. The chain must snap, the weak links beginning to appear in my mind. I need to learn and make an effort to repair the damage. Or let it rust away and break in the shower of my feelings, so that someday it will fall off in bits and pieces allowing the new to manifest.

11/3 - Back to my favourite spot on the ledge. 28 days to go, the writing has lost its ongoing flavour. The routine has resumed, all things and experiences come to pass. A day begins and ends, leaving me wondering what ever did really happen? First use of the bedroom air conditioner last night, the fan's not working since five days. Heated muggy room, so sleep broken time and again. An occasional dream of Vaishnavi farms and Ransai lake, it was everything yet nothing to me.

Substance generated and now emptied, transient and fleeting are both the joys and the anxieties. Back now and dragged into the trivial, rising and falling and reaching NOW-HERE!

12/3 - Two more haircuts to go, the measure of time here now dwindling, soon to become zero. A time well spent, not a single regret if any I guess, at ease with what has passed and what remains to come. The unfolding of a state of complete rest and the beginning of a hectic activity of my professional life abroad. More and more comfortable now with this lazy phase of life. It suits me and I somehow know that life has become increasingly richer during this trip!

The poverty of my thoughts becoming poorer, disturbing me less. A sense of calm replacing anxieties of the past. A fruitful romance ended, imagination leaking away. The bucket filled with catalytic agents emptying on its own. The burden of this leaky bucket had its own pitchers of anticipation and joy. Now its level below the reach of my mind, the well springs shifted to the heart. That heart has been replenished last week living in an ambience that allows for a shift. A transference from nature to human, an experience that will stand in good stead and allow maybe a meditative quality to arise in its wake!

My craving has gone missing. It feels like a fall from a gentle slope rather than from a cliff into an abyss. Easy to negotiate and navigate it. Yes, time is consumed but comfortably so. It is allowing a deep seated patience to take seed and sprout when the cracked shell breaks apart completely. Will the source of this spring have enough water to nourish the apparent enduring calm, or will it gush like a torrent to drown these peaceful moments and leave me just as I was a few years ago? Will it dry up instead from unknown passions and its heat, will it exist like the scorching heat of the sun or will it wax and wane like the phases of a cool moon?

I write no longer knowing why and for whom. Maybe just like my incessant walking, my hands need this flight into the sky as much as my feet need the embrace of this earth!

Any such love affair brings in its wake a pain that is inevitable, as my cracked painful sole (soul) reflects. Yet, I carry on enjoying both aspects of it. Same too, with these words, at times delightful, at other times a reflection of torment.

Chapter 23

Here she comes, the source of my ongoing self-torture. I sit almost bald having had my second to last haircut. Wish it were as easy to cut her out of my imagination. But just like my hair she keeps revisiting, growing, disturbing my nerves unevenly and I keep trimming her out of my fancies. But just like my hair, the pruning is superficial, the roots buried deep and impossible it seems to uproot totally. For though I cut the foliage of my illusions, I keep watering them at the same time...

First time in three months, back-to-back days in half-sleeve tops. Otherwise every alternate day she has been seen in her three-fourth sleeve top. My exposed parts since last week's stay on the farm and my unending walks in the sun without the protection of a hat or sunscreen have given a hue to my skin that closely matches her complexion, maybe mine is even darker now. She left looking at the ground. Must have been relieved all of last week at my absence here. Wishful thinking on my part, for the reality now is that she is completely indifferent to my presence or absence. I fool myself thinking I exist for her in her subconscious that makes her consciously avoid any accidental meeting of our eyes.

My nephew's sandals returned. Await instructions about the size and type he needs before I go to the store to exchange it. "If it doesn't fit, you must acquit," a very convincing argument that set a possible murderer free in the O.J Simpson case. If you do not know the answer yourself, never ask that question of a witness in a court of law! A hand in a glove, feet in sandals, just like the layers of clothing covering the essential, a protection at times, a tease often. The allure of what is concealed being more riveting than what is revealed.

My writing similarly revealing a hidden agenda, a conversation of sorts that will end the imaginary is essential, a much needed closure and a graceful exit from her life!

Two strangers passing each other often many times in a day, many weeks in a row, months even, barely having had any exchange of words. Silently passing by, one leaving a fragrance, the other, a stink. My meetings with her, real and imagined, have always created waves of opposites between us! Sound and silence, joy and sorrow, delight and anguish, attention and indifference etc. All such opposites either of feelings or thoughts are complementary and reflect the duality of life, manufactured by just one of the parties concerned.

My party time over, bittersweet will remain the final parting. Yet there is the desire and a lingering expectation that I will find her still across from me at the end of this year when I return, single and still cross with me!

A dialogue from *Anand* pops into my mind, and I again borrow from its brilliant writer with utmost gratitude and put it here for your perusal:

Gurudev (Master): So, *chela* (Disciple), taking an exit before me, are you?

Chela: What to do, all my dialogues are over.

Gurudev: Okay, get your team together, I will be coming soon too, and then we can have our competition of dramas upstairs.

Chela: It will still take me a long time to learn Gujarati.

Gurudev: Okay, I am going now, will see you again.

Chela: Where?

Gurudev: Here, Jaichand. Here. I will meet you here, again. I will not let the curtain fall so soon!

Goes out, sobs and sobs!

For the sake of the message I have condensed this scene to a few snippets of the exchange between my all-time favourite actor Rajesh Khanna and Johnnie Walker with BabuMoshai (Amitabh Bachchan) hovering, listening with his own silent tears.

Chapter 24

13/3 - 26 days to go. A trip to Karjat tomorrow. Pending issues surfacing repeatedly, but largely ignored. Not just the clean-up and discarding of stuff from home, but of my return trip needs. Leftover days at a premium, the repetitive nature of each day synonymous with my obsessive routines of three months. A chance vision of her on my walk, thoroughly ignored by her, crossing each other on opposite sides of the lane. A one-sided attraction, so close yet just like the horizon unable to attain, as like many other tasks that will remain unfinished. The totality of an ending to this saga will remain partial. Then comes the awareness of a missed opportunity to conclude this, missed, almost more than a month ago. By design I guess, for then life might have become unbearable in the final days. The sheer hope of hopelessness dominating, the procrastination of things and events, now so much my second nature.

The walks are more enjoyable now just from the pervading thoughts and feelings that surface time and again, nullifying attempts to be just a witness on my walk.

Nothing now attracts my attention as vividly as the hands playing by the window. The first experience of that sight ever fresh, ever new for me, yet so much a part of her unconscious daily routine, maybe. I doubt if she is aware of the charm she exudes, a hand inviting, leaving me full and empty. Her silent gestures like music to my ears, like stars in my eyes, a breeze generated that floats across and caresses me, the water falling from her copper pot like a soothing rain that mingles amidst the hidden tears of my longing. She generates an allure that mere words are unable to capture or convey. It's a puzzle with a most important ingredient missing. Truly speaking, that ingredient was never created, the puzzle incomplete to begin with. And I keep arranging and rearranging the pieces of my broken heart. In this recurring display of the unattainable, unreachable, is a leaking heart that continues to bleed and replenish daily.

Yet it feels like a frog does, when being brought slowly to a boil in water, degree by degree, getting accustomed to a slow death rather than like a volcano suddenly erupting without warning, its lava burning everything around, like a frog being immersed into boiling water suddenly. That so-called philosophy has been a myth for generations.

How fortunate are those who see her every moment in her activities. Converse with her, feel her presence close at hand, wear the clothes she washes and maybe irons, the meals she often helps prepare as well as cooks for them, the smiles that must light up in every nook and cranny of her home.

My thoughts emptying on this diary of sorts, yet in her absence is a presence that emanates from me, thrills our plants that repeatedly and unexpectedly shower new petals and flowers to replace each dying one!

And isn't that what this is all about? My thoughts and feelings alive each morning and dying each night, no longer any dreams of her; they were very few and rare to begin with.

Dreams come from unfinished tasks and unfulfilled desires, so why then does she not appear in them?

A wise reader would have gathered by now, that this ongoing fire was kept ablaze by the mind fanning the tiny spark that erupted in my heart months ago in that first seminal vision at the window.

It was pure and simple dreaming all day, so no reason for it to be continued in my nights, where I am slowly becoming more awake and aware for moments.

She keeps appearing and vanishing, just like the emptiness between and within my words. Too poor is language, the richness of her silence replaced by a plethora of my words.

I wish her all happiness and the comfortable life she so richly deserves wherever she finds it (I know full well, it isn't and can't be with me) and knowing that she has found it will bring some peace to my pen. Yes, too bad, that there is someone just across from her ready to bring it to her on a platter, though nothing concrete was ever offered in the moment that passed between us like the blink of an eye.

Yes I will find solace in knowing that she has done well. It jogs the memory of two dear ones whose lives turned around from my continuous adoration, untouched admiration, adulation and pure romance without ever having taken any advantage of them, also never having touched them physically. My selfless attention perceived as enough of a threat that made other suitors jealous, fearful, making them take concrete steps to marry and remove them from the daily drudgery of dancing at night for their livelihood in full traditional Indian dresses. That is a story necessitating if not a short book, a very, very long chapter by itself at some time in the future, should I continue my writing in a different vein.

This story is far different. Her simplicity, natural acceptance of herself, no costumes or cosmetics, her innocence and continuous daily hard work as honestly as the others did too each night into the early hours of the morning, is surely deserving of an equally bright and safe happy future. A contentment that is surely her right to reach for and find. Fortunate and lucky will be the one who can give this to her, for she has tremendous unrecognised gifts to offer (new pen, the other pen ran out of ink at the word offer. What a moment to do so!) for the one who can have the eyes and vision that seems to have been generated within me! But she has missed out on the romance of her life; it will come from somewhere else in far better measure hopefully!

I missed her going out to water as I went inside to get a new pen. But saw her returning, prettier and serene, her qualities, they just keep growing on her. A few words exchanged with the watchman, my first view of her half smile in about a month or more. But it wasn't for me, the bucket and tumbler empty, entering her home, leaving the knowledge for me, that she has nothing to give to me!

Chapter 25

I switch on the radio in search of songs I like, as I haven't been listening to music over the last three years. This desire to listen now is going back on what I had written much earlier I guess. A subterfuge of letting the songs of my heart drift across to her and convey the feelings that no direct conversation is able to do so, for lack of a meeting again. The volume not enough to reach her given her morning noisy chores, they do not leave her unoccupied to listen or dream. I find that the cassette deck is not working, adding to my agony, for I have every possible song and *ghazal* (rich poetry set to music) to convey my deepest feelings. Everything now seems like a crutch to help support and give voice to my feelings to stir her indifferent heart.

I laugh and I cry, each sentiment overflowing into the other. In this stupidity too there must be a lesson unlearnt. Things that have dropped off from my life can still come back unannounced. Either please me or give rise to sorrow momentarily. Yet there is no longer an attachment to them, it is but a temporary use for my own selfishness!

ALL IS FAIR IN LOVE AND WAR, ISN'T IT?

I LOVE HER AND I AM AT WAR WITH MYSELF!

Radio India, time for breakfast. I set my tea on the stove, bread in the toaster. One a flame, the other a filament. Both with enough heat to complement my own apparent coolness. In comes my nephew, searching for new batteries for his camera. Suddenly erupts one of my most favourite songs that I last heard two weeks ago and kept humming on my walks. The tea comes to a boil, the song fires up flames of passion and carries my pain across my window. No one listening but me, interrupted by a phone call from my brother just when the last couplet was playing. My silence disturbed, the toast lying idle till the song finished.

TOASTED AND ROASTED, CHARRED WAS THE FEELING OF MY ROMANCE!

As I finished eating, and was having a smoke outside, another song about life came on. Its ups and downs, its duality, its play of light and shadow, of hopes and fears, success and failure and most other opposites you can think of, yet complementary to each other, the deeper you go into them. The program ended, the last song not melodious enough to match the musical harmony of the previous two songs.

Two hours of writing over, the futile exercise of one hobby ending, replaced by another one: reading.

She, however refusing to read my love and affection, it having no effect on her attitude or demeanour, stoic as ever and irrepressibly distant!

14/3 - The day disappeared. Saw *Aradhana* on television, reading stopped, songs touching. A short nap then phone calls for planning Karjat visit. Met Arham and Hetal while sitting, saw her as if she was purposefully glancing across. Just a bit of her face, the beginning of an aborted smile. She too, I guess has heard the songs of longing now, either with a longing for me to disappear to a foreign land or reach out again to make a home here. An evening at Chinmaya School, Chapter One of the Geeta, a discourse by Swami Swatmananda, gifts for Tina and Dk *mama* and dinner with them, after which I returned home. Then I called Bandhu (Saumitra Biswas) and his wife Reshmi's son Jishnu (Nikhil) in USA for his birthday, giving my greetings, wishes and blessings on this occasion. Given the time difference between the two countries, it was now day-time there. I do this each year as his birthday falls while I am always in India. Saumitra and Reshmi are very dear friends of mine. He was a trainee under me during his years of neonatal fellowship at McMaster in Canada. They now have three wonderful children - Oishaani the eldest daughter, then Jishnu their son, and Sharika the youngest daughter, who was a most welcome surprise addition. In fact for years they had been trying for a child, so the arrival of Oishaani more than a decade ago was a joy difficult to describe in words, not only for them but for me as well as all our common friends abroad. Bandhu and Reshmi are the most laidback, happy-go-lucky friends I have been privileged to know, and some of their qualities over time I hope have rubbed off on me too.

A trip to Karjat, Kadau, return via Panvel. An evening with Tuks and Umi at their home with Professor Bvd and Pabi. An 18-year-old Glenlivet, onion *bhajias* (fritters), *bhel* and other snacks. As Tuks said about the malt, nothing but the best for my friends. A great conversation touching many aspects of life again with Professor's reminder: "Hey dadhi, *Aata gup bas*! Now keep quiet." I reiterated, I am quiet at home generally. Since we meet just for an hour each week, I have to make it up to you all! A call to a village in the south, Shankar's kid's medical issues discussed. Shankar was my elder brother's assistant at the workshop for automobile repairs. He had moved back to his village a few years ago. His kid had repeated episodes of cold, cough, and breathing difficulties, necessitating frequent visits to doctors as well as hospital admission. I discussed at length the symptoms, the tests, the treatment given to date, spoke to the doctor also, gave advice regarding potential triggers and their elimination, suggested remedies and then follow-up calls as needed.

Confirmation with Bharat Somani regarding a property visit and a call to my dear friend Bawa, and then my day ended.

The trip in search of a countryside retreat somewhere in the vicinity of Mumbai only served to bring me back to reality. An eye-opener of sorts; some were way over the range of my own already inflated budget and affordability. Inaccessible, cumbersome, insecure, so far out of reach, nevertheless, a worthwhile journey that has in some way helped temper my dreams and illusions. *Bhabhi* accompanied me after finishing her household tasks in time, obviously waking up ridiculously early to finish them, so that we could get out and reach in time. A whole day exploring options served partly as a disappointment also for us, given the conclusions derived. Not a total waste however. This endeavour was a fruitful learning expedition. The search will have to be directed closer to home and in easy reach. But besides increasing the costs dramatically, it will lose the charm one derives from a place that is distant from the city, not too far but not too close either.

Like many other things in life, the search for your own self or "No self", the Buddhist concept of 'Anatta', is after all the most defining of life's journey. Yes, that too seems distant, yet in truth, always hidden inside one but we do not have the eyes to see nor the ears to hear, or the touch to feel.

Halfway into my last month. More and evermore crops up a desire in me to return to my roots. They seem to be quenching their thirst slowly, steadily as I keep watering them. But the sun and heat of my split mind makes it evaporate rapidly leaving them thirsty for more. She looks and turns away before she can see me close my eyes gently. Early to water and earlier removal of dried clothes, an indicator of how a day begins and ends earlier for her as the season brings a heat wave that saps one's energy sooner for most tasks and chores.

She returns uncaring for me, a smile to the *dhobi*, rings her bell, enters and exits in this game of hide and seek that I play with myself, neither a victor nor any one in defeat. The joy of my writing, ending each day in the sorrow of the unfulfilled. 24 days to go, 24 hours at a time, most of it spent daydreaming or asleep, writing, reading and walking. She is off to iron clothes, a task of hers I have not realised till now as she is out of sight for more than an hour but not still in the bathroom for the laundry.

She seems to me at least, to have no respite from her duties, obviously neither from my looks. Someday, I hope I can read this to her, the inspiration of my perspiration. English not something she understands probably, so to translate it into Hindi or Marathi may be the only option. In which case she can read it herself but doubt that she ever will. This ink is not easily removable, but the words devoid of much meaning can easily be subjected to an erasure just from the neglect of them.

Chapter 26

It started out as a reasonably uneventful day. Music on the radio, finished reading Kabir, a surprise lunch of *pani puris*, long walk, and final visit to my roadside booksellers, buying something from all of them. Evening dinner with family - spring rolls, nuts, snacks, dessert, already having had a sumptuous lunch. A visit from Arham late last night as he was unwell, taken care of. Trip to Murli's farm today and tomorrow another visit to Karjat with *bhabhi* and Jaju, a friend of Bharat Somani, an engineer and also very well versed with land issues and opportunities for retreats in the areas I am interested in. Very generous of him to pick us up in his car from Panvel station for the trip to Karjat. Another weekend will be over, leaving one more with an Easter weekend vacation out of town with my family and Dk *mama* and family and his son Neil (Biddu) and kids, they coming from Washington, also joining us for that outing.

Unfortunately a wonderful evening later marred by a small heated argument spoiling the pleasant family get together momentarily. My irritation got expressed in anger, an apology tendered immediately but damage done. Awareness arose and subsided like a wave after the event but the winds of anger released continued to fan the trivial argument that ended amicably soon enough though. A lesson learnt and forgotten easily too.

Consciousness disappears and my reactionary mode takes over. A persistent inability to always be responsive is troubling me albeit the situations leading to it are diminishing rapidly. Often a culprit myself, I try to protect my aloneness and avoid being the trigger. But one episode arising thanks to me, however infrequent they may be is one too many. It is still a humble reminder that this journey to awareness has barely begun.

Wasn't ready to make the trip to Chinmaya and NSCI with Dk *mama* and family, so tendered regrets. Two more farm visits pending, one more haircut, a plenitude of tasks to be finished in the next nine days to avoid a mad scramble at the end once April rolls around.

The romance will automatically be pushed into the backseat of my mind, the writing will become utterly ordinary, doing injustice now to what has seemed at least to me, an extraordinary occupation of my time here.

I see new flowers, new soft leaves, bright green, white, pink, red, purple, lilac and yellow *turi*, a bouquet of colours, and a whiff of fragrance at the tail-end of the morning. A renewal of my spirits after a gainful rest and better sleep. Waking either with the song of the birds, or the broom sweeping the courtyard or occasionally the alarm of my brother's mobile. And then comes the faint outline as I sip my first cup of tea.

A one-dimensional day is the barometer of a one-dimensional life. Just the geographical borders adjust themselves, smooth or jagged, the content essentially unwavering; moments of calm and moments of turmoil exchanging their relative importance and presence each day. Having fought to establish territory and might, they both retire to resume their fight the next day.

I pretend to laugh at this drama but my mood remains serious. This disease constantly nagging but not manifesting in its full glory nor cured enough to move on.

And in that process, I partake of an existence that is either at complete rest or in an ecstatic dance.

The cat returns daily searching for a rat. Her movements are stealthy and quick but unwise, as no rats venture out in daylight. It leaves always without its prey to resume its futile search the next day. It has just decided to take a sip of water, crouch and sit under a car thinking of seeking a new pasture. It is a reminder of the futility of what I go through each morning with my writing, returning empty. Though nothing achieved, nothing was lost, as I did not have it in the first place! Her hand reached out, filled the maroon flask water bottle and I missed seeing the hand putting the pot back in its place.

The new fern leaves, soft and gentle, a matter of time before they harden from their experiences and learning, just like the innocence of a young child is lost when it embarks on formal schooling and disappears completely as it begins to grow and learn the ways of society.

She left and returned, a few papers in her hand. Her three-fourth sleeve top not seen for many days now. Given her tasks a wise choice realised much later by her, as her sleeve would get wet and soiled during her duties of washing and cleaning.

But for me, her forearm half covered is more appealing to my senses than her appearance in her half-sleeve top. For, now my vision drifts on occasions to her upper arms away from her hands whose delicate dance was the ultimate tantalizing gesture that captured the attention of my heart, culminating in the subsequent harrowing tension of my mind. I will learn to appreciate this too. Three weeks is all I have and it will fade away as other pressures and work will prevent these lapses in judgement, the ending of a romance that had never begun.

Isn't that what life is in between birth and death?

She returns from another errand. The rays of the sun, briefly causing her left nostril stud to sparkle. Upright and hurried she is today, aware, possibly taking some delight too in the manner she continues to haunt and torment me. A continuous unending play in which she has never relinquished her upper hand. As if she is just directing this drama, refusing to participate on the stage of its performance. She hasn't put even a solitary brick to lay its shape. My edifice built, reshaped, already crumbling under its own weight of thoughts and feelings, missing the glue to hold it together which only she possesses and refuses to part with.

Ready again to come out, no, not really. I am as mistaken today as I have been for the past three months. This mistake, a continuous one, in perpetuity, not ending in any resolution. But it is not as if this mistake is being repeated, it still has to end its one life, and that is the vicarious delight of its continuance.

It is way past her watering time, given that I now take cues from her to water our own indoor plants. I will have to vacate my seat soon and do what my plants expect of me. Done! Phone rings and disconnects the moment I say hello. It feels more like a goodbye and good riddance, her back to the window, the tease continues, unawares on her part. An hour to the radio program, a rediscovery of music, the motive possibly selfish though. I doubt she pays any attention, nor does she seem to care, rightfully so! A visit to the farm, a late arrival given an accident on highway, stuck in traffic for hours. So just three hours on the farm. Mangoes taking hold in good measure, may get to eat some before I leave. Snacks, food, *baksheesh* to all the help on farm and Junaid and Tukaram, I return with a big bag of produce, and find it's Hetal's birthday, so my wishes to her in plenty.

17/3 - She was visited by presumed family, relative or friends. I was wondering how come she was ready in a new attire by 12.30 pm instead of the usual 1.15 pm. *Ghazals* from 2.00 pm to 3.00 pm, three ones of Murli's favourites. Another trip to Karjat, unbearable prices for non-agricultural plots. The curtain drops on my wishes; everything seems to be unaffordable in Karjat. I will need to set my eyes farther and lower. Kalhegaon near Lahuchiwadi and Karnala also, no property in sight. So it is unlikely anything will materialise. At a crossroads now, a desire to work less for income, split time between India and Georgina, do what I can and also enjoy my renovated home here and these long lazy hours of sitting on my ledge.

This trip has gone by too quickly for my liking. I have enjoyed just about every moment of it. A lifestyle that has suited me, prompting me to rethink my life in Canada.

Come back! Is the advice of my dearest Dk *mama*. Be happy as you have been on this trip.

One week out of the remaining three will be consumed, with a few days included for preparation of the vacation with family and the last week drowned in a sea of anxiety.

Chapter 27

All my energies and enthusiasm are fully devoted to my passionate activities, including helping in the home and at Surya hospital. Early to bed often, dreamless sleep, maybe this home is the place where I will awaken and make the efforts needed towards growth, maturity, more silence and responsiveness. Then why not begin that NOW?

My first look at her this morning while reading. Noticed that she does now voluntarily look across, before shifting her gaze and herself away the moment our eyes meet. Is this a welcome change or just the fiction I have chosen to create? Some songs whether she likes it or not must have reached her ears. Unlikely that she would have strained her ears to listen deliberately or dwelled upon its poetry. I too realise that it is just a fraction of her unintentional look that unleashes a fury of words on these pages.

Is it all a product of mere coincidence? The coincidence of being in a place right across from her, almost 24 hours a day, otherwise, maybe there would have been no possibility of this indulgence. And also, without my home renovation, there was previously no possibility of such imaginary engagements with her.

All is chance, without her this visit would have lost something indefinable, with her too, this visit has suffered a loss that now appears quite tangible. In between these two is left a saga of pages over pages. Read one and you have read all, read none and you haven't missed anything of value at all.

It is all just a fool's meandering in an attempt to be wise. The real lesson will come only when I understand this to be ignorance masquerading as knowledge.

The knowledge of being rejected daily is obvious, this then, a creation out of nothing. The journey from one page to another, unending. The beginning and its conclusion all encompassed in the first seminal vision of a pot emptying its contents into a flask bottle. One becoming spacious, the other filling up, how come then, I feel so full and empty together?

Will there ever be an opportunity to translate this into a language she can herself read or be read to and explained, when she hasn't felt nor read anything from any of my silent language. My eyes drift repeatedly as my pen conjures up words upon words, a mirror of my existence she reflects back to me, my echo adding basically nothing of herself in return.

A mistaken conclusion, as all of yesterday she has engaged momentarily with my eyes. No expressions whatsoever, a blank face like a mirror, no movement of any kind, just reflecting the dust and veil over my eyes.

Anyway, it started with her hanging clothes earlier each day. I had to stop right in front of her sight as someone stopped me requesting directions. I found her standing looking at me, I nodded and carried on. Came back and switched on the radio, a favourite *ghazal* of maestro Jagjit Singh from *Sarfarosh* came on. Unsure if she heard, for she had obviously finished her noisy tasks and the song must have breached the distance between us for her to still ignore it. The rest of the day was my usual Monday with no real happenings.

The day ended, another morning came rapidly in its wake. The ink getting darker, telling me that this pen too has not much left in it, just like this visit of mine which hasn't much left in its measure of time.

A reminder maybe, that in fact this whole story has not much of anything in it.

The fourth pen in use now, fourth month of my stay and the recurring dream continues to dominate my waking hours. Time has changed in Canada last weekend. Spring forward, as it is called. A phone call for Princess Avery's (one of my former pre-term patients in Canada; a delightful child of multiple miracles who occupies a very, very special space within my very being!) birthday last night, to my cousin Hemant this morning and time spent seeing a patient. Plans fluctuating for next weeks' vacation spot but it will likely be Matheran. My plants watered, hers remain thirsty, but the thirst is still mine only. She seems obviously at ease with her lot in life, while my craving is increasing exponentially. The page on this diary is now the plot number of my second home, 221. A file from Canada will have to be tackled soon. I keep delaying the inevitable disturbance of Canada from polluting my last days here. Yes, there is a sense of comfort, it will bring clarity to dispel my confusion and replace my doubts and fears with some decisive action regarding both my work and life.

Looming is a choice while I keep weaving webs of fiction. The drift endlessly carrying on, the web swaying back and forth, too strong in its fibre to snap and collapse on itself. A scissor or knife is needed to cut across and reach the open space without allowing its sticky threads to cling onto me.

There she comes to the window, leans partially across and looks. My gaze lifts, she retreats immediately. My advance remaining progressively steady, anchored and unmoving is she, in spite of my innumerable cues. She is aware that I continue to seek her in spite of her rejections and denials. If a spark is being lit in her, albeit late, it will fire up of its own accord, all I can do to help it is to be the gentle cool breeze around her.

There isn't any passion of lust, just the purity of an affection that is loving and kind, maybe generous too in its giving. For I have enough of it for both of us for now, until she can bring some of it, of herself to this momentary fragmented relating.

The cat arrives on schedule refusing to learn, returning empty every day after a fruitless search. I too, am not much different in terms of results achieved from this imaginary pursuit. The cat has probably smelt the rat from the latter's visit the night before having left its odour to fool her, and having disappeared sometime before dawn to a safer haven.

Four months of seeing the same faces, and the birds, dogs, cats, etc., yet I doubt that I am noticed any more on my perch. I have merged with the landscape given my monotonous routine. It was a novelty earlier given that my window ledge was new, now it has no freshness or excitement to charm anyone, while it still continues to amuse me.

Are their lives any different from mine on a daily basis? Seems as if nothing substantially new is happening on this stage, barring a few rearranged props and decorations. The same players on the same stage, same audience with some temporary additions and subtractions, continually aging, changing every moment without it ever being perceptibly noticed. The conversations circle around the same broad themes, its content must vary bit by bit, but the story clearly stuck going nowhere in particular like this effort of mine, nothing gained but an irretrievable lesson lost.

Tedious and boring for the spectator, but seemingly not so for any of its players. Yes, there is a satisfaction that comes from being a participant in life, which is neither small nor big, which is as it is, carrying on to live another day.

Very few desires requested, very few accepted, there is in life a provision that seems endless though in its giving.

In all the hardships, I continue to see laughter and gaiety amongst the working class of the poor, enough frustrations pile up, but except for the materially well off, I have yet to see outbursts of anger from the former class who continue in perpetuity to work for and serve us, the so-called well to do people.

Anyway its past 10.00 am, I am bewildered today as her imagined routine is out of whack. No movements, no vision, no watering, all is quiet on the southern front! Something is amiss; her life so within the realms of predictability, that I can feel a change in her routine is an omen for me, but still very much a nagging mystery.

Peeled pomegranate, half spoiled as it was left aside for too long, so I threw it away, my delay contributing to its rot, whereas delays here adding to a possible sweet harvest or a total destruction of my fictitious orchard! The gate of this orchard now open for a long time yet no one seems to be entering or exiting. All is in a state of suspended disbelief. From the corner of my eye, the shadow of a hand reaches to replace the copper pot into its position as if it is a sentry to her heart. It isn't my lucky day, isn't time for the music yet, maybe I too should depart from my routine and create a disturbance.

This saga taking an unseen toll on both you and me. However there is a silver lining, this affection has enveloped me and made my attitude even more loving and responsive to my circle of family and friends. But it remains ignored by the very one who has brought about this change. We see each other briefly always, but her expressions do not change from the mask of almost total indifference that she has put on for me. I continue to look at her, which she knows I do and as always, everyday ends without relief, for another chapter to unfold the next day.

Chapter 28

20/3 - A day less than a score left. The cupid's arrow has taken flight ages ago but it feels as if it happened just this very moment. It continues on with its own energy without landing on its intended target. So the score is still zero. There is maybe a perceptible shift, undoubtedly an inclination on her part to look at me and turn away the moment I catch her looking. Also now the songs I hum on my walks often appear on radio or television channels within a day or two of my remembering them. Last evening a favourite from *Khamoshi*, of course starring Rajesh Khanna, a mental asylum inmate. My eyes closed, my hand assuming various gestures, I am sure none as enchanting as her still hands that erupt suddenly in a dance that seems out of this world. Anyway, I am in harmony with that song. It seemed as if to resonate and get released from within me, unaware if she ever glanced during that brief moment of ecstasy within me.

I sat imagining how she loves her work; my labour is just my love trying to reach her via umpteen dimensions. It haunts, it caresses, it remains injured, stutters, and tries to fly with a broken wing, the distance small but the destination of its flight may take a lifetime of waiting. But the wait will have to be undertaken here. I am so much in tune with the lifestyle generated on this visit, very much at ease being unoccupied, time flying, hopefully with no other regrets whatsoever.

The call is loud and clear, it is maybe time to return home. Temper my needs, make my expenses even more judicious, arrange pending matters and pursue the longing of something more productive in nature. If the love is rewarded the tensions will be many, some known, some unknown.

Appealing is the prospect of a career of voluntary work. Make a bare minimum to survive and meet undeniable expenses with the income generated from my investments abroad. Utilise free time to engage in what I love most, take concrete steps towards solidifying honorary work at Surya and grass roots services in the tribal village of Lahuchiwadi that I have been blessed to know of and cherish. I would still live in two countries, settled in Georgina and Lahuchiwadi and see my India alone.

The magical moment is revisited as I lift my gaze. It still creates butterflies in my stomach on a daily basis, every morning and night. My sleep will reduce as my time draws to an end, the waters of my well utilised and replenished, but leaving me as thirsty as the day before.

She has refused to even glance at me today. Her *patla* (wooden board for rolling dough) on the wrong side of the grill, an indicator that I am on the wrong side of age. There is no possibility of fruition; the seed will remain buried in her rocky soil. Her hair is never seen in a free flowing cascade, but the vision of her hands just now adjusting her hair band is equally delightful to see. Early to water, looks and moves, her shifting balance immaculate, every nuance still upsetting my balance.

The story of a lost first love and a one-sided last one, a multitude of innocent flirtations in between leaving each one's dignity intact, but leaving now an emptiness that is filling me up repeatedly, culminating in this last romance. She returns too quickly as if she has left her plants as thirsty as she has done with me. There will have to be something lasting, something tangible to materialise from this abstract posturing.

Whether it takes the form of a rock or flower, both are quite acceptable. However one will seem dead and secure, the other very much alive yet fragile in every moment of its existence, death ready to arrive any moment.

This mind has replaced one subject of its repetitive thinking with another. This one more painful but more welcome. In this is the working of my heart and mind in tandem. Difficult to know where the feelings end and thoughts take over, the words only an indication towards truth but not the truth itself.

Truth requires no proof. It is or it is not! Whether it materialises towards norms of society as a surrogate, or remains without, this experience has been one of totality. For love is the ultimate flowering, whether received or not, reciprocated or not, the giving of it has been real.

This morning in the paper is the ultimate *sutra* from Nietzsche and I take the liberty to reproduce it:

"To love is to suffer; to survive is to find some meaning in the suffering."

Chapter 29

One thing too is real: She has brought music back into my domain. I have never heard it come from her home. Maybe it's because they do not listen to it or more likely the sound hasn't travelled across. It leaves a sinking feeling that my songs haven't travelled across to her either! Am I listening for myself or is it just a ruse to make my feelings known to her? Soon this music too will disappear again as I move away from her physically, to resurface again if this story has any legs left on my visit later this year.

These romantic sad songs of my morning and in the gaps of the evening television serials of my brother's viewing often take me into the world of my past obsession of it. It is nice to know that it can come and go without taking deep roots again. It is the time of music heard, songs silently sung and released from my grasp to create a harmonious melody in the space that keeps us together yet separate.

The writing continues, and in between I try to accomplish minor tasks so that my looming journey back does not leave me scrambling and floundering because of the compassionate passion indulged in daily.

It is comforting that there is more than an ounce of pleasure which has demanded more than a pound of pain of an unrequited love.

A generally uneventful day except for my 15 minutes of play with my nephew - a break from his studying for exams. This visit has been one of my most relaxed ones in a long time. A long walk, then an evening at Nehru Centre for ADAPT charity function and program followed by NSCI for drinks and dinner with Dk *mama* and family. Interesting last two and a half weeks, the juggling of time and tasks will begin if it hasn't already. The heat in the daytime picking up, the nights still pleasant enough. This evening too she will be missed due to an outing with my family. And the wait will suddenly be over like the unexpected leap of a cat. It will be April, the month of my departure. It will hit hard, my softness temporary, but the depressed mood will return later than usual.

A papaya cut, she comes out, pretty in anger as in half smiles, even in her indifference. It seems as if my imagined life with her is like the preparation of a brief as this treatise reflects, a work in progress eternally, the final script as elusive as her. A slight chewing of her lip, a smirk it seems knowing full well that I am a puppet with the strings in her hands. I dance all day to the tunes she sets, my walk often occupied with her thoughts. Remembering some of my favourite songs from the golden oldies, suddenly the months of attempts at meditative walking lost in memories, my remembrance lost like her.

As I step out of my reverie, she is seen cleaning the balcony grills. The act in utter purity fully absorbed in it. I sit transfixed looking at her arms, her face coming into view off and on. Her smile for the fruit seller, the use of a fine brush and even blowing with her lips to clear the dust and dirt in her sliding window tracts. It is as if she is brushing me off. A slow almost a standstill motion of sliding the windows closed, feels like the shutting off of a door to my dreams. But, she looked often, finding me morose now, I am sure. Hers is a beauty beyond my imagination.

The fabric of my love not being woven with any conviction nor with any help from her, is slowly tearing my heart into unrecognisable pieces. She finishes cleaning and the next song is not to my liking. I changed the channel, but she will not hear my songs now for an hour or more. Then a song comes that echoes my pain deeply, only I hear it and a silence descends upon me.

I was mistaken again as I have been on most of these pages. I find her back at her cleaning looking across the road, the curtains lifting and dropping, an unending drama, then a sudden joy that maybe she heard the last song too. This is a fire that refuses to die out, burning me repeatedly in its wake. What a misfortune! My old favourite *"Pal pal dil ke paas"* came on, but she was long gone. I was left ruing, if it had come on a few minutes earlier, she would have heard it then, as all was silent across us. This song has many memories that surface every time I hear it. Some of my best and not so good moments are embedded and buried alive in this song. I had waited for days for it to come on and when it did, I was left alone again amidst the ruin!

The spring equinox comes and goes, songs filter out with no receptacle for them to settle. Weekend rolls around, two more to go after this. How many days should I keep playing the songs that convey similar if not the same messages to her? It will soon become tedious for both of us. Repeating a message three times is one of Buddha's sayings, if she hasn't listened by now, it is unlikely that it will ever reach her heart.

On and off, she continues her silent, expressionless, momentary observations of my observing her. A bit of my longing has reached her like the whiff of a fragrance. It's up to her to hold on to it and crave for more or let it pass by for a better appealing and fresher one. The most sensible thing is to continue in silence and avoid the music lest it become overbearing. Her tolerance has been tested enough, yet, I can't shake off the feeling that she has begun to show some interest in what I would do next.

What is that last straw to break her resistance, the last blow of the hammer to drive the nail completely in? Time is not enough, her busyness at odds with my laziness, the clash leaving no common ground for a meeting of our hearts.

Chapter 30

I can sense her day today will be different. An early closure to recoup energy from yesterday's taxing chores and late night. I wonder time and again what sustenance she possesses to go on like this day after day at such a tender age compared to most people her age who don't need to work at a means for a living. They would have so many other interests, colleges, outings, entertainment, maybe a desk job, etc. somewhat carefree lives provided for by their well-to-do parents. She, on the other hand is barely exposed to enough sunlight and fresh air, nor significant outings with friends or a suitor. Maybe also no time, as I have never seen her reading newspapers or books. Here, living across from her is someone who wishes a different life for her altogether and will miss her terribly soon enough. She is totally oblivious of such an option.

Hers is a story similar to countless millions in this country. Often engaged in never-ending labour for others, and sometimes meeting the barest of any decent living standards. Aging or ravaged by chronic illnesses and pains of the body, disappearing into the unknown leaving behind the briefest and limited remembrances amongst the survivors. Yes, some are lucky not to be in the madness of city crowds, while others are cocooned working in one or a few homes, moving from one deadline of work to another all day. She is very lucky being cared for by her employers' family as a family member, a live-in housekeeper obviously respected by them and them dependent on her. Others often make do in the corridors of buildings, away from family, each of their days arriving and departing with a regularity that leaves no room for anything unexpected or any change that can be considered eventful in their lives.

Often found in the barest of daily wear, each necessity of my life is a luxury for them. Even though their basic needs are few, they remain difficult to fulfil. Wants unrecognised and unknown, we move oblivious to it all barring an occasional piece in print, a sound-byte or image on the radio and television. A lot remains to be said, a lot remains to be done.

All this touches me, percolates down, rises as feelings and erupts into meaningless words of self-indulgence on paper. Action will soon come I hope, like in the movie "Field of Dreams", If you build it, they will come, a baseball metaphor.

Pest Control in my building reminds me of how much of a pest I may have become to her...too bad, for I am not going away easily! The smoke filling up my home, all vision obscured, the mirror of my existence in a fog. I breathe this in too, the smell sickeningly sweet, this episode now over ripe. It is in danger of becoming rotten unless swallowed now or discarded into the garbage bin.

I refrain from playing music which now seems even to me like undue noise given my ulterior motives. I see my *khakra* order has arrived, a huge storage bin obscures my view of her completely, an omen of some sort, an understanding awaiting its dawn in my being.

A cyclone here, a mini volcano upstairs. Circumstances plenty and justifiable, our acts at times of non-cooperation, and taking things for granted. Indecisiveness, lack of expressing gratitude and appreciation, burdens and frustrations common like in many other families, nothing new there.

Impatience transforming into anger generating words that cast shadows all around, yet linger on even when the sun is down. Things however are quickly resolved, misunderstanding cleared, an air of expectancy about the upcoming vacation brightens the day again.

Heat making sleep difficult, I wake up early at 5.45 am, surprised to see her light on. I saw her, she saw me, a never-ending similar occurrence often leading nowhere, and I went out for an hour's walk. As my imminent departure looms, sleep is less and less, her day will begin earlier and end similarly sooner. My last visit to Murli's farm today, Matheran next weekend with family and relatives. Then reality will hit home as my last week will bring all the weaknesses I go through about my departure.

When will I ever find her alone like myself to have a communion of sorts? Easter weekend in Matheran, Gudi Padwa - the New Year - after my departure, cannot wish her on either occasion.

I am now left wondering at the rise and fall of her waves, the ocean disturbed time and again yet reaching nowhere.

Ekadashi today: Watermelon cut, other fruits, juices, wafers provided, all in good store for my brother's family upstairs as I will be gone most of the day. Come to think of it, for about the past two months I have gone missing, often not present, mind and heart in tandem, subject to vagaries of time itself. Seeing the last morning star disappear, few floating clouds, last evening the colours at sunset. A week ago the flame of a disappearing sun at Haji Ali bus stop, mangoes on branches, parrots whistling and similar sights enthral me now. Many delights come surfacing in a hurry as I find little time left to enjoy nature's beckoning call in this part of the world.

My return to my rental condo and my hospital and university, an environment so very different, will bring a lingering doubt about everything that I missed during my four months here. Majabira Cottage on Georgina will make up for some of the losses, however.

Chapter 31

I can sense a desperate clinging to my last days here. Gone is any advance made towards non attachment. The desiring mind and the hopeful heart are creating one conflict after another. Confusion reigns, procrastination raising its venomous hood, clarity now a myth and a horizon unable to materialise.

The flight of birds reflected in the windshields of the cars parked in the courtyard, voices of children waking up, yet the voice I so long to hear is silent as ever for me. My song just about finished, the end of such a melody seems to have become a disharmonious ending. The cat arrives to remind me of my broken heart as she too will have to leave on an empty stomach. I feel this emotion now in my gut, the unending cries of a love that has possessed me insanely only to disappear into emptiness.

Empty and full has been the norm each day, a clean slate now just an illusion in reality. This narrative now seemingly full of nouns and adjectives, the verbs that are symbolic of something alive and living have gone missing. Its loss felt more deeply by me today as I find my hand quivering, the writing of words just fodder for the sake of filling empty pages, as the message is emptying itself without meaning or substance.

The irresistible urge to still pick up the pen repeatedly, is mute testimony of the fact that it is her on and off appearances that lead me into insanity time and again!

The look of my eyes may be considered jaundiced by most as my hours spent on the ledge almost guarantee an ongoing vision of her. Her routines are familiar, yet they surprise me on a regular basis, when the clock of my time is determined by her activities. Time and again it moves either too slow or too fast for me to catch up with it.

A chance vision of her in a gorgeous new yellow top with three-fourth sleeves in sheer black chiffon and black leggings, must be a special occasion. Yellow isn't her colour, yet it takes to her like a second skin. The beauty you may say is the product of my eyes - to me she simply looks wonderful in whatever she adorns herself with.

A cool day on the farm. No plots for sale. Swimming pool planned to serve as a storage tank for irrigation mainly, but also for the joy of swimming, which Murli knows I love a lot. It will be ready on my next visit later this year. He is making sure that his place becomes the ultimate combination of Georgina and Karnala with the benefits of Sawragaon farm too. No place else I will need to search for my Utopia. If I can't find it within myself wherever I am, he is making sure this surrogate will help me in the search for my own being! A very charming evening, some unexpected medical issues amongst my relatives and friends will keep my upcoming week busy enough.

This morning too there is a gentle cloud cover here in the city, like over the farm yesterday. Puffs of cotton ball-like clouds, a remarkable display of nature, in two places and on two separate days. A soothing breeze not letting any of us sweat on the farm even in the early afternoon. A long story of missing cashew packets amongst the snacks. Due to Narayan's oversight while packing, it was found when I arrived home, in the bag containing soup that Daxa had sent for me. A parting gift unintentionally for me, this being my last visit to the farm and cashews being the ultimate favourite nut of mine. News of Murli's family and many friends' trips to USA and Canada aborted for this year because of certain extenuating circumstances for them, so they plan to go to Europe instead. They will be missed by me of course in Canada.

A lazy Sunday morning, a memory of some long since heard Jagjit's *ghazals* played by Murli on the way back yesterday. Enjoyed and fondly remembered those days! The songs now disappearing fast, my message already disregarded and now stale. The weight of my expectations receiving no shoulders to support, the imaginary house crumbling. In every piece of its ruin is the glimpse of a spirited broken heart.

But every bit of this romancing my mind was worth it. I did nothing, yet a lot did happen and pass away, leaving me better off than on my arrival.

My departure this time feels bittersweet, the pain as much a part of the pleasure, yet seeped with a suffering of an unknown nature. I camouflage this pain in the tender feelings of the heart and the dancing monkey of my mind. There is a sense of relief in this surrender of effort. The message will hang around in my absence. Waiting for an embrace of arms other than mine. If not, I will be back to hug it myself!

She will be unmoving like an axle, my wheels will continue to rotate and revolve around her, leaving her dignity untouched, unblemished.

Does imagination become real or does reality become imaginary? Am I an emperor dreaming I am a butterfly or vice versa?

I see her very briefly at night back in her old outfit; the orange top with three-fourth sleeves and white leggings combo has disappeared now for about three to four weeks. Somehow it feels like a metaphor of her rejection of me. Discarded... but then I have never been fancied by her, never worn so never discarded, just ignored. In which case a subtle hope prevails of this ongoing tug of chain, with longing as its fetter on one side and resistance that is distant, from the other side.

Not so nice a morning. I missed her everywhere. Now this afternoon saw her unexpectedly looking at me, but with my returning look, she just seems to evaporate away. Wish I could say that she melts away; that would be a wonderful meaning, wouldn't it?

This is a classic tale of being on the horns of a dilemma. If I choose to see her she doesn't engage and rapidly moves out of sight. The rare occasions of her looking at me also make the moments fade away. How then to be certain that there are not more times and moments of her looking at me without my knowing of them! A catch-22 situation! My attempts to know will be the reason of their demise, especially if she is developing an uncertain interest in me.

One thing is certain though - she has become the center, the source of this writing for months now. Once the inspiration goes with the loss of proximity, the writing if it continues will appear manufactured. All this up until now has been natural, spontaneous, seemingly not in my control even though it is related to my feelings of deep love towards her.

Page 242, mathematically becoming the Number '10'. She the 'One', me, on the verge of being her zero!

In this missing has been a glorious living of sorts. The petals opening each day and closing each night. My sleep again generally unburdened, the flower continues to survive waiting to blossom fully or to die suddenly! Withering is no longer its nature it seems, either it will persist or desist from existence.

Chapter 32

25/3 – It is Dr John Watts' birthday in Canada. He is a mentor and a friend. It is also the death anniversary of my mum's eldest sister Manjumasi, her death happening in front of Dk *mama* and me, the only family death that I have witnessed till the present moment. Yesterday a family dinner together, a disturbing movie of the events of 26/11 in Mumbai so awake till late. Spoke to Rima, voicemail at Avery's. I woke up half an hour early and having finished my morning routine, I was on my favourite perch much sooner than usual. A golden opportunity let go last evening on my walk. I saw her from a distance, at the first garden making her way towards Gandhi market, via the main road of Sion. I was near the Mata Lachmi Hospital, a bit surprised. I quickened my pace to catch up, she slowed down. Her back to me unaware I was now so close behind her. I came to a standstill three times lest I overtake her and create the feeling of it being on purpose as it is not the route of my daily walk. Maybe hoping she will turn around and I can greet her. Saw her trying to call someone on her mobile unsuccessfully four times. She kept walking slowly, window shopping at pavement stalls but not interested in buying anything. I was barely a step behind her all the way but she seemed miles out of my reach.

Too crowded the pavement, the mind fighting with itself. Almost approached with a prepared apology and a request for three minutes of her time for the three months of my longing. She never looked back and I faltered. Was it destiny at play or did I miss the opportunity to make a difference to this 'relating'? I will never know now what could have been the outcome if I had kept my courage, listened to my heart and let my prevailing sense flee in that moment.

I turned, went back to my usual street of walk in the Kikabhai Hospital lane, which is behind the main road of Sion, hoping to run into her on her return. But the traffic was heavy there, Sunday chaos, and it ruled my walk also. She kept coming into my thoughts persistently. I was left fumbling, disappointed at my lost attempts to seek a fortuitous meeting. Remember, Kikabhai Hospital lane is where I had first seen her last year without knowing of her whereabouts and I did wonder about her at that time too!

So also lost my brief moments of so-called meditative peace, now replaced by the feelings of love which by themselves are meditative, aren't they!? But now a prayer is needed I guess or a sense of prayerfulness to make the impossible, possible.

This happening like a boat adrift, its moorings lost. The anchor of my expectations too heavy to cast away and move to a point of stability amidst these stormy waters. I reach nowhere, awaiting the moment of my drowning. A song comes to my lips and dies that very moment.

She will find this ocean of love sweet whenever and wherever she wishes to taste it from. I will find it salty however, for it is mingled with so many of my silent tears unknown to her, yet very much being shed every day!

But the ocean that separates us is quite indifferent to where its salty nature comes from.

Chapter 33

I struggle to finish my tasks, deferring them daily. They keep piling up to leave my last week here not one of rest and relaxation but with a multitude of deadlines to meet. That in itself will put an end to this vacant obsession of mine. The imagined scenarios take shape daily only to disappear each night. They recur each day with the same intensity with barely any perceptible change to their quality or quantity. Influenced only by subtle nuances of her activities that still continue to amaze me, each new gesture making my heart skip a beat.

Today, I wonder when the last writing on this trip will be and what it will be!

This puzzle is not just for you, it's for me too.

Have I succeeded in making the imaginary real or will a perceived reality get dismissed as an illusion or delusion?

The proof, as they say, is in the pudding!

To taste or to feel it, it has to materialise first, isn't it? This writing reminds me of the opening scenes of my most loved movie of all time *Anand*. An award ceremony where a doctor's novel is the winner of one of the highest honours in the land. It is introduced as a conception of the author's mind, done so and written in spite of a very busy clinical and academic practice. The doctor corrects this notion in his few words of giving thanks for the honour bestowed. I paraphrase the essence of his words, not obviously as eloquently as the writer of the scene:

"If you have perceived this novel as fiction, a product of my imagination then the fault rests solely in my writing ability. This book is based on a real character and events I lived with and experienced myself. He became my dearest friend and we his family and friends. The version of the story of his life in front of you, are just the pages of my daily diary!"

An emotionally breath-taking answer bringing tears to all eyes. Dispelling eloquently the notion of it being a myth, he reminds the audience of it having been his immediate reality and experience, which unfortunately the jury panel and readers thought of as fiction.

Fact or fiction, this journey has been a teacher in many ways. The lessons soft and hard, soothing and harsh, sweet and bitter, to ignore them is not easy. The richness or poverty of it is a matter of opinionated judgement. In this language is hidden a seed that is unprotected, unsheltered, alone, daring and courageous enough to die any moment in the rocky terrain or to live eternally in the fertile soil of a loving heart.

Can this writing similarly transform my life? Isn't it true that the process is on its way already but the awareness is still lacking?

For instance yesterday was the first day I realised how to mark the later tasks of her morning routine. The light in the bathroom around 11 am is the surest indicator that she will not be in the kitchen for almost 90 minutes to two hours. The cleaning of clothes done in instalments, the amount of time taken determined almost weekly by a surfeit of extra loads and so a prolonged absence in the morning.

I am much aware now of the routines of her waking hours as I am of my sleeping hours. Right now occupied with the preliminaries of washing clothes, the light goes off, soon she will emerge to hang the first load, go back, light on, clean her own clothes, take her bath, light off, come out in fresh clothes and go hang the remainder of the wash. In a little while she will be found in the living room, re-enter her kitchen for final lunch preparations and her meal, often she is now out of sight for most of that time. I bet you aren't enjoying this litany of details. But I am; it is after all my writing.

Unless you have ever felt like I have, you will never get it!

Her family is out this morning, the daughter will soon to go to her College and she will be alone. It is quite tempting to observe, wait and defer the task I had planned to do this morning, try to instead step out for small tasks and run into her should she too step out on an errand of her own.

Does she miss the music that I played for her? What is the message of the occasional looks that keep my temptations alive? Neither deaf, mute nor blind, how come it is becoming so difficult to clear the air between us! The initiative again will have to be mine, the scorn and indifference will have to be faced and tolerated again, sweet will be its pain. Holi coming and its colours and festivities this year like many previous, will not add much to my life.

I am left with just the purity of white of my daily attire, the marks and stains will clearly show the failure over and over again about the weeping of a bleeding heart!

An hour into writing. The calculations of my mind like an upturned apple cart. Nothing has happened as per my thinking. Good to know however that the heart is slowly trying to master the mind, the being still aloof from both. For her presence within me has always been without her acceptance. Her new top worn for a short while is not amongst the clothes hanging out to dry but it has done its job by leaving me hanging. I will have to leave on errands, will miss her watering. It probably doesn't matter for this thirst is without the source to quench it anyway!

Her door has been open for a long time, the invitation obviously not for me. Nowhere is she to be seen. Then I suddenly found her with a large garment in her hands in the kitchen, nothing going as per my visualized plans for her. Is it the Monday morning blues? Even this hesitant writing is a relief of sorts. Now a big utensil, her work seems to be never ending. And today in Hindustan Times an article detailing the life of a household maid caught my attention. Yes, the drudgery mixed with the benefits for them, albeit they are the keepers of the convenience of a few.

Money, we all know, buys a lot of things, but not humans hopefully in this day and age! This writing too, a form of drudgery, inconvenient I guess for both you and me alike, a labour futile and unrewarded.

I left, bowed at her window, returned with my shopping bags. Her mistress is back within and can be seen at the balcony window; heard her conversing. I glanced across at her house while entering my courtyard. She in a regal, majestic pose in the garden, shearing scissors in hand, a half smile on her face as she saw me looking at her. So tempting but the feeling generated was as if her scissors were toying with me, cutting me to pieces. A leash of my own making, fraying with each pull and give, yet remaining bound to her by the slenderest of threads.

Way past my breakfast time. I wait for her to finish and return. This might be an intense prolonged wait, her garden work may keep her occupied for the better part of an hour, a faint hope lurking that she might have started the work very soon after my leaving, so maybe I just need to be patient, it may not be too long now. This ink stronger in full ferocity, like the darkness before dawn or the twilight at dusk before night. Either way it is symbolic of *sandhya* - the in-between time of utter silence. The ink is on the verge of running out, the birth of a new pen waiting in the wings, the words however unlikely to be any different though.

How much more magic and mystery can I create? If the feelings and thoughts only seem to gather a depth, their void and emptiness is the same, just sinking deeper and deeper into a morass that allows nothing to grow!

Chapter 34

She goes back and forth; I find two songs to give extra wings to my flight. Her amusement at my stupidity can be felt, a vicarious pleasure though, is felt by me in this. She is back inside having finished her outside work and I, summarily left on the outside of her life. Soon will come a moment when I will feel as if I am fading away, trying to gain her reciprocation. And in that moment will come the friendship of my loving towards myself. Unable to contain it, it will continue to flow in other dimensions of my life.

Yes, there have been so-called moments of love a few times with other women but never during the whole course of my marriage. In that there was absolute love and fidelity without any extraneous romances or flirtations, to the one who still chose to leave me, in spite of caring deeply for her. Now a more constant love with nature, my solitude and my aloneness will continue to grow I hope. Last night, on television, two songs back to back again, a repetition of my previously humming them. Coincidences coming much too often, but not really so. Is it because I have a deep seated feel for a few melodies so near and dear to me, while music channels on radio and television are far too many? It is obvious that these songs will be found playing somewhere every day? So is all of this just a manufactured coincidence of my search for good music? There is a selfish motive lurking behind this kind of satisfaction and apparent mystery on a daily basis.

One more Tuesday left, today being Holi, a painful reminder of my holiday coming to an end. Yesterday's song too bringing a delightful romance to its natural ending. Mine just wasn't real enough to sprout, no instruments left to till this soil. My hands bare and empty, no place to put the seed or water it anymore. Suspended in mid-air it can only gain nourishment from an occasional shower of rain now.

She has gone missing since yesterday morning! Just the day after the parting romantic song from *Do Raaste* (Two Roads). Her path and mine, parting ways after a meeting of just the one with himself. Strangers of day and night, a journey never taken together, a separation that was already written in the meeting itself.

That song, which followed the one about life from *Safar*, was about love being sacrificed because of material circumstances, only to be richly gained at the end. Such is not the destiny of my love - it has left me humbled yet richer in spite of the poverty of her response. Two days of Holi, she is likely with family in her village or city, hopefully not a long holiday. No one I know has the kind of holiday that I do. Except when I was away for five days at Murli's farm, my eyes have seen her every day and always so by my being when away from her. Today is my first morning here with no meeting of the eyes. The day awaiting the eruption of colours, a muted Holi with drought raising its ugly head in many villages, the water there unfit to drink even for animals, let alone humans. A collective consciousness is trying to make this a waterless Holi with limited use of colours that are often laced with toxic chemicals.

A haircut this morning. Suddenly, having re-read most of my Osho books and magazines, there is a lack of interest to read anything else. Though I keep buying more books in plenty, no change on that front on this visit too. Again, and now really my last trip to my vendors, a parting until I resume going to them on my next visit. An outing with family to Matheran in 48 hours. I hope to spend time today in silence, hearing and feeling every bit of nature and society. Listen, understand, and rejuvenate myself for a long hard stint of work abroad in two weeks or so.

The ink is not dry yet, maybe it is waiting for her sight to give out a sigh and a last gasp for an unrealised yet very fulfilling romantic interlude.

In her absence I found none of the songs appealing enough to play them. Maybe they too realise the purpose of my playing and chose to take a well-deserved rest from being the medium of my message to her. A feeling of ruthless apathy prevails, my activity at a standstill. How much unknowingly I have come to miss her across from me. Writing a mere substitute to while away my time. Both courtyards empty, the revelry of Holi not evident for now. Birds missing, a mild breeze providing some solace to a forlorn heart. She will never know of this nor would she care. Someday though she may find out, by then, it might have been too late. Not her fault by any means. I have failed utterly to seize the moment, to make my intentions explicit, simple and direct, without allowing the opportunity for any doubt to take hold and germinate within her.

Then, either my love would have sown roots or died to live another day!

Chapter 35

Holi over, it is now the wedding anniversary of Arham's grandparents. A little red *gulaal* leftover, my gesture of showing her my honourable intentions lost to time as she hasn't come back yet, and the dish is cleaned. Family dinner, *kajukatri* and *mohanthaal* shared with Arham's family at night. No KEM buddies meeting today as Tuks' son Nikhil leaves for USA. And, another day gone. A beautiful *saree* bought by *bhabhi* from an exhibition, I was correct in guessing its price, however its value and beauty priceless, handmade, one of a kind. A three hour walk on Holi, drenched with pistols of water from Krishna and Nikki from their balcony. The dry *gulaal* smeared by the water now colouring my *peran* (white thin cotton short *kurti*) in blotches, the evening breeze was cool so it dried in no time. Phone calls to Canada, friends, relatives, superintendent Franca and my patient Clark, where I could only leave a voicemail. Hardly any reading all day, bits and pieces of eating, sitting, doing nothing. The mind kept roaming in its labyrinth, its maze difficult, almost impossible to extricate myself from. Circling around albeit much slower than before, some gaps seen as windows but the door to escape remains elusive.

The morning after Holi, the city is reflecting a certain serenity, after the boisterous activity at least in some areas, a balance is now restored by nature. The energy and enthusiasm to write is dissipating in her absence. I just wish to sit on my ledge and see how long this discontent lasts. Her reappearance unlikely till next week, as also will be Arham who greeted me and said bye as he is on his way to Saputara.

Everything happens in its own time and season. Spring comes and the grass grows by itself. Her absence too likely an indicator for this aimless, circuitous writing to cease. And then, it may be the way for me to come back and reclaim my silence. The noise will undoubtedly return with her coming but this lull in between must have its own reasons that I can't understand yet.

April 1 – Gone missing is the inspiration. A week's absence leaves me feeling weak, reading stopped, a weekend now in Matheran at 'The Byke'

Little tyke on his bike, His understanding just right!

A great time with family, immediate and extended one amidst nature and plenty of monkeys. Swimming endlessly, eating way too much and too often, games, swings, walks, music however went missing from my life. Did she miss me during my absence and stay at Murli's farm the way I keep missing her? Hope all is well with her family. Maybe it's her first break in some time to go back to her village, hopefully not to get engaged or betrothed. She would never know that I was away again for three days only this time around. Maybe she won't be back before I leave for Canada. This going will be muted but her presence may make it even more painful. Best not to have a glimpse of her before that, it might just then make it a wee bit easier. Who am I kidding?

Newspapers, Osho, Speaking Tree all left by the wayside. A chanced glance at the television on my return from Matheran yesterday. While I was shaving, my brother found *"Anand"* while surfing channels on the television in the late afternoon. Already halfway into the movie, it wasn't the same watching it, yet the tears did flow as they have always done every time over a lifetime of repeatedly watching it. It was also March 31, my ex-wife's birthday, so what a day for it to come on when I had been waiting expectantly for it the past four months. It came as an indicator of half a life, the major part of humour over, leaving only tears; somehow such incidents trigger coincidental memories of my life.

One more Monday morning and I try to find ways to stretch my last week as much as possible. Arranging, rearranging events and tasks to finish on a day to day basis.

April 2 - This is the day when a deep funk begins. Next week on this day I will be missing my sleep at home here, sitting at the airport and trying to sleep in space. More and more is the pull of returning to my roots and restarting the missed life here. As memory starts to dwindle again with my deliberate attempts to do so, and a romance over before it even took birth, it is a painful reminder that even if the body and heart feels quite young, my age is stamped on my face and mind, noticed by all and myself.

Lest I forget, it may be of use to begin from my earliest memories, create a jungle of events, circling various paths at random and see where I reach. Last month of this trip was somewhat occupied in the search of a retreat out of town, which ended without any encouraging results. At least, I came to the conclusion that it is unaffordable for me, hence it is futile to waste further time over it. But overall, I am quite okay by myself anywhere here or abroad. A serious look at the ramifications of committing such a huge corpus of my savings to this endeavour, maybe quite foolish at this stage in my life, something in common parlance called as taking over a white elephant. On the other hand, it would be more feasible to use my investment and interest income proceeds for family to enjoy short vacations at different places on weekends once or twice a month or when convenient for them.

As for myself, Murli's farm is home for me, a deep solace and the ultimate dwelling for my peace and calm. The pros and cons of life and work, Georgina and Karnala, Ancaster and Sion, keep churning over and over again. A trigger is needed for the bullet to fire so that there is no longer any turning back from a decision reached. Either it will find its target and goal, or miss it and be spent and lost, but any result from it would be acceptable to me, if my decision is total and not stemming from the split mind of mine. For my survival and a balanced life, just 60 to 75 percent of my current working lifestyle would be enough to earn and live like I have been doing in two countries for 20 years now. A significant drop in my savings would occur, but that shortfall can be made up hopefully by income generated from investments. Barring an unforeseen calamity, I think the means at my disposal may guarantee a comfortable living.

This writing is fast losing its freshness, charm or ability to sustain even my attention. A U-turn is needed to re-navigate, create small abstract pieces full of meaning again. It might then avoid this all-pervasive feeling of either boredom or seriousness, both primary diseases that hinder the living of a good life. Humour is missing, this tragedy a comedy of sorts where no one is laughing.

Reaching a state where it seems I am content doing nothing, this trip has gone a long way to push me towards a decision. But it is hampered and weighed down by the nitty-gritty of the various practical and other unavoidable problems and pitfalls that would need sorting out; every aspect of such a decision, its aftermath and hassles throwing a monkey wrench in my plans.

My thoughts keep going on and on like a squeaky wheel, the oil being sought not just as a lubricant or catalyst but as a means towards the smooth stoppage of the wheel itself.

And so I return, always back to my nature, a procrastinator par excellence!

Chapter 36

April 4 – I came back from my walk, cleaned up the afternoon utensils, showered, and while drying the utensils saw her and it seemed as if my breath had stopped. She is back! A recurring nightmare!

Her mistress returned and saw us exchanging looks, and she quickly looked away. Then a song played for her but she had left her kitchen. In the week that she has been away it is as if the music that had reignited itself disappeared again from my life. As if my heartbeat had stopped like a clock whose battery has run out.

I will leave before the opportunity to wish her new year's greetings, as Gudi Padwa falls on the day after my departure. The signals that are left to send across, now few, and the moments of engaging far too fleeting to hold her gaze. A cold shower takes care of the sweating I subject myself to on a daily basis. At least with her returning, I have been able to pick up my pen and write again, to do her the justice she so richly deserves.

Five days to go, my feelings refuse to allow me any clarity, neither do they allow a decision to manifest by itself. A calm has descended, maybe it will evaporate once I return back to Canada and resume my real work. An early dental appointment, my subsequent hours still in a flux. The evening location to spend time with Dk *mama* and family is still undecided, my travels uncertain now except for the imminent departure to Canada.

At least with her return my leftover mornings will recapture the flavour of the past three months. Just looking silently on and off, brief glimpses are enough to fill my emptiness. Her memory carried over as an ever burning slow, cool flame within my heart. She will appear time and again even in her absence, unannounced, that I am certain of if nothing else. Whether that just comes as a thought or a feeling to savour remains to be seen. It could also well be the source of everlasting pain not followed by any pleasure, lingering on as a sorrow that too is still welcome.

Either way, I will never be indifferent to her. This writing is circular just like time, nothing new happening, just the rotation of ups and downs carrying on. The ink ran out, an omen as she returned looking down every step of the way, her message suggesting the water isn't for me. I am condemned to remain thirsty even though the source is so near to me.

Twice seen while hanging clothes. I stood there, my feet refusing to move, looked and looked, she refused to meet my eyes. Though she was quite aware of it as I noticed a brief sideways movement of her eyes, which seem a dark black.

I left for Dk *mama's* clinic a bit early so as to have some time near Gamdevi to search for the book "*Jurassic Park*" for my nephew, my own copy given away ages ago it seems. I was unable to find either a new or used copy in my area in spite of searching for a month. The decision paid off and I found it close to DK *mama's* clinic in an old newspaper shop and bought it for him. My touch up done by Dr Aditi, who along with my *mama* has taken utmost pains to keep my teeth healthy so I can keep chewing this narrative of nails without trouble. Anyway, pleasant news of her engagement to her long-standing sweetheart Nilay. My heartiest congratulations to both. I had a gift of a designer *kurti* for her like my previous few years, but was unaware of her engagement. I hope it fits her for she appears taller and not very, very slim as I had imagined her to be from my visit a year ago. Dr. Aditi is like my cousin Biddu (Neil), who was the first to ever clean my teeth patiently and gently, soft hands and a long sitting with never any pain or discomfort, way back in 1985 when I first left this country is still vividly etched in my memory. In 25 years plus I had never been to a dentist, so my Dk *mama's* son Biddu, during his training and registrar post at Nair Dental College, did my teeth. I may have been one of the first family members he ever treated and his handiwork on me was so great that I immediately sensed the remarkable potential he had during a career that has now taken root in the USA, and a gentle, meticulous, thoroughly artful and immaculate bedside manner continues to impress each of his patients. Yes, he inherited it all from his father, my *mama*, genes do run in the family across generations, some too for me from my father, also a family physician and my mother an avid reader, human and compassionate always.

Dk *mama*, Biddu and Dr Aditi, their skills and manner bring back the memory of my dad. Family members would rave about his skills as a clinician and also at intramuscular injections, they were barely perceptible to those who were fortunate to be treated and have it administered by him. I too seemed to have inherited that sleight of hand, as after my graduation, throughout my internship and postgraduate years, I would be called upon by family and friends alike in need to get treated by me including both intramuscular and intravenous injections. They used to fondly comment, that Jay has inherited his father's hand. Yes, I at times had to administer Intravenous Aminophylline to my father in emergencies when he would have a severe bout of asthma, and he would recover in minutes and I could see the pride and joy, the relief and tears in his eyes behind a faint smile. I then knew I had made it, in his eyes and heart he must have felt the torch of his legacy carry on. I just hope I have been able to be a fraction of the compassionate loving clinician he was. Not only family and friends, even colleagues at work in Wadia Children's Hospital would ask for me to administer injections to some very challenging and frightened children, instead of getting the nurses to do it as was the norm. I remember distinctly when the adopted little girl left in my ward at Wadia became sick with fever and diarrhoea requiring intravenous fluids, none of the nurses were willing to poke her. We all loved Neha so much that no one wished the slightest discomfort or pain from their hands to pass on to her. So, given that I had taken the responsibility to raise her in the hospital, it was me they looked at to deliver. Yes, that day starting her intravenous therapy to give her fluids and medicines and for a speedy recovery, and her first year vaccinations were left to my gentle hands by the nurses. Anyway, Neha's story is a separate one for a later time in my life's writing, if another book is in the offing. I just hope that you do not take this interlude as a boast of my skills or the pampering of my ego. It was solely an attempt to emphasize the humanistic skills of my Dk *mama*, my cousin Biddu and the talented hands of Dr Aditi being groomed by my *mama*. My father's hand well remembered amongst the family.

A visit to Awadhesh at Flora Fountain for some books to read in my spare time before my evening resumed with *mama* and family. I spent an hour chatting with some old friends, Dr Naomi and Dr Amrita, a gift of a book requested by her, bought and inscribed with a message and two haikus written at Ransai Lake. Then Swami Swatmanada's discourse at Chinmaya, evening at Bombay Gymkhana and return by train. Two trips in the same day to Flora Fountain, can't remember ever having done that before. Lucky to be able to congratulate my childhood friend Gautam at the Bombay Gymkhana award ceremony. I reached on time to witness the honour and accolades being showered on him. He, singlehandedly over a period of two days indulged in a marathon game of badminton, winning 9 out of 11 matches to give Bombay Gymkhana its inter club city badminton tournament championship. Gift for my cousin, DK *mama's* daughter Tina also. My last meeting with *mama* and family on this trip, to be continued in the USA in June/ July again after this parting.

A supreme honour is in the offing for Dk *mama* on April 29, I will have left though. Impossible to enumerate his endless awards, honours, prestigious doctorates and a platitude of recognition given over many decades by national and international bodies, organizations and universities. None of us will ever reach the level of esteem he is held in across the world. Singlehandedly, he has given the family innumerable moments of pride and privilege. His numerous distinguished orations, exemplary clinical practice, profound academic and epidemiological research excellence in the field of oral pathology and oral cancer, long standing prestigious grants from NIH in USA and similarly from India and Europe, numerous peer reviewed publications, book chapters and a comprehensive book, along with talents and services in other fields such as Bhartiya Vidya Bhavan etc., you name it and I will still have missed many of his accolades and feathers in his cap. I could go and on about his achievements and talents, one of course being my *mama*! Jokes aside, he is a friend beyond the pale of friendship, a guide for me and a world renowned leader in his field.

But then, this is about the lady across from me, and my ego trips over past four months emptying on these pages, with the hope of exhausting it over time. Four more days to go, this diary will have empty pages left over. My crossroads is coming closer. Do I pick up the pace or slow down a bit, continue this status quo or just be natural and surrender to whatever lies in store on my return to work in Canada?

Only a hand is seen opening the windows. Seems as if she is purposely not letting me have a glimpse of her face. She stretches her hands across as if to shove them open. However, at night she has to lean out slightly to reach and close them and a profile may be visible for a second. Soon she will figure out a way to prevent that glimpse. It can be easily done by just holding the frame closest to her, slip her fingers around and shut them so that her face would never come in view from my sitting place on dad's chair. It does not matter to me, for she has no idea that it was just the hands that started this saga months ago and they are still visible often. No deliberate looks from her now. It is a goodbye or good riddance I guess for an interlude that never began with greetings of any sort.

Two courtyards, a wall in between, two iron grills on either side keeping this love caged. She with total freedom to choose, accept or reject. Mine was never a choosing, the feeling just happened in an instant, thoughts came much later on. Now the exercise of this debate is pointless. Love has failed the test of logic but I feel that I haven't lost anything so far.

No longer since her arrival back has she taken a good look at me. Why this continues to traumatize me is impossible to explain. Our lives so separate, unbridgeable, a generation apart but love remains the only feeling that breaks all barriers and boundaries. My cup of it has overflowed daily, yet there isn't someone ready to take a sip.

My last evening with KEM buddies. Gudi Padwa gifts for them, drivers, secretaries and waiters' *baksheesh* also. A lavish dinner at home with two desserts, *aamras*, *shrikhand*, ice cream. Indian Premier League T20 match on television at home. Sleep not calm, stretching time when awake, a way to prolong the ending.

Tuks intuited in our last meeting that *dadhi* will be in love by this October with someone totally unexpected. A genius he is in our profession and otherwise, but his power of intuition I wasn't fully aware of. How close he is to the truth he doesn't know yet, but he will if he reads this, the truth that I am trying to make appear in words now. Unfortunately this love is not reciprocated nor did I ask

Tuks whether that someone will love me in return. Love is after all a sharing not a demand from someone. So he is right for the one half of the story, absolutely right is his intuition, albeit delayed in his telling of it.

Almost missed her coming back. Her hand covering her face from the glare of the morning sun in her eyes. A half smile to the watchman and for the first time I notice a dimple developing high up on her cheek. Slim long fingers without nail polish. Her complexion appears fairer than mine now actually.

She returns each day with the bucket empty. A reminder repeatedly that she has nothing to give to me or share with. But I have enough love for both of us, yet I can fathom no way now to deliver this message. 96 hours left for me and I will step out of her life, maybe never to see her again unless on my return she is found single and still working in the house across from mine. The way she has worked over my heart and mind will remain a fond memory of time well spent.

Chapter 37

April 6 – It feels as if all my dialogues and monologues are over, but most people have felt that I talk too much anyway. So one can surmise that if the monologue is over, then this writing too has to stop.

A nice evening family dinner. Didi missing though. Then at 11 pm, a surprise visit by Arham and his parents with cakes, brownies and a candle to wish me a safe journey. 'Be happy,' says Arham, innocently asking that if you are sad to go back then why are you going! A child's simple question with a touching smile that I listened to with loving attention. Difficult to explain to him in the short time that I have, why my professional work abroad is still so critically important and a joy to me. But this will prompt a re-examination of how much more time will I devote to my career there. The call to call it quits is slowly beginning to gather a momentum of its own, a risk to be taken and a headache may need to be undergone, the heartache ever so present, unlikely to disappear. Otherwise I will never know what life would be on a long term basis of pursuing the 'Art of Doing Nothing' before it becomes too late. A waiting for the slow growth process that this visit has encouraged to materialise.

The agenda remains a dream: Living in four different dwellings spread across the year. Seriously take up my passion of writing side by side with my reading, walking, swimming and rest. That way I can turn this living back into a comedy with humour again, eliminating the bit of seriousness that has crept in and kept somewhat building over time in my aloneness. Yes, in company for short periods everyone still recognises the old *dadhi* with the ready wit, the gift of the gab as my Biddu says often, and the one who gets the last word.

84 hours to go, 24 in sleep, 12 in walking, another 16 in evenings and errands, 4 in bags packing. A few phone calls and even fewer conversations, leftover 28 hours of unfixed time will deepen this loss. This journey will end and another one will begin.

Time and again this coming and going back is creating a sort of tension difficult to describe. It comes from deep within and dies before reaching the surface, only to keep recurring again and again.

I have had the greatest of times, the love of life, a frightfully delicate romance beginning and dying on a daily basis. Emptying and filling my heart, aimlessly occupying my mind, no purpose, no goal except for its thrill and uncertainty overlapping each moment after another, often throwing me back to the present, tempting and taking me back into my past or an imagined future, before it can settle down into my being.

Why, when love is so fleeting, does loving seem so permanent and unchanging? Any love that is reciprocated between humans is necessarily going to have hate as its shadow alongside on occasions. It may be prompted by circumstances or by moods triggered, whereas loving is its own mood creating a climate with a fragrance that is everlasting.

I consider myself fortunate and grateful to have experienced its feeling and some of it as thoughts on this visit.

I have a long way to go before I can reach a state where only the experience is and the 'experiencer' no more. "The observer is the observed" is how the master Jiddu Krishnamurti says, and so do many other great masters. Having learnt a lot in this visit, it will translate into knowing someday. I prepare to leave but this time there is a cultivated calm about my departure in two days. Tomorrow is my dad's death anniversary and Clark's birthday in Canada. Someone dies, someone is born, and the cycle continues eternally, age old wisdom replaced by young fresh innocence.

A Sunday morning, cool, pleasant, new sounds reaching me. Moments when the senses are alive, sensitive to all the joys and pains felt, seen, or heard. Man made chirping from the toy seller and his trumpet mimicking the song of the birds. The horde of children still asleep on a lazy morning, he will pass by without sharing his toys. Too early he has come, too soon I will depart from the life that has been in between, seemingly prolonged. The green leaves taking on a golden hue, the petals in a rainbow of colours. A symmetry in nature, a constant dissolution and renewal. We have lost the eyes to perceive its grandeur and the ears to listen to its silent music. But music played in my heart, an endless song repeating every day, destined to remain incomplete, its melody ever fresh, and continues its silent humming within me.

A sumptuous family dinner with dessert again and a trial run of the living room air conditioner was successful. A win by Mumbai Indians in IPL cricket tournament, late to sleep, a call wishing Bennett on his birthday in Canada. As the night ends, my day begins with the persistent unerring monotony of a lazy existence now disturbed by my imminent departure.

Made some attempts at writing poems and haikus during the days spent on Murli's farm and Ransai Lake. This is a ridiculous prose generated in an attempt to regain solitude in this urban sprawl. Perched on my ledge far removed from the noise my ears hear, my eyes just see the One repeatedly. Every moment appealing in itself, a sincere attempt to still my chaotic mind. But my every task still done mostly in unconsciousness, thanks to my continuous preoccupation with her.

Yet, there are often imperceptible moments when my awareness is brief but total. Sitting silently, slow breathing, a gently paced walk when a parrot's song briefly captures and holds my attention, absorbing me. Each moment's preciousness is beginning to dawn on me, yet my mind is too often ready to drag me away. It is still the labyrinth of recurring identical thoughts, stealing away the moments of spontaneous exhilaration.

A deep pain though surfaces every morning. The watering visit and return, exit and re-entry barely lasting a minute or two. It pulls my heart strings hither and thither. No longer any meeting of the eyes, no longer the exchange of a smile. A slow measured walk with downcast eyes, a sombre look. My prayerful gestures neither noticed nor heeded to, yet I continue to care deeply for her simplicity and labour. She a teacher of many lessons for me, each one more precious than any of my book knowledge. At such a tender age, her life seems to be solely devoted to her employer's family, who in turn no doubt treat her as one of their own.

Nowhere is seen her very first outfit and the last new one! One discarded, one reserved for special occasions, I party to neither, still left searching for metaphors in her very essence that makes my life richer.

Chapter 38

April 8 - Another morning rolls around. I listen silently to its silence. Two telephone calls to Clark and Nina in Canada, a large platter of *sev puri* for dinner and dark chocolate and ice cream for dessert. The night falls quickly, its darkness covering up my romance with life. The loving carried over in hope of more footsteps in the morning. Just like today, tomorrow will come with the message that my last sleep here is done. And in its loss will come a feeling of what it is that I have gained from my time here. A sense of patience, often a reconnection with Nature, a calm less easily disturbed, a lifestyle without haste or hurry, yet my time just burned away.

Two young butterflies last afternoon playing over the flowers, a captivating sight of an innocence and presence that I am finding hard to bring back into my life. (Ink is getting lighter, may need a new pen, maybe not!). The news of another day around the world, a rehash of ills and disasters on a recurring basis with hardly anything substantially new except that the players involved are different though on the same stage. Maybe it is because I have become stale without fresh eyes or a new sense of listening. Moments of bliss come and go unawares until the moment itself has passed and just become a memory. My storehouse empties and fills up again, none of it could be called essential.

A desire remains for my loving to become a deep friendship and kindness towards all. A radical U-turn in a one-way street, a search for clarity in my remaining years or moments left. A deep embrace with myself, allowing what is a practice now to become a more spontaneous existence. Yet my conversations will die out, very little left to say.

To the 'One' whom I have a lot to say has refused to hear even my silence. That was the music and a song ignored, what use would any words be for her?

If that is the case, why do I write so much? As someone has said and I quote, "Talk is cheap because supply exceeds demand." With my written words or my inner talk both supply and demand are mine alone. So an exercise either of words or of silence is fruitless.

Yet I hope there are plenty of flowers amidst the weeds and thorns for a careful gardener to peruse. Today, I am left without any water to make my story grow. Sun and wind still embracing, caressing the earth, soon to disappear into the empty sky.

Yes, it is over. I just hope I am left somewhat better than when I arrived here. Can it sustain itself over time? Can her absence continue as a presence, a friendliness even in her continued indifference towards me?

She saunters back uncaring of the pain she generates, though I have no regrets and even welcome its continuance. Not surprising, given most of us continue to live in pain and misery refusing to drop out of it. For it is the only thing we seem to have or know.

Afraid of the emptiness, we wallow in the negativity. We forget that a gap will come in a short or a long while before the seed of anything positive emerges. The earth of our feelings longs to fly up to the empty sky, yearning for the courage to embark on an uncertain flight. Take the gamble and risk not knowing whether it will ever reach anywhere.

But just that longing and an effort will give a new dimension of the vertical to manifest and make us drop out of the horizontal and circular thinking of time!

April 9 – So now is the day to leave. The change in ink may be a metaphor for the birth of a new leaf, as the old in me leaves!

MY TIME IS UP!

P.S. To paraphrase from the Holy Geeta: She is a part of me but I am not a part of her! Was this all a lie or the truth!

I leave you to figure it out, for I have already done enough of my share of it.

P.P.S I move effortlessly from one life to another. In between will come the death that I am seeking while still alive!

AFTERMATH

April 10

Six pm and it all seems so unbelievable. Back in Canada, being welcomed by a cold, cloudy, windy, rainy day. Slowly completed my chores in a daze of sorts to get my house up and running again, while my escape has come to an end.

My pen was left behind; a marker for the grave, a tombstone for a trip that some may think of and remember as having never begun. For not much was done or achieved if viewed and judged by the eyes of others.

So a new pen as I sit wondering silently about what had come to pass. A couple of phone calls to my dear little ones in Canada brought some enthusiasm back to this arrival. But I was unable to reach my dearest friend BabuMoshai on the phone.

Ate a bagel, a mango, and some fresh groceries kept in my fridge by Hemant and Sudha. Emptied my bags as if emptying the memories. My parked car filled with daily needed stuff for my work, and then came the urge to write again.

Back to black ink amidst a touch of blue and red, an unintentional suggestion of my mood. Yet the writing not much different in one colour or another.

The purity of white unable to be captured, if it can ever be. For that, best to leave the page empty!

Plan to retire early, a day of cold freezing rain to look forward to tomorrow, so errands will have to be kept to the bare minimum that is essential. Half an extra day this time as I had booked an earlier flight from Frankfurt, yet a full day likely to be lost tomorrow.

Just like my life. Half a step forward and a full step back, moving nowhere yet everywhere in my mind.

Unable to reach Dafne's mum to wish Dafne a happy birthday, now two years old, a miracle of sorts.

Anyway a roll of thunder struck note the moment I had entered with my bags, a steady light drizzle, the sounds of car tires on wet roads, an occasional voice of a bird, yet no human voice heard from the courtyard and the street below.

THE WORLD SEEMS SILENT, YET THE NOISE WITHIN ME IS BECOMING DEAFENING!

Four hours on, the mind still chattering away. This time it's different. It is likely going to prove far more difficult to resume my usual routines of work and other activities; she has made it somewhat impossible is what I feel right now.

April 11 - Gudi Padwa

A 12 hour sleep, phone calls to wish New Year greetings to relatives and friends. Freezing rain, picked up my mail, cash, and a few groceries, a visit to the public library walking the 600 metres, picked up some good books but frozen on the way back. I am as stupid as ever at times, having dared to walk those two blocks in such horrid weather.

Suddenly, she too being a Maharashtrian surfaced, this being her new year too. The one person I would most want to wish deeply can't be reached by phone or by sight. So a song for her is the best I can do. I found *Baazigar* on tape, set it to play and waited for the song to appear. The music that I had given up a long time ago has come back into my life with some sort of vengeance.

But this time it is for me alone. She is too far away, in a separate world, asleep. Maybe she will have a few hiccups in her sleep, as my remembrance caresses her, with my emotions and feelings taking a long distance flight...

Given this weather I am almost tempted to fly back. The song comes on and I am still for a moment...

THE WARMTH OF AN INTIMATE PAIR OF HANDS BECKONING IRRESTIBLY!!

"In the missing embrace for my living

Is the embrace of my dying"

'REFLECTIONS'

Attempts at poetry during my days on "Vaishnavi Farms" and the banks of "Ransai Lake"

March 6, 2013 to March 10, 2013

6/3

1 Whispering hot wind,

Green leaf falls on stone,

Thunder on the ground,

A small bird takes wing

2 Green mangoes in a bunch

Green tomatoes on vine

Scorching heat, green chillies, waterless fields

Electricity gone, pump silently watches

3 Butterflies humming, flies buzzing

Birds crying, ants crawling

Bites many, legs dry itching

No water for wash

4   Mother shouting, child crying

Wind stops, all is quiet

Car honks!

5   Mosquito bite wound

Band-Aid peeling

Flies smell blood!

7/3

1   Swaying palms, rooted trunk

Wind dies, dance incomplete

Picks up, dancer succumbs!

2   Dogs lazing, lunch eaten

Cat late but alert

Missy missed, dogs hovering

3   Clear sky, hot air

Balloon burst

Sound shocked into silence!

4   Old and young leaves

Both falling

Mango fruits hold, flowers wither

Burnt by heat, taken by wind

5   Water comes, so does power

Friends rejoice, celebrate

Work begins again

6   Power goes, hide and seek

Ice melts, water again

Nature at rest, silent

Drama over!

7   Rooster and hen

Majestic black, Earthly brown

Crowing at sunset

Hen observes, amused

Dogs and cats sleeping

8/3

1   Sun rises, mist evaporates

Cigarette into smoke

What a waste!

2   Soles cracked, feet black

Forearms burnt, dirty hands

Salt of sweat stains

Flies gather!

3   Silent night, early to bed

Stars galore, laughing

Day just begun

Mosquitoes feast

4   Bucket bath refreshingly cool

No mirror, unruly beard

Salt and pepper hair, face black

Clothes fresh

5 Heat sizzles, towel dries

Water for body

Being still thirsty!

6 Thoughts few, writing halted

Feelings many, words minimal

Lost it all!

7 See contentment in utter poverty

Laughter in rest and work

Hopes none, ties many

Innocence dripping!

8 Big *jamun* tree, small birds

Pecking away in gay abandon

Flowers eaten, fruits lost

Chirping laughter and glee

9 Cotton clouds in sky

Trip ending, anxiety returns

Noise of city looming

Peace and calm distant

10 White clouds turning grey

Such is its mood

Nature sensing mine

Existence is all or none!

11 Children playing, lady sweeping

Animals expectant, pots empty

Just like words

Namaaz heard, food is the priority

12 Nature rests, man begins evening

Tuning out of existence's rhythm

Day and night

Cycle squeaks, stumbles, falls

13 Sun down, lights on

One hears the night

Cat demure, dog aggressive

Meal over, Missy misses again

14 Intruders, dogs howling

Peace disturbed, driven away

Barking at own litter mates

Is this not man also?

15 Ferocious guard dog

Young barking incessantly

Biscuits to divert

Sentry's job, food ignored

16 Small jackfruit falls

Ripe ego downed

Sound becomes silence!

17   Two brothers unalike, docile, restless

Lorry traffic on highway

Hum of existence drowned

Float and hear!

9/3 night (No such night at home next month)

1   Crescent moon, triple helix fading star

Light grey, orange horizon, three over

Fire lit, one to go

Temple bell rings, sliver moon

2   Moon vanishes, plane across

Tea on boil, pink mountain top

A flame lights

Sun says hello and goodbye!

3   Day in night out

Grandeur of existence

Too sad, monotony of humans!

4   Ransai shore, Banglawadi shore

Feet in water, boat takes life

Fishing canoe in lake

Net is cast, take the jump!

5   White heron, B&W dive bomber

Dam across plantation surrounds

Heron, patience personified

Existence renews dissolves

6 Still waters running deep

Content jumps, awareness waking

Live, eat, work, rest, die

Feast over, lose it!

7 B&W dive bomber on rock standing

I sit on rock

Its food fish, me searching

A moment lives, a moment dies!

8 Green bird in green valley

Green *chunri* waving, pink *saree* drying

Fishes crying and dying

Heron takes flight, patience like my mind

Missing eternally!

9 A famine and a feast

A recurring theme

Senselessness prevails!

10 Stop this dreaming

Swallows aplenty

Sugar coat this pill

And chew on it!

11 Magarwadi, a whistling in trees

No instrument, bird, wire or wind

Tune in, tune out!

10/3 Ransai Lake

1 Electricity hum carrying across

   Wasn't a mystery, stupid

   Mahashivratri Sunday

   Laze, no cares for livelihood

   Achieved and yet lost!

2 Birds few, songs many

   Fishes surfacing, no fear

   Predators on holiday, except man

   Pump takes to life, shatters idyll

3 Father and son

   On bank and in boat

   Lessons for livelihood

   An education that is wisdom

4 Father alights, son takes over

   Colours of India flag on boat

   Pretty you think

   Shadows for its children, dark unending

5 Feet in cool water

   Fish lost its cool

   Up and out on a wave

   A savoury lunch

   Pump quiet!

6

Solitary bird in sky

Mirror image in lake

Life upside down

Death laughing!

7

Mother on boat

Elbow on knee, hand on cheek

The caress

Of a missing breeze!

8

Bird skimming on surface

A skater on thin ice

A whistle from the treetops

A warning for the fishes

9

Father, a break for snuff

Son takes over

Lucky, catches one

Mother equally adept

10

Pregnant woman on bank

Fish thrown by husband

A new life taking hold

A death in her hand!

11

Pair of dragonflies cavorting

Play is their romance, mine imagination

Words aplenty, romance none

Long live the romantic fool!

12
Two hands of grace

Two poles silent

Eyes gazing serenely

Here comes the reward!

13
Young girl in pretty pink

Naked boy eating fruit

Net covers vegetation

I slip under!

14
A fishing net, embroidery of death

Volleyball net, a play

Somewhere sorrow, somewhere joy

I partake neither!

15
A centenarian at well

Walking stick, bucket in hands

Solitary alone defeated

Dreams none, surrender!

16
Magarwadi mother consoling child

Husband and her, silent fight

Face stern, no recognition

On purpose, chocolate opportunity missed!

17
Viman's noise

Hum in valley, you fool

A simple villager's knowing

Shatters city man's delusion!

18   I am here now

Though never present anywhere

All done, time to go

Temple bells have rung, I asleep

19   Ransai lake, no waves

Dead like the mind of mine

A river of thought

Feelings of a churning lake Simcoe!

20   Rest and respite at an end

Month till departure

That too will pass like this here

A mad rush!

21   My time hanging by a thread

Tread softly and gently

First do no harm

Then let the good disappear too!

22   Grateful to have been alive

Gratitude too when I die

Life so easy

Its living that is arduous pain!

23   Somebody fishing for hours

Playing for hours

Cooking for hours

Cleaning for hours

And some just laze around

How come it keeps eluding

Flying away from me!

24   A plenitude of stars

Polaris, Orion, Cassiopeia

Whether in Georgina or Karnala

Spectacle of sky same

Seasons only differ

Am I like seasons or the sky?

Moods mine, existence is all!

'Carrying books not load on body/mind

It is only after reading them, that

They become a burden!'

'MEDIUM'S MESSAGE' MOVIES AND SONGS

Saajan

Tu shair hai main teri shaayree

Mera dil bhi kitna paagal hain

Bahut pyaar karte hain tujhko sanam

Jiye toh jiye kaise bin aap ke

Anand

Maine tere liye hi saat rang ke sapne choone

Kahin door jab din dhal jaaye

Zindagi kaisi hai paheli haaye

Safar

Jeevan se bhari teri aankhen

Zindagi ka safar hai yeh kaisa safar

Hum the' jinke sahare woh hue na hamare

O nadiya chale chale dhara

Blackmail

Pal pal dil ke paas tum rehti ho

Mere Jeevan Saathi

O mere dil ke chein

Deewana leke aaya hain dil ka tarana

Daag

Mere dil mein aaj kya hain

Andaz

Zindagi ek safar hai suhana

Do Raaste

Khizaan ke phool pe aati nahin bahaar kabhi

Anupama

Dheere dheere machal ae dille bekarar

Baazigar

Chhupana bhi nahin aata

Sarfarosh

Hoshwalon ko khabar kya zindagi kya cheez hai

Khamoshi

Woh shaam kuch ajeeb thi

Humne dekhi hai un aankhon ki mehekti khushboo

Bandini

O re manjhi, o re manjhi

Kudrat

Humein tum se pyar kitna

Aandhi

Tere bina zindagi se koi shikwa to nahin

Kati Patang

Yeh shaam mastani madhosh kiye jaaye

Pyar deewana hota hai mastana hota hai

Aradhana

Mere sapnon ki rani

Aan Milo Sajna

Koi nazrana lekar aaya hoon main deewana tere liye

Kanyadaan

Meri zindagi mein aate toh kuch aur baat hoti!

Acknowledgement

February 10, 2015. 11.15 am.

If you have chosen to read this far, you can afford to read this too. There are some important people to whom I wish to express my gratitude, because their effort was for me and not for their own gain. My labour was just out of pure love, both of the subject and my resurrected passion to write again, albeit what I wrote and its apparent conclusion has remained somewhat a difficult ending to come to terms with.

I owe a lot to each and every one of the people I now wish to write about, for without their support or their critique, this story would never have seen the light of day. It is a difficult task not to miss anyone, so to make it simple I will express my thanks in accordance with the chronological order of the steps taken to fulfil this journey, to the people who helped it along its way to a destination that still remains elusive for me.

Some of you may have read this book fully so will have no qualms about reading this too. Others may have begun and left me somewhere along the way, some would have flipped through the pages and reached the ending, and still some others may have bought this and left it as a decorative piece in their well-stocked libraries or on their coffee table out of a sense of loyalty to me, not really wanting to read it. I thank all of the above buyers of my book.

It is difficult to persuade all of you to read this section also. But I implore you to do so. In this effort of not missing any of those who helped me in some way or another, even friends who pooh-poohed my work without even knowing its subject or content prior to its publication, they all deserve a generous round of applause from you. You, the readers are most welcome to leave all the brick bats for me alone!

As the mystic Kabir once said, and I quote the translated version, though it may not be completely accurate: "When you build your home, make a cottage for your worst critic in your own courtyard; that person will be the one who will help you grow!"

This process of expressing gratitude hence begins with the genesis of this book to its completion and release into the world outside of me. A special thanks to all of them especially the characters featured in the book, who have no real knowledge of their own presence within this book as yet!

1 My immediate family and my housekeeper for making any of this possible. First and foremost to my *bhabhi* for the vision, the design, the planning, and the ideas both small and big, her patience and perseverance that sowed the seed for the renovation of my deceased parents' home. To her and my elder brother and housekeeper, who worked tirelessly suffering enormous inconvenience and disruption of their daily routine silently, allowing for the renovation to proceed and finish over a period involving three phases of work over two years and more. They created what became my favourite spot on the ledge in the day time, my dad's chair being the spot for the evenings, or else, the book you hold would not be the one I could have ever written, maybe not written anything at all!

I feel humbled at their repeated apologies for making my vacation not a holiday, but filled with hard work and multiple daily inconveniences that I never voiced to them. The reward has come later without any expectation of it during those times that all may have felt to be most painful. In addition, they allowed me the time and space, the privacy and help in getting the manuscript on to the computer and my attempts to make it in a digital form thanks to my younger brother and his family's computers. Also they respected the confidentiality of my manuscript totally. Any of them could have chosen to read a part or the full work at any time. My original diary and the re-transcribed manuscript in paper and digital format were easily accessible to all of them in 2014 during and after my leaving. Though written in early 2013, as you will recall, the diary sat in my handbag in Canada till I returned back in late 2013. I myself had neither read the whole work or even a part of it till nearly nine months after having written it. So I am eternally grateful for their respecting my freedom and privacy.

2 My close friends and colleagues, here and in Canada, who sincerely lauded my attempt of this work, especially Tuks who wanted a soft copy of it last year, willing to pay any price for it, and even offering an additional amount to book a copy in advance. I felt deeply touched by his support and encouragement. He never failed to raise the issue on every one of our weekly meetings on Thursdays.

3 My friendly critics who warned me that not one book will sell and rightfully questioned me about its substance, which I have not divulged to date. In the same breath they said, there are a dime a dozen books published every day but if you are serious about it, then give it your best shot leaving no stone unturned. For me, lacking in much effort or will power this sounded surely like an omen.

4 To the two brothers Vipin and Sanjiv Mendiratta, my neighbourhood friends and owners of a press called 'La Concepta', they immediately and generously offered their help and the services of their talented artist, Amol at my disposal. Amol helped to bring the vision in my heart of the book's cover in a draft form on his computer using Corel draw and his expertise so that I could present the manuscript in a more appealing form to the publishers. He took

precious time out of his busy schedule over two sittings to create and give me the file and a print copy of the same.

That draft has subsequently allowed the new and final cover to emerge thanks to the tireless and patient effort of the brilliant artist Rathi Varma, senior Executive of the Design arm of 'Wordit CDE' the publisher of this book, along with the sister concern BecomeShakespeare.com. My hats off to her; she is an aesthetically gifted artist. Just seeing the cover was so appealing to me that I would have bought whichever book the cover adorned, even if the book had been written by someone other than me.

5 To Chandubhai, a family friend and owner of Ratnadeep at Sion Circle – my gratitude for personally being there for me at his shop and directing his assistant Venkat to make a printed copy of my manuscript and attaching the draft cover in a spiral bound book form, so that I could begin my journey to the publishers with a serious intent.

6 But first to my relatives Arunmasa and his wife Sudhamasi and their daughter Sangeeta of the publishing house, "Vakils Feffer & Simons Pvt. Ltd." for their time, patience, generosity, advise, support and above all delight that I had written a book and that too, a non-medical one. I learnt a lot about the insides of this industry, the pros and cons, traditional versus self publishing aspects of it, the promise and pitfalls, the expenses involved, the hassles and marketing issues and many other subtle nuances that have proved to be a wonderful lesson for me. As Sangeeta remarked after just reading the disclosure and Introduction, "You still write beautifully Jaybhai!" They immediately offered that they would be willing for the self publication of this book but also asked me to explore other major publishing houses in Mumbai who could do a much better job at marketing and distribution in North America, two areas where they themselves may not be able to do full justice to the book They advised me not to seek others with offices in Delhi and elsewhere as

it would result in significant delays given my need to have this done in the short time at my disposal on this visit. I have no words to fully express my eternal gratitude to them as any volume of words will fall way short of the sentiments I wish to express towards their help.

7 Now again to my dear friend Tuks who seeing my travails, troubles, frustrations and delays in getting this going with publishers who could provide me with a totality of services needed, spontaneously called his friend Madhavi Purohit, an Editor in the traditional publishing business in my presence, and the process just took off. He had suggested this to me in 2014 but I was not yet ready to follow up on it. It was the in the middle of March 2014, which left me very little time to proceed with the demands it would require.

8 Madhavi, after a conversation with me and a follow up email message the same day immediately arranged for my meeting with Malini Nair, head of self-publishing at Wordit Content Design & Editing a sister concern of Leadstart Publishing and BecomeShakespeare.com. Malini too, like my relatives at Vakils gave me her valuable time and patiently engaged me through the process involved and I knew right then that I had found the people and place to bring my work to life. Yes, I consider myself fortunate now to be part of their family as I have been with those at Vakils too.

9 I took a dummy contract home to read and signed the official contract the very next morning and paid for the full amount of their services at the same time, instead of in instalments that they suggested. The cost is all being absorbed totally by me. I have no intention, nor desire to claim any proceeds from the sale of this book, not even a penny to recover my own cost of this. All the proceeds are to be shared totally amongst a few characters and other worthy causes as already mentioned in the introduction. (Yes, I hope the book will sell enough to make such a sharing be of some material substance to them!)

FOR ME THE BOOK IS PRICELESS, THE ONLY REWARD I CLAIM IS OF IT BEING A GIFT TO MYSELF!

10 To the family of my publisher, Malini Nair, Pallavi Borkar the project manager, Niyati Joshi Senior Executive-Editing, Rathi Varma the aesthetic artist, Shruti Bhiwandiwala, for the due diligence in proofreading this manuscript, her painstaking effort and perceptive eye not leaving any room for errors (If you spot any, they are mine alone) and Rinky Gopalani in charge of the final process of getting the book ready for printing, marketing and a host of other relevant administrative issues. I thank all of you for your unwavering support, guidance and help.

11 Most importantly to Roona Ballachanda, the appointed Editor for my book. A remarkably astute, patient and talented Editor with a very keen eye and in sync with the nature and the flow of my narrative. She has worked tirelessly, asking very good questions, making important suggestions, correcting my written English and its woeful grammar yet preserving my sentiments and my words almost in its totality for the final manuscript! I truly appreciate your hard work. You are the most important person in finally bringing this book to the table.

To the whole team of such an energetic, dedicated young and talented family, my utmost thanks for adopting me! I am humbled and privileged to be a part of you all.

12 A special thank you to Dk *mama*, his wife Rajanimami, and their daughter Tina for their undying support, encouragement, help and advice to get this off the ground with the underlying sentiments of deep care for my work as well as their understanding. They are the first ones to listen to a few snippets from the main body of my work on one of my weekly visits with them last year. They listened with full attentive silence as I spoke and then stopped. In that gap DK *mama* said, "You write very well", "Wah!" said Rajanimami, "Great.

Jaybhai!" remarked Tina. They congratulated me and then my *mama* said, and I will always remember his words, "Creativity can never fail, it will make its mark in its own time and season." "So proud of you," they all remarked spontaneously.

Besides them and Sangeeta, I have only read the preface and a bit of the cover's words to my dearest friend Murli one evening, in the presence of my elder brother at our home last year. They listened and offered their best wishes too.

I may have missed some other key players and my apologies if they have gone unnamed here. I doubt there is any such omission though. I still unfortunately possess a photographic memory, but I hope there is some blurring of its totality, as I am desperately trying to learn the art of forgetting!

Sorry, but a kudos to myself too is in order, only because, this book is being published by BecomeShakespeare.com. The travesty of it brings a smile to my face just now, as I have never ever read even a word of the work of the great Shakespeare!

Don't you think I deserve this smile, for haven't I shed enough tears till now?